New Beginnings

A SHORT STORY ANTHOLOGY

ANNEMARIE BREAR

ANNEMARIE BREAR

New Beginnings: A Short Story Anthology

ISBN: 9781520260235

First Publication: November 2010

Second Publication: February 2016 AnneMarie Brear with Smashwords.

Third Publication 2021 AnneMarie Brear

Cover design by Image: AnneMarie Brear

*Warning story contains sex scenes.

Kitty McKenzie

Kitty McKenzie's Land

Southern Sons

Marsh Saga Series

Millie

Christmas at the Chateau

Prue

Cece

Contemporary

Long Distance Love

Hooked on You

India Dreaming

S weat dripped off my nose. Not a good look, I grant you.

Relentless, the sun burned down from a cloudless peacock blue sky. My clothes, a simple lightweight white skirt and sleeveless yellow blouse stuck to me. This was one country where bikinis should be the national dress. My hair, I knew, looked lank and unwashed, even though I had shampooed it only that morning.

I checked my phone again, wondering why Brett had rung me to meet in a café not far from our hotel in Agra. We said our goodbyes, very satisfactorily, in bed this morning. We'd had only twelve hours together. Brett arrived in Agra late yesterday evening, while I'd only booked into the hotel that morning after leaving Mumbai the night before.

The heat, which sucked the air from your lungs, hung heavy, waiting to knock unsuspecting tourists off their feet. The physical squash of people, the innumerable mass, swarmed around me. Everything was done in a hurry here. I felt I should be running to keep up, but even if I'd wanted to my body refused to move faster than a walk.

Was I walking? Could the shuffle I did through the open-air market be called walking? I doubted it.

An ancient local held up a woven basket full of some delightful red spices and for a moment my nose was filled with something other than the stink of unwashed bodies and the tang of overripe fruit flattened on the road at my feet. India was exotic, colourful, over-powering, yet enchanting.

I felt a tug at my skirt, and instinctively clutched my bag and camera tighter. A gaggle of barefoot children with tiny limbs wearing clothes too big for them jostled about me, their inane chatter ringing in my ears as they held out small groping hands for money.

In a frantic moment, a lesson learnt on my arrival in Mumbai a few days ago, I dove into my skirt pocket, pulled out a handful of jingling coins and threw it all behind me. The result was a mad dash of spindly children pushing and shoving each other for the bounty. I quickly picked up my pace, eager to put distance between myself and the horde.

After a glance at my watch, I left the market and crossed the road, weaving between a boy on a decrepit bicycle and an old woman carrying a basket on her head.

'You made it then?' Brett asked, sipping a cool drink, as I stepped into the dingy café. His wry grin made me catch my breath.

After giving him a kiss, I slid onto a plastic chair at the table. 'Yes, I did. I hope this mystery adventure is worth it. Don't you have to catch the train to Mumbai for your flight tonight?' I sighed. Despite Brett's good looks and devilish charm, I had planned a day of snapping photos for the travel magazine that, as it would happen, paid my bills. Just swanning off whenever I felt like it wouldn't earn me money. But, when Brett smiled at me with that cheeky, little boy smile, how could I say no?

'There's been a change of plans.' He leaned back in the chair, his eyes alight with some inner sparkle. 'I'm not flying to Dubai now and instead I have a week before my next assignment.'

'A week? You can stay with me for a week?' I dared not think such a thing was possible. 'How marvellous.' My heart pounded with the thought of Brett and I waking up together, sharing breakfast, lunch and dinner with him day after day. It was such a rarity.

'Would you like a drink?'

I shook my head, knowing the lack of availability of clean public toilets here. 'I'm fine for the moment. Seven whole days. I can't believe it. Why did the plans change?'

Brett shrugged one shoulder, his gaze on a woman who entered the open front cafe with a small child clinging to her back like a little monkey. 'Head office called me after I left you this morning. They want me to go to Afghanistan, so there's heaps of paperwork to sort out first.'

'Afghanistan?' A small fission of fear trickled down my spine. 'You were there last year. Isn't it someone else's turn?'

'Apparently not.' He took my hand and smiled with reassurance. 'I'll be fine, Lauren, don't worry. This is what I do.'

I pasted on a smile. 'Sometimes I wish you weren't a war journalist and instead had a normal job, like working in a bank, or in some corporate high-rise were the only excitement was ordering Chinese for your lunch and not a sandwich, or playing golf and—'

'And you'd be bored with me in a week. Besides, your job isn't normal. Why should I have to stay home while you travel the world?'

'Because taking photos for a travel magazine, is safer than interviewing leaders of guerrilla armies, or terrorists.'

He reached over the table, lifted my chin up with a finger and kissed me softly. I knew this tactic. A kiss would shut me up whenever I became too concerned with his crazy and unpredictable lifestyle.

I gripped his hand tighter. 'I'll be quiet, I promise.'

'I know you worry, and I love you for it, but you know this is what I do. It's my job and I enjoy it.' His serious expression changed; a smile played on his lips. 'So, you've got me for a whole week. Shall I be your slave and follow you around lugging all your camera equipment?'

Leaning forward, I eyed him suggestively. 'The only slaving you'll be doing is in the bedroom.'

His blue eyes darkened. 'I suppose I can force myself.'

I laughed, knowing exactly how keen he was in that department. The old saying 'Absence makes the heart grow fonder' was also true for sexual frustration.

Brett swirled his drink, his gaze becoming sensual and brooding. 'How long have we known each other?'

Surprised by the question, I frowned with thought. 'Two years? No, two and half years. We met in Paris, remember?'

'It was raining.'

'Yes!' I was astonished he would remember that detail.

'And it was your birthday.'

Blinking, I grinned and sat back in my chair. 'Yes, I was leaving a restaurant after having a birthday lunch with Suzy. She had an appointment and left me waiting for a taxi.'

'In the rain.' He winked.

'In the rain,' I echoed. 'You were standing on the side of the road waiting too,' I whispered, melting inside again, just as I had when I first bumped into him and looked into his gorgeous face.

He nodded. 'I had finished a media junket in a nearby hotel.'

'You were heading for the airport you told me.'

Brett grinned, flashing even white teeth. 'I never got there, did I? Well, at least not for that flight.'

'We never got our taxi either.' I sighed wistfully, reliving that heady moment of falling in love with a stranger.

The heat and sounds that surrounded us faded as I recalled that cool winter's day - the day I started another chapter of my life. 'We sauntered in the rain along the Seine, not caring how wet we got.'

'Then the drizzle stopped, and we found ourselves in a side street with the little café on the corner. We sat and drank numerous cups of coffee and ate pastries and talked for hours.'

'I talked about my childhood in Australia.'

'And I talked of growing up in Maine.'

'Just two foreigners in France.'

'Who happened to meet.' He finished the rest of his drink and stood, holding out his hand to me. 'It was the best day of my life.'

'Ditto.' I stood, too, and stared at him, deeply touched that he had remembered our first day so well. I shouldn't have been surprised though. As a journalist Brett relied on his memory for details and he often surprised me for remembering small things I had completely forgotten.

Brett whistled suddenly, taking a risky step out into the busy road to hail a green and yellow tut-tut. The energy-sapping heat assailed us once more and the crush of the people brought me back to the crowded noisy street away from the dreamy memories of wintery Paris and falling in love.

As Brett and the friendly taxi driver conversed, in halting English on the driver's part, I sat back and wondered why Brett had started such an intimate conversation in the middle of a rundown café. He was never one for discussing such things. We were often apart, our jobs taking us separately all over the world and when we did manage to find time to be with each other, we always had so much new stuff to say and share that reminiscing never happened. So why now?

'Where are we going?'

His answer was a silly grin.

'Brett?'

'You'll soon see.'

Within moments we were trawling along the narrow alleys and clustered streets towards some unknown destination – unknown by me, at least. I tried to take an interest in the passing crowds, but clinging humidity and ear-splitting noise of so many cars and people made it impossible to relax.

Brett brought my hand up to his lips and kissed it. Again, I stared at him. What had come over him? Another public show of affection? Who was this new man and where had he hidden my hard-hitting journalist boyfriend?

'Is everything alright?' I whispered, loud enough for him to hear over the constant tooting horns of the traffic.

'I hope so.' Brett winked.

He hoped so?

What the hell did that mean?

I hoped he wasn't building me up to something...like he was dreadfully sick, or seeing someone else, or anything nasty as that. Was that why he reminded me of our first meeting, so I could remember the good times before the hammer blow? I now had no moisture in my mouth, but I knew my face was an unbecoming shade of beetroot as the heat of the midday sun threatened to suck me dry.

The driver slowed the tut-tut and gestured wildly to a boy leading a laden donkey in front. The boy turned and gave a cheeky salute and slapped the animal's rump to move it on.

Brett pulled his wallet out of his jeans pocket and gave some notes to the driver. 'We'll walk from here. Thanks.'

I tumbled from the taxi, nearly colliding with an old man pushing a hand cart piled high with carpets. People were everywhere. I looked around at the shabby buildings, the ugliness of the ramshackle huts. A slum. Brett has brought me to a slum area. I held my bag and camera tighter. 'Where are we?'

'Agra.'

I raised an eyebrow at his smart reply. 'I know that.'

'Come on.' Brett took my hand and we weaved through the mass of people, carts and animals.

The sun burnt down and reflected off the tin shanties hurting my eyes even through my sunglasses. The noises and smells of so many people living so closely assaulted my senses. A lone cow sat in the middle of the road, forcing people to walk around it. The wretchedness of the area no longer alarmed me, instead, I wanted to capture it.

Keeping an eye on Brett, so I wouldn't lose him in the crush, I slowed to pull out my camera and began taking shots. My breathing calmed, the heat ignored, I saw a fascinating and tragic world through my lens. I took pictures of an old woman, who smiled widely at me, her teeth all gone. I caught the soulful look one a young woman's face as her baby cried in her lap, of happy children playing with a ball, a thin man holding a long stick over his shoulder guiding several goats.

'Laurie!' Brett stood further up the road. 'I swear one day I will lose you for good.'

'Sorry.' I gave him a helpless look. He knew me well enough by now that if I had a camera with me, all else grew unimportant until I finished capturing the shots I needed.

'We're nearly there,' Brett said as I reached his side. 'Only just up the road.'

I looked around as we walked, noticing that there were more westerns in the crowds now. 'Where are we? Why did you bring me to this area? If you wanted to go somewhere, we could have gone to...'

He paused before a red bricked stone structure and put his fingers to my lips. 'Don't say anything for a moment.'

We lined up in queue with others all heading in the same direction. Then we walked under the arch of what looked like a gateway and into open gardens. It was like stepping into another world. Quiet and peaceful, it was the exact opposite of the shanty town we'd just left.

'This is the Taj Ganj.' Brett gave me a knowing smile.

Ahead of me, dominating the skyline, was a three-story red brick building with four white domes and a white centre facing. Something at the back of my mind told me I knew this place, but yet I didn't.

Intrigued, I silently stepped alongside Brett as we crossed the gardens surrounded by a red brick wall. 'The Taj Ganj...' I murmured.

Soon we were passing under the dome-topped construction. It was a beautiful creation, standing tall and powerful. The press of the crowd was nothing when one could look upon such architecture. I grabbed my camera and quickly took some shots.

'Wait. This is only the forecourt.' Brett smiled and taking my hand once more, he guided me under the imposing arches.

'The forecourt of what?' At that moment I knew where we were.

Abruptly, Brett stopped. He swept his hand wide. 'The forecourt to this.'

Stunned, I held my breath, mesmerized, until the urge to breathe made me let it out.

In front of me in shining white splendour was the Taj Mahal.

The tiny hairs on the back of my neck rose as I stared at the vision before me. It felt like I was standing in someone else's shoes.

Was I truly here?

The rising white greatness of the Taj eclipsed even my wildest dreams. I'd wanted to see this for such a long time. It was, in essence, why I had begged my magazine editor to allow me to photograph India. And of course, India meant the Taj Mahal.

'I know it was on your itinerary this week.' Brett broke into my thoughts. 'So, I decided that you couldn't see it unless I was with you. I wanted to share it with you.'

Love for this man overwhelmed me. I threw my arms around his neck and kissed him. 'Thank you. I can't believe I'm here, that *you've* brought me here as a surprise.'

'I've wanted to do this for a year or so, because I know how much you wanted to visit this place. Only, we are never together long enough in one place to organize anything.'

'I wish we could spend more time together.' I sighed, holding him around the waist.

'Well, wishes sometimes come true.'

'What do you mean?'

'I love what I do, but I think I'll only do it for a few more years and then I'll take up some of those offers I've been getting to work for a newspaper or even freelance for a current affairs TV show...'

'Which one?' My heart raced in hope. 'Maybe the one in Sydney?'

'Yes.' He frowned and looked into the distance at the Taj. 'You're based in Sydney and staying in one place, putting down roots, is appealing.'

'You want to give up travelling to war zones?'

'Not yet, but I've been giving it some thought, yes.' He gave me another kiss. 'What do you think?'

I knew my happiness was bursting out of me. 'I think it would be wonderful, but what about returning to your own home?'

'With Mom and Dad gone, there's nothing for me to go home to. You are all I have.'

I felt sad at the mention of his parents. They had both died of different forms of cancer within six months of each other. I had met them once, last year, and regretted that the holiday had been short for they were nice people. 'We can make our own family, Brett.'

'I'm looking forward to it.' He nodded. 'Let's walk down to the pool.'

Arm in arm, we strolled in awe along the path through the gardens to the edge of the shimmering waters of The Al-Kawthar, The Celestial Pool of Abundance. In amazement I stared at the stone bench seat, on which famously Diana, the late Princess of Wales had sat alone.

We wandered, hand in hand, down the length of the gardens, the watercourse beside us, until we stood before the most recognizable building in the world.

The magnificence of the white marble against the blue sky dazzled our eyes. It was all so bare, enabling the building to stand alone and proud. We crept inside the mausoleum, hardly daring to breathe. The cool, quiet serenity entered my soul. I wanted to look at everything at once but did not move in fear of breaking the spell of wonder.

'Let's go look at the river and then we can come back and inspect everything again,' Brett said and before I had chance to speak, he ushered me outside into the sapping heat once more.

The murky river Yamuna swept by in an arc, the flow slow and lazy. Few people lingered in this area, tourists taking photos mainly.

Brett shifted from foot to foot. 'There's something…'

I turned from gazing at the small wooden boat chugging its way up the river. 'What?'

Brett knelt on one knee and pulled from his pocket a small black velvet box.

My mouth dropped open.

'I'm as nervous as hell.' He swore softly and wiped the beads of sweat from his forehead. 'I'm not this nervous when I'm reporting in a war zone.'

I blinked, totally unable to speak.

'So,' he smiled wryly, 'so, Lauren Howard, I was wondering if you'd do me the honour of becoming my wife?' He offered up the box for me to take.

Tears spilt over my lashes. Holding the small box, I opened it and stared at the beautiful single diamond on a gold band.

'Well?'

'Yes,' I whispered.

'Thank heaven for that!' Brett stood and swooped me into his arms and swung me around. We kissed and hugged, laughing and crying at the same time. Tourists clapped and cheered, and I felt like I was in a movie.

Lowering me down to the ground again, Brett then took the ring and slipped it onto the third finger of my left hand. 'I love you.'

'And I love you.' I kissed him again, my heart swelling with emotion.

'Shall we go back inside?'

I looked at the Taj Mahal, built because one man had loved his woman.

Here, before the most romantic building in the world, the man I loved had asked me to marry him.

Here, under the Indian blue sky, I had lived out more than one dream.

Walking into the Sun

Courtney lowered her suitcase to the floor. She gave one last lingering look around the comfortable apartment that overlooked the sun-dazzled Sydney Harbour. It had been her home for nearly ten years. Ten years of dreaming, believing she lived the life she wanted. Would she miss it? Most probably, at least to start with, but it wouldn't take long to find the old Courtney again.

She gazed at the teak wall unit. Gone were the few ornaments that she'd received as birthday presents over the years. They were packed in boxes and stored at her parents' house, along with other personal belongings she wouldn't be taking with her. The furniture was staying. All the pieces she had loving selected and paid for, arranged and taken care of, were all staying in the apartment. A fresh start meant exactly that. Besides, it was only furniture and could be bought again.

Above the television a large gold-framed photo of her in her wedding gown hung from a golden hook. Her own eyes stared back at her smiling. How happy she had been that day. Who would have thought that it would all end in heartbreak?

A noise from behind caused her to turn.

Stewart, the man she once loved, stood in the doorway. He left the door open and took a step inside, his eyes not meeting hers. 'So, you're going then?'

'Yes. I told you it would be today.' Her heart thumped in her chest. How was he going to react now the time had come?

'It doesn't have to end.' He shrugged as though they were discussing the merits of the weather.

'Yes, it does, Stewart.' God, why did he have to act this way?

Stewart threw his keys on the narrow hall table. 'We can talk about it!'

'We've talked until we're blue in the face. It never does any good and things always revert back to us being miserable.'

'I've never been miserable,' he accused, walking into the clean modern kitchen.

The open plan of the apartment meant from her position in the sitting room she could see him open the refrigerator door and take out a can of cola. 'No, you weren't miserable.' She sighed. 'You had no reason to, did you?'

'I do love you, you know.' It was a statement not a question.

'The love you have for me isn't enough.' Courtney collected her handbag from the cream sofa, hating herself for still feeling hurt by his lack of affection. 'It's not the kind of love I want or need. I realise that now.'

'What the hell does that mean?'

'It means you don't love me enough. You love your beer and your mates more. You live your life like a single man not as a husband. Now I'm just making it official. '

'Listen, Courtney...'

'No, Stewart. Say no more and neither will I. It's over. It has been for a long time. Only, I was too stubborn to see it and too scared to do anything about it.'

'We can work through this.'

'No, we can't. I've tried, Stewart, and I'm tired of not being happy.'

'I'm sorry I'm not what you want any more.' He sulked like a little boy who'd lost his favourite toy.

Stewart's self-pity left her unmoved. Not so long ago it would have made her put her arms around him and forgive him for his lack of interest, but no more. Too many tears had been shed and all the lonely hours spent by herself, while he had been drinking with his mates had killed her love for him. Her feelings for him had waned until they diminished altogether. The dreams she built while on her honeymoon were scattered to the wind. She was only thankful that her vision of having children had not come into fruition. Stewart's immature attitude being a husband was bad enough, but to be a father as well would have been disastrous. He didn't want the same things she did, and she understood now that he never did.

She picked up her suitcase and handbag. 'There is nothing left in the apartment that I want. I've only taken my personal belongings, you've got everything else. Later, I will apply for a divorce.'

'A divorce?'

'Yes, of course! We discussed this!' Courtney fumed. It was typical of him not to listen to her.

'I remember it was the reason for our last fight.' He flopped onto the sofa and switched on the television.

She took a deep breath, not wanting to be reminded of their heated arguments. She hated confrontation and their fights had left her crying and sick at heart. 'There's food in the cupboard and all the bills are paid up.'

'Whatever,' he mumbled, flicking through the channels.

'Yes, well... Bye then.' Did he really not care, or was he acting the tough man?

'Where are you going to be?' Stewart quickly asked, eyeing the suitcase with distaste.

'I'll be travelling for a while...'

'Travel? What about your job?'

'I've resigned.'

'Can I ring you?' The self-pity surfaced again.

Courtney sighed in irritation. 'No,' her tone was firm, as she bent to pick up her case. She put her own keys onto the small table. They lay side by side to Stewart's. Courtney averted her eyes. They made it very final.

'Goodbye, Stewart, take care of yourself.' She left without a backward glance. Enough. She'd done her best and no one could say she hadn't tried to make her marriage a success.

Walking out of the apartment building she made for the sleek black BMW parked across the road. An enormous sense of relief overcame her, and she felt light-headed with the impact. Taking a deep breath, she steadied herself to meet the rest of her life.

'How did it go?' A tall, dark-haired man with handsome features opened the car door for her.

'Okay.' Courtney gave him a shaky smile. 'Thanks, Mitchell.'

'You have everything you need?' he asked, taking her suitcase from her and placing it in the boot.

'Yes. You don't mind doing this? I really could have managed on my own. I could have got a taxi or even the train.' She slid onto the front passenger seat, eager to be gone.

'We're going to be spending a lot of time together. I want to be there for you and help in any way. I'd like us to become friends.'

'Thanks.' Courtney's eyes filled with tears. Blinking rapidly, she stopped them from falling. Lord, that's the last thing she wanted to do – cry in front of Mitchell Crompton.

'Nervous?' He fired the engine to life and pulled away from the curb in a smooth action.

'A little.' She gripped her hands together to hide their shaking.

'You have a right to be. It's not every day you make a life-changing decision. The housewife and shoe store salesperson turned travelling magazine photographer is a huge step!'

'Yes, I know. I realise now that it should have been one I made years ago.' She watched the familiar streets flash by and felt the excitement begin to stir in the pit of her stomach.

'You'll do a fantastic job.'

'Thanks. You have been wonderful and have given me the chance to make something of my life.' She glanced at him as they merged with traffic heading for the airport. 'You took a gamble.'

He grinned cheekily. 'Oh, I believe the risk is worth it. Your portfolio was impressed for a hobbyist.'

'Photography has kept me sane for years.'

He pulled the car to a halt in the airport terminal car park. He retrieved her suitcase from the back seat and held it. 'Want me to come in with you? Maybe we could have a coffee?' He glanced at his watch. 'You've got time.'

Courtney bit her lip, hesitating. His good looks and easy manner made her comfortable, but she didn't want to appear eager for his company. In truth, she didn't want to be alone. She had been alone in her marriage for so long that the thought of having a male's attention made her slightly giddy. 'Thank you. That would be lovely.'

After checking in her bag, they found a small café tucked into a corner of the airport and Mitchell ordered them both hazelnut lattes. Courtney watched him answer his buzzing phone with practised ease. His sophistication was such a contrast to Stewart's beer swilling antics on the lounge in front of the television.

'Sorry about that.' He smiled as the waitress placed their lattes on the table.

Courtney watched the waitress preen under Mitchell's smile. Something swift and lethal pierced her heart. Was it jealousy? No, it couldn't be! Heavens, that's all she needed, to be attracted to the first man who is kind to her. And he had been kind. From the first time she met him at the job interview, four weeks ago, he'd been warm and friendly, making her feel relaxed. The second interview had gone much the same way and she'd been so happy to make the shortlist for the position. Then finally, last week, he'd called her and told she'd been successful in getting the job. He'd invited her to come to the magazine office and meet everyone and go through the paperwork. After two hours together huddled in his office, they'd gone out with other members of staff for dinner. She liked Mitch. How could she not? He was handsome, sexy and intelligent.

Mitchell turned his phone off as it rang for the tenth time in as many minutes. He turned towards her and gave her his full attention. 'You'll like Brisbane.'

'I'm sure I will.'

'Do you know anyone there?'

'I have a cousin who lives near the river. She has promised to take me out to all the nightclubs.'

He leaned back in his chair and studied her. 'Watch out Brisbane,' he whispered.

Courtney fiddled with the cup's handle. His lazy appraisal fired up her blood. How long had it been since someone showed an interest in her? Stewart had stopped years ago. She glanced at him from under her lashes. 'The photos you sent me of the apartment and the city itself were great. I also carry the list of the local facilities you sent me too. You've been so kind.'

'I know the apartment is only small, but it's not like you'll be there a lot. A travelling photographer lives out of their suitcase.'

She sipped her drink. 'I know I'll enjoy it. This is an enormous opportunity for me.'

'Your first assignment is the south of France.'

'France!' She shook her head in wonder and gave him a brilliant smile. 'I can't believe this is actually happening. I never dreamed my hobby would one day become my career.'

'From the standard of your photos, I'd say you have a very long career ahead of you.'

She lowered her gaze, knowing her cheeks flamed from his comments. She had to get a grip of herself. He had her blushing like a schoolgirl on her first date.

Mitchell half rose out of his chair and took his wallet out of his jeans pocket. He extracted a business card and gave it to her. 'Keep this with you at all times. That has my email, phone and home number on it. If you ever need me, just contact me. It doesn't matter what time or day it is. Okay?'

'Thanks.' She took the card from him. Their hands touched and she experienced a shiver of excitement tingle all the way up her arm. Her heart thumped like an engine piston. Need him? She wished it were as easy as that. To simply ring him up and say, hey could you take me out for dinner tonight and maybe afterwards we could share a bottle of champagne in the spa? Courtney cringed at her wayward thoughts and knew she was blushing all over again. She had to stop such thoughts. She needed time and peace after Stewart. No men. Just travel, visiting interesting places and meeting new people.

A bold voice rang throughout the airport announcing that departure of the Qantas flight to Brisbane was ready for boarding.

Courtney stood as Mitchell went to pay the bill. She watched the way he moved, sleek like a jaguar. His black leather jacket fitted his shoulders well. His jeans hugged his cute backside. She turned away to gaze at the surrounding shops and tried to think of something else. Everywhere she looked were posters of hunky males modelling watches or cologne. What was wrong with her? Perhaps she was sex starved. After all, she'd not had sex for many months and when she had slept with Stewart it had been very unsatisfactory. He was a taker, not a giver. He was so bad that she had started leaving women's magazines around the house which had tips on how to seduce your woman, or *Top 10 Tips on Improving your Woman's Pleasure*. Sadly, he never read them.

'Ready to go?'

'Yes, all set.' She smiled up at Mitch, liking that he was a good five inches taller than her. Without a doubt she knew he would be a good lover. Shocked again at her thoughts, she hitched her handbag strap higher on her shoulder. 'I can manage from here. Thank you for everything.'

'You sure?'

She gazed into his soft grey eyes and nodded, suddenly unable to speak for the emotion clogging her throat. She felt like he was her only friend at that moment. Here she was leaving her family, her home and her old way of life for something totally new and strange. She admitted, if only to herself, that she was a little frightened of what lay ahead.

'Is your cousin meeting you in Brisbane?'

'Yes.' She felt relief at that. Her cousin Suzy was married with three children and led a hectic life, but she'd phoned only the night before saying how thrilled she was that Courtney would be in her city soon and there was so much she wanted to show her.

Mitch walked with her to the boarding gate. 'I look forward to seeing your work. Email me when you have settled in your new apartment. I'll be in Brisbane next week. We'll go out for dinner and discuss the south of France.'

Her eyes widened at the suggestion. 'We will?'

'Of course, didn't you know that's what bosses do?' he joked.

Courtney grinned, feeling better. 'See you next week then.' She walked away with her back straight and head held high. She had left behind a life she thought she would have until she was old and grey. Her stomach clenched in sudden fear, but she fought it and outwardly showed composure and calmness. Ahead was a world of new opportunities and the promise of excitement. Who knows, maybe one day a new love too?

In the Blink of an Eye

Eloise slammed on the brakes. The wet road took control of the steering wheel out of her hands as the car spun. She watched as her car and a large black shape in front of her collided in slow motion. Her stomach lurched, her hands gripped the wheel harder, but she was thrown to the right and banged her head on the window. The grinding, sickening crunch of metal hitting metal was terribly loud and suddenly all was still.

She sat staring out of the windscreen at a tree that was mere inches away from the front lights. The windscreen wipers swept away another deluge of rain. The car was sideways on the road. She turned her head to the way she should have been facing, the way she had been facing only moments ago. The bent end of a black 4X4 filled her vision. At eye level the car's badge winked in shining splendour untouched by the crash. Mercedes.

The passenger side door was wrenched open. Wind and rain lashed at the interior before a man stuck his head inside. 'Are you hurt?'

Dazed, she gazed at him, hands still gripping the steering wheel. 'Err…no. I don't think so.' She peeled her fingers off the steering wheel to lightly touch her head, it throbbed. Was she hurt? Probably. But trying to ascertain if she was badly injured or not was beyond her at that moment.

'I'll move my car up a bit and see if we can get you out.' He withdrew and the door closed.

Eloise shivered. She'd been in an accident. Great. The thought was so bizarre she didn't know if it was actually true or not. Eloise Foster in a car accident? Never! She had an impeccable driving record unlike her sister, Penny, who managed to average a crash every year or so. No streetlight or fence post was safe with Penny behind the wheel.

Her hands shook as she reached to turn off the engine. The wipers stopped mid-way across the windscreen and the rain fell harder, obliterating the view. Dusk was falling. Darkness came earlier enough in winter without bleak grey rainy days.

The driver side door jerked open again and a blast of cold air filled the car. Eloise blinked, feeling rather silly, hoping to God that she wouldn't cry. That would be worse than having crashed the car. She hated crying. She wasn't a good crier – not the type that cried silently with angel-like faces that melted the fiercest heart. Not her. When she cried it's the full-blown red eyes, running nose and hiccupping sobs of gigantic proportions. Ugly.

'You okay?' The man's tenderness calmed her somewhat. He spoke nicely. Lord, what a thing to think of right now. She must have hit her head harder than she thought.

The solid width of his shoulders blocked most of the rain from hitting her. 'Can you undo your seatbelt?'

'Oh…er…yes.' But her fingers were numb, the messages from her brain weren't filtering at all well.

'Here, let me.' The man reached across her stomach and unclipped the buckle. 'It's awful out here, but there's a bus shelter a few yards away. We can wait there for help.' Gently, as if she was made of spun glass, he assisted her out of the car and across the grass towards the shelter. Rain splattered her face, making her blink and shudder.

Once seated on the timber bench in the shelter, Eloise took a deep breath. Raindrops drummed on the roof, and she shivered again from the dampness seeping into her clothes.

'I've called an ambulance just to be safe.' The guy flashed a brief smile. 'I'm so sorry.'

'I don't need an ambulance.' Dazed, she turned to look at him and her breath caught in her throat. He was handsome. Not just the average guy next door type, but knock out handsome, the kind that are in movies or in magazines, modelling briefs - all chiselled jaw and sensual eyes.

'It was an accident,' she mumbled, forcing herself to stop staring at him.

'Here.' He stood, took off his long black coat and wrapped it around her shoulders.

'Thanks.' Eloise blushed. She wanted to refuse his offer, but the words wouldn't form. She was wearing jeans, a baggy jumper and muddy boots, her normal attire as a country veterinarian. Not a pretty picture especially in comparison to him, who was dressed smartly in a black suit. The warmth from his coat relaxed her. The spicy smell of his cologne clung to the material, and she breathed it in until she felt giddy. What was she doing? She had definitely hit her head hard.

'I'm Tom.' He smiled, revealing a slight dimple in his left cheek. 'Tom Shepherd.'

'I'm Eloise Foster.' She returned his smile, liking the way she felt at ease with him.

'I'm really sorry for this. I'm new to the country and these little lanes with blind corners just appear out of nowhere. In the rain I didn't see the dog. Thankfully I didn't hit it.'

'You do have to drive slower in the country.' Why wasn't she angry with him? Her car was a wreck, her day ruined. How on earth would she get to her clients now? It was all his fault, yet here she was chatting to him as if they were waiting for a bus! She had interviews to conduct in an hour for the vet position and people relying on her. What a mess!

'Are you sure you're not hurt?' Concern clouded Tom's blue eyes.

'I'm fine, honestly.'

'Your cars will need towing.' He grimaced. 'Mine should be okay, but I had better get it checked out.'

'Jackson's garage is the closest, about three miles away in the next village.' She heard the ring of her mobile and stood to go get it out of her car, but Tom held her arm.

'Stay here. I'll bring your bag to you.'

Eloise watched him go back out into the rain. He was behaving like a perfect gentleman, which completely threw out the argument that gentlemen were a dying breed. When he returned, her phone had stopped ringing, but that didn't bother her. She searched through her bag and brought out a small wallet full of business cards. She flicked through them until she found the right one. Jackson's Garage. 'Here.' She gave it to Tom. 'Do you want to ring them?'

He nodded. 'I'll ring the police too.'

While he made the call, she rang the Veterinary clinic and told them what had happened. After assuring everyone at work she was fine, Eloise hung up and realised a headache was building.

'You look a little pale.' Tom stared at her intently.

'Just a small headache.'

His expression altered and he glanced up the road. 'Where's that ambulance.'

'It's okay, really.'

'No, it isn't. You could have a problem.' He walked out into the rain to glare up the road as though that would make the ambulance immediately appear.

'We'll have to swap insurance details and all that.' From her purse she dug out her own business card and handed it out to him.

Rain dripped down his face as he sat beside her again. 'My insurance will cover everything, please don't worry.'

Her hand itched to wipe the water running down his handsome face.

He read her card, while at the same time taking his wallet from a pocket inside his jacket. 'You're a vet.'

'Yes.'

'If you don't mind, I'd like to go in the ambulance with you.'

'There's no need, honestly. I'll ring my dad. He'll come and collect me.'

He frowned and gave a slight cough. 'I couldn't rest easy not knowing how you were.'

'Someone will have to stay here and sort the cars out.'

'I'll take care of it...' A smile played on his lips, and he gazed at her.

'What's so funny?' Eloise frowned.

'Would you believe I was on my way to a job interview.'

'Can you ring them and let them know?'

'I could...but I can save myself the phone call and just tell you.'

Head throbbing, she didn't understand what he meant until he held up her business card.

'I don't think I'll make the appointment. Sorry.'

Eloise's eyes widened. 'You're a vet, too? You were coming to see me about the job advertised for the clinic?'

'That's right.' Tom's smile turned wry. 'I hope the accident hasn't put a cross next to my name?'

'Well, I'll have to think about it.' She smiled back, knowing in her mind he already had the job. He had already been put to the top of her list just from reading his C.V. last week. She could handle
working with someone as nice as him, and he was easy on the eye too.

He shifted on the seat as though suddenly nervous, her card dangling from his fingers. 'You know, it's true what

people
say.'
  'What's that?'
  'That your life can change in a blink of an eye.'
  'Yes, I guess so.'
  'My life has, by this accident.'
  She scowled, not understanding. 'How has it?'
  He looked her straight in the eyes. 'I have met you.'

Remembering

Shannon slowed the car carefully, not wanting to skid on the ice, though the village streets looked well cleared by a recent snow truck, but black ice was an invisible enemy. She turned the engine off and climbed out of the car. Weak sunlight captured the ancient street, highlighting the piles of dirty snow shovelled off the pavement outside of the shops.

Her boots crunching on the packed ice, Shannon walked down the street, passed shops she had visited so long ago. She peeked through the window of the chemist's before continuing on past the small hardware shop, the butchers, and a clothes boutique that hadn't been there when she lived here and then finally the newsagents on the corner.

The same brass bell tinkled above her head as she opened the door and walked in. The same smell of newspapers and all manner of things that hide on shelves tucked away in corners.

The shopkeeper, now an even older woman than she remembered, gave Shannon a long look. 'Shannon Watts. It's been a many a year since you were last in this shop.'

'Yes, it has.' Shannon gathered a bottle of water, a chocolate bar and a magazine and put them on the counter. 'How are you, Mrs Turnball?'

'Still living.' Mrs Turnball added up the items on the register. 'Five pounds, ninety.' She put them into a plastic bag and exchanged that for the money Shannon handed to her. 'How's your family?'

Flinching, she hesitated. 'I lost Mum recently.'

'Sad to hear it.'

When it looked like Mrs Turnball was ready to ask more questions, Shannon gave her a fleeting smile and headed for the door. 'Goodbye.'

Once on the street in the cold air, she put her head down into her scarf and hurried back to her car. What a fool she'd been to come back. Stupid. Stupid. Stupid!

What was the use of dragging up old memories? Where would it get her? Didn't she have enough heartache in her life without wishing for things that were long buried?

One more stop, she promised herself quietly. Just one more place and then she'd leave this town and never come back.

Ten minutes later she was turning into a rutted dirt track, edged thickly with snow drifts. The windscreen wipers cleared away another covering of sleet. Shannon wiped her fringe out of her eyes and peered through the foggy windscreen. The tyres skidded on the ice and snow. She hated driving in such conditions. With a sigh, she turned off the engine and opened the door. A blast of cold air hit her face - a deep bone chill of mid-winter on the moors. Heavily burdened with its load, the sky hung low and grey. Shannon pulled her coat tighter, lifting its hood over her head. The crunching of snow underfoot was the only sound to fill the air. The bleak moors were devoid of wildlife and human presence - save her own.

The shepherd's hut stood alone on the rise, braving the harsh weather like it had done for years. How was it still standing after all this time? She trudged up the slope looking neither right nor left. Her whole attention was on the shelter. It had aged, she noticed, yet in her heart and mind it remained the same, as it had been the day, she had run from it, twelve years ago.

The door was not locked, only jammed tight with age and snow-covered hinges. Shannon hesitated. It was the final barrier. Should she take the ultimate step and enter? Inside, were memories that haunted her, sadden her. With the slightest of shrugs, she put her shoulder to the door and pushed. The door squeaked open, and she stood teetering on the threshold, as she had stood teetering on the threshold of adulthood, so long ago. Gingerly, she stepped into the dim interior pausing to let her eyes adjust to the gloom.

Grime covered the two small windows, filtering out most of the daylight. Mustiness tickled her nose. Thick coatings of dust covered every surface and in the corners of the roof hung fine necklaces of cobwebs. From the holes in the roof, rainwater stains created a patchwork on the walls and floor. Beside the black pot-bellied stove, a cardboard box held sticks and short thick logs. A yellowing newspaper sat on a wooden shelf built along one wall. Shannon grinned. It hadn't changed. She reached up and her fingers felt a box of matches on top of the newspaper.

It wasn't long before the flames caught. The cheery crackling of the fire consuming the wood made her feel better. She held her hands out to the warmth, refusing to let her eyes wander to the iron bed in the corner. She had been able to dismiss the large object while busy lighting the fire, but now it drew her to images she wished to forget. Telling herself not to be silly, it was only an iron bed, Shannon firmly turned her head to stare at it in accusation. Her shoulders sagged. Its mattress was gone, and the springs were bent and rusting, but once it had held soft pillows and warm woollen blankets.

She made a step towards it, when suddenly she heard the sound of crunching snow. Someone was here. Mesmerised, she watched the long door handle turn downwards and the door slowly opened. A man in a huge blue coat, blue jeans and black boots stood silhouetted in the doorframe. She searched his face. Her stomach clenched. Her throat became constricted when she looked into his pale blue eyes.

In her heart she knew he would come.

'I saw the smoke. I knew you were here.' His voice was deep, sombre.

'How did you know I was in town?'

'You know what this place is like. You were seen at the service station. You were remembered. I must have pulled in right after you left. Old Pete was talking ten to the dozen trying to tell me you were back.'

'I bet he was!' She sighed, going back to the fire, turning her back on him.

He seemed to dwarf the hut's small interior. He shut the door and came to stand beside her. 'It is cold in here.'

'Yes.'

'You haven't changed, Shannon.'

'Yes, I have.'

'Not to me. To me you will always be sixteen, young and carefree.' His smile was a little shaky.

'I cannot remember being young and carefree. All I remember is the last years of struggle.'

'I tried to find you, but I couldn't. They never told me where you went. No one spoke of your family again.' His eyes bored into hers with hidden pain.

'Why would they? The whole town was glad to see the back of us.'

'Life for me was unbearable without you. My parents despaired of me ever being normal again. How could they understand that they had broken my heart by forcing your family to leave the village!' His voice was harsh, and she gazed up at him. 'I hated them for phoning the police.'

Gently, she placed her hand on his arm. Heart full of emotion, she swallowed back her tears. 'They were protecting you. My father was a petty criminal, my brother a fool. They didn't want you mixed up in such a family.'

'I cared nothing about that! It was you I wanted!'

Shannon bent to the cardboard box and picked up another log throwing it into the embers of the fire. She didn't look up, couldn't trust herself to be calm if she saw his gorgeous eyes linger on her lips like they used to just before he kissed her. 'Did you become a lawyer?'

He let out a breath and pulled off his gloves. 'No, a doctor.'

'I'm glad.'

'And you? What happened to you?'

'I'm a social worker. After leaving here, I went to live in Manchester with Mum. She divorced Dad went he went to jail. I went to college.' She stood and steeled herself to look at him.

He smiled. 'Are you hungry? I have a thermos of coffee in the car, and we can share my sandwiches. I was on my way to do house calls, so I packed my lunch and brought it with me.'

She nodded, her throat too tight to talk much.

He left the hut and Shannon shivered as the opened door let in more cold air. Closing her eyes, she tried to shut out the memories that wanted to crowd her mind. For years she had successfully blotted out the happy memories of a dry hot summer when she had fallen in love for the first and only time. This hut had been their haven, the one place they could meet away from prying eyes. But she should never have come back here. She was mad to think that she could return to a place that had meant so much to her and not feel anything. She was a fool.

For a while they were silent and ate half a sandwich each while drinking hot coffee sitting on a blanket, brought from his car and placed over the bedsprings. Then, slowly they began to talk of mundane things. Hours ticked by as they talked about all sorts of events happening in the world today. Not once did they talk about their past or the love they had shared, at least not until they were down to the last log in the box, which Shannon put onto the fire with an ache in her heart.

'Why did you take so long to come back?' he asked, from the bed.

'Life doesn't always turn out as you plan,' she murmured, watching the flames.

'So, you had planned to return?'

'No, not until last week.' She turned to him and hesitated before speaking again. 'My mum died two weeks ago. It was an impulsive thing to do, coming here, but I found myself alone for the first time in my life.'

'You never married?'

'No. I... I was content to have Emily and Mum.'

'Who is Emily?' He frowned, in confusion.

'She was my daughter.'

'You had a daughter?' He looked incredulous.

'Yes. She died two years ago. She... She'd had leukaemia since she was two.'

He stood and went to her. Placing his hands on her shoulders, he gazed into her eyes. 'I am so sorry, Shannon.'

Shannon shrugged off his hands and went back to sit on the bed. 'I don't know how I'll go on without her. She was my life.'

'I don't know what to say. It must have been awful for you.'

'It was, still is.'

They fell silent again, each consumed with their own thoughts, then Shannon spoke again. 'What about you? Are you married?'

'No. I was too full of anger at my parents and the world in general to attract anyone to me.' He chuckled at himself. 'My parents wanted me to be a lawyer. I wanted to backpack around the world and live as a hippy on some South Pacific Island.' He laughed. 'In the end we compromised. I told Father I would become a professional something, as long as I moved out of home and had no allowance from him.'

'And you decided to be a doctor,' Shannon stated, pleased that he had put his intelligence to good use.

'Yes.'

'Do you see your parents much now?'

'Once a month, or so. We get along better now that they are old, and I am wiser.' He chuckled again. Then, his smile disappeared as he gazed at her sitting on the bed. 'I can't believe that we are here in this hut again after all this time. It's a little eerie.'

'It's hard to believe,' she agreed, suddenly nervous. She did not want the conversation to stray into hurtful territory.

'I never thought I would see you again. I so wanted to find you. I wish I had,' he said, softly.

'It would not have worked. We were too young. Too much had happened.'

'Maybe, but there was no need for it to turn so...so ugly!'

Shannon played with her empty coffee cup. 'Our parents were doing what they thought was right,' she said, defensive. 'I couldn't hurt my mum anymore. She had enough to cope with in Dad and my brother.'

'I thought your father was going to kill me when he found out about us.' He shook his head in amazement at the memory.

'He would have if your father had not called the police. My dad was more worried about being finally caught by the police than us two. They had wanted him for a while.'

'I will never forget that last day when I came here after searching the whole village for you. I found you crying on this bed. The very same bed we had...made love in so many times. I never wanted you to leave me.'

'It was hard for me too.'

'I thought I would die.'

Shannon averted her gaze. She did not want to see the same longing in his beautiful blue eyes that had made her wild with desire all those years ago. 'We were so young,' she muttered.

'Our love wasn't. It was as old as time.'

She looked at him, grinning at his eloquent way of words. 'You always made me weak with the things you used to say to me.'

'Did you know, on that last day, that your father was taking you away from here?' He spoke with an edge to his voice. He wanted her to know the pain he had suffered. He had thought his life to be over.

'Yes.'

'But yet you didn't tell me. You went away knowing we would not see each other again.'

'I had to.'

'Why?'

Shannon stood up and walked to the dirty window. She stared sightlessly out of it. Her throat thick with emotion and her eyes blurring with unshed tears. 'I couldn't say goodbye to you. I wouldn't have been able to leave if I had.'

'We could have gone away together, Shannon!'

'How would we have survived?'

'I would have found work!'

'I was sixteen. You were eighteen.'

'So, what did that matter? We would have been together!'

'I was pregnant,' she whispered.

He stared at her in shock. His mind trying to absorb her words, but he was having trouble believing them. 'Pregnant?'

'Yes, three months.'

'Why didn't you tell me? Why didn't you write to me and let me know?' he cried, in agony. 'You shouldn't have kept it from me.'

'You had your whole life ahead of you. You were going to be a lawyer or a barrister or something great. Your family was wealthy and powerful. I was the daughter of a petty thief and sister to a thug. It was made very clear to me that I was not welcome in your family and that I was leading you astray.'

'But to have a baby without me? How could you do that, when you knew how much I loved you?' His pain made her wince.

'It was because I loved you, that I didn't tell you. You would never have become anything if I had asked you to take care of the baby and me.'

'As if I cared about that!' He paced the hut. 'I can't believe you've kept this from me!'

'I'm sorry!'

'Christ, Shannon! I was a father...' He suddenly stopped talking and looked at strangely her. 'Your daughter, the one who died, was she...?'

'Yes, she was yours.'

'Oh, God!' His face revealed his inner torment. Anger and loss fought for control. 'You shouldn't have kept it from me. I had a right to know.'

'I'm sorry, really I am.' She gulped back a sob. 'I didn't know what to do. Suddenly, I was a mother and it freaked me out.'

He ran his fingers through his hair. 'I can't believe you didn't tell me.'

Tears trickled down her cheeks. Guilt raked her body, and she wrapped her arms around her waist. 'I'm sorry.'

He strode to her and pulled her tight against his chest.

Together they cried for their lost daughter and their lost love. All their pent-up emotions and buried feelings surfaced and engulfed them. Through her tears, Shannon told him of the hard years she had spent studying and looking after a baby. She told him how they had lived off her mother's meagre wages, who had become a night office cleaner to support them. She told him of the days and nights she had cried for him, especially when Emily was diagnosed with leukaemia.

Finally, she pulled from her pocket, a creased photo of their daughter sitting on Santa's knee when she had been about three years old. The image that smiled back at them was the double of her father.

'You see? I still had a part you.' She cast him a teary smile. 'I had you in my heart and in our daughter.'

'Look at her.' His eyes widened in wonder. 'She's just like me. That's how I looked as a child.'

Shannon squeezed his hand. 'I was wrong in what I did. I should have written and told you about her. I was selfish, but also afraid. Now I realise that both you and Emily missed out on so much. I'm sorry. Please forgive me, though I doubt I'll ever be able to forgive myself.'

'It's all been such a shock.' He shook his head as though to clear his mind. 'First, you turning up here after all these years, and now you tell me I was a father. I had a daughter. It's unbelievable.'

'I did what I did because, at the time, I thought it was for the best. Do you believe me?'

'Yes.'

She sighed deeply, glad that he finally knew and that he understood her reasons. 'I wish I could change the past, but I can't.' She gazed down at her boots. 'So, what do we do now?'

'I don't know.'

'I feel like I'm sixteen again, all undecided and lost.'

He placed his finger under her chin and raised her face to stare into her eyes. 'I will not let you disappear from my life again, Shannon. I feel like I've been waiting all this time for you to return.'

Her heart pounded as she gazed at him. 'I don't feel like running anymore.'

The fire died out and the hut resumed its cold musty air. They left hand in hand, walking away from the special place that had once been a sanctuary for them to be together, to take refuge from the world. Now, it featured once again in their lives.

A simple hut that had drawn them back and given them the chance to heal their wounds and look to the future - together.

In Paris, with Love

Poppy paused to listen to the sounds around her. A couple strolled past, arm in arm. The man said something to make the woman laugh and Poppy's heart constricted.

There was the general noise on traffic, the constant blare of horns, the rev of engines on the city streets, but it didn't distract from the happy atmosphere of Paris on such a hot day.

'Come on, Poppy.' Her best friend Leah had turned back to face her with a deep sigh. 'It's too hot to stand out in the sun. Look, the queues are getting longer.'

Poppy glanced towards the crowds milling beneath the Eiffel Tower. 'I don't want to go up. I told you that last night in the hotel and again this morning at the cafe. I'm not good with heights.'

With a frown, Leah glared at her. 'Don't be a spoil sport. You can't come all the way to Paris from Australia and not go up the Eiffel Tower. Besides, it'll just be like being in a hotel room and looking out of a window. I'm not asking you to bungee jump off it, for heaven's sake.'

Searching the park, Poppy pointed to a bench. 'I'll wait over there. You go up.'

'No. I can't go by myself.' Leah frowned and hitched the strap of her bag higher on her shoulder. 'You know, I read that people find their true love on the observation deck of the Eiffel Tower.' She grinned at me.

'Don't believe everything you read.' True love indeed. Poppy took a bottle of water out of her bag and drank deeply. It was nearly two o'clock and the heat was pooling in the city with no cool breeze to refresh the citizens.

'Please come up with me, Pop.' Leah tilted her head and gave Poppy a doe-eyed look. 'Please?'

'The crowd is huge...'

'So? It won't take long, I promise.' Leah grabbed Poppy's hand and dragged her towards the lines of people. They dodged a group of Asian tourists and then stopped to allow an older man to take a photo of his wife touching one of the thick steel beams of the structure.

As she and Leah waited in line for the elevators, Poppy watched a young couple kissing and cuddling. She looked away and blinked back threatening tears. That should have been her and Nick. He should have been here today. They'd planned this holiday for two years and as a surprise on his birthday last week she'd bought the tickets. Then it had all gone horribly wrong...

Leah read from a pamphlet. 'The Eiffel Tower was built in 1889. The Prince of Wales, later King Edward VII, officiated at the ceremonial opening. The design—'

'I have to go.' Poppy began to push through the queue.

Grabbing her arm, Leah pulled her back. 'Wait, what is the matter?'

'I can't do this.' Sniffing, Poppy ducked her head and let her hair fall in front of her face so the people around couldn't see her cry. 'Nick was meant to be here...'

'I know.' Leah hugged her tight and then let her go. 'I'm sorry he's not here. He's a pig to put work before a holiday of a lifetime with you.'

Poppy rummaged through her bag for a handkerchief. 'Damn. Do you have a Kleenex?'

'Yes. The line is moving. We'll be on the next elevator.' Leah passed a small packet of tissues to her as they shuffled along in the queue. 'I know this is hard for you, but I really want to Paris from the observation deck. They say it's incredible.'

'Okay...' Unimpressed, Poppy tried to forget her heartbreak and enjoy the day for Leah's sake. After all, her best friend had dropped everything to come on this trip with her when she and Nick had the huge argument on his birthday.

Putting her arm about Poppy's shoulders, Leah grinned. 'If you give me the chance to find my true love up there, I promise to go to all the museums you want.'

'Really? You'll come with me to the Louvre and Sacre Coeur and—'

'Yes, yes, yes!' Leah rolled her eyes. 'We'll go everywhere you want. I swear.'

Poppy took a deep breath as they entered the elevator and were squashed in the corner behind a large man with bad body odour. 'I'm telling you, it's just a tourist slogan, that's all. People don't *find* their true love on the deck. They are supposed to *go* there *with* their true love. We aren't in *Sleepless in Seattle*, you know.'

Wiggling for room, Leah smiled and nodded towards the large man just inches from them. 'I think I've found him.'

The doors opened and Poppy held Leah's arm as they spluttered with laughter. The large man frowned at them, and they laughed even more.

'Oh, he's nice.' Leah pointed to a tall good-looking guy standing to the right of them. 'Paris is full of hot guys, have you noticed?'

'Wow. This is fantastic.' Poppy walked away from the crowds a little bit and stared out at the magnificent view. Paris lay before her in the brilliant sunshine. Below, the river Seine shimmered like a dark blue ribbon while the city buildings stretched as far as the eye could see in all directions. Poppy fell in love, not with one of the many men Leah was goggling, but with the city spread out before her like a colourful blanket. She wanted to see it all, to feel and smell, touch and taste all Paris had to offer. Her pulse raced at the magic of being somewhere special.

Leah touched her arm. 'Look at him, he's rather lovely.'

Distracted, Poppy idly glanced at the man Leah indicated and then she smiled as his partner came up and offered him a drink from her water bottle. 'Aww, better luck next time,' Poppy murmured in Leah's ear. 'Try to find someone single.'

'Let's go over the other side.' Leah tossed her long dark hair in the careless way she had. '*He'll* be here somewhere. I only have to find him.'

'Don't bet on it.' Poppy followed her while taking her camera out of her bag and getting it ready to take photos. She wanted to capture every moment of this trip. Who knew when she'd ever come back? And she'd need happy memories to think of once she returned home and sorted out the mess with Nick. Her heart constricted at the thought of him. She wasn't proud of the way she acted that day during the argument. Losing her temper and behaving like a crazy woman wasn't going to get her far, but there were times when saying what you mean helps to relieve the stress. Bottling everything up was stupid. Communication. All the self-help relationship books said couples had to talk. Well, she'd shouted, screamed, yelled and finally swore before walking out. Twenty minutes later she arrived at Leah's in a flood of tears, and then proceeded to get very drunk - so drunk she threw her phone into the fishbowl when Nick rang.

She knew Nick had a heavy work schedule, but just once, she wanted him to put her first. Just once, she wanted to be in the forefront of his plans. Did he honestly think that working 24/7 was healthy for their relationship? Did making money give him comfort at night when he was alone in their bed?

She sighed and focused on the amazing scenery before her. But it did no good. She ached for Nick. Longed to see him, feel his arms around, hear his voice and see his cheeky smile.

'Hello.'

As if she'd dreamed him up, she blinked and stared as Nick suddenly stood in front of her. 'Nick?'

No, it couldn't be. He was back home, in Australia, on some business trip...

'Surprise.'

'Nick?'

'How are you, gorgeous girl?' He smiled the smile she loved and the way he said the nickname he called her sent tingles down her body to her toes.

'I... what... how...' Poppy frowned, not able to think or speak. The shock of seeing Nick here sent her mind spinning.

'After you left, I realised I'd been an idiot.' He looked sheepish. 'I made a mistake. I'm sorry.'

Tears burned hot behind her eyes. 'I thought you couldn't get away, some big deal to sort out...'

'I did.' He let out a deep breath. 'But nothing is worth losing you over. I stuffed up. I let work take over my life, but once you'd gone, I soon learnt how much I love you.'

'I can't go back to how it was. I won't be put second again, Nick. I'm tired of going to functions by myself, of spending nights in front of the TV alone, or cancelling dinner reservations. I want to be in a relationship where I actually spend time with my boyfriend, not see him when he can fit me in between appointments.'

'It'll be different, I promise. I'll cut down my workload. It doesn't have to be that time-consuming, I just thought you wanted all the good things money can buy.'

'I'd rather have you, actually.'

'I love you, Pop.' His tender gaze tore at her emotions.

'I love you, too.' She gave him a shy smile.

As one they stepped forward and hugged each other tight. She closed her eyes, filling her senses with the feel and smell of him. It was heaven to be in his arms. It was where she belonged, where she was the happiest.

He suddenly dropped to one knee and from his jean pocket brought out a small black velvet box.

Poppy gasped as he opened it and there, on a white satin bed, sat a diamond ring.

'Will you marry me, Poppy?'

She heard Leah scream with delight from somewhere in the group of people who were openly watching Nick's proposal.

'Poppy?' Alarm was written on Nick's face, alarm and fear.

'Yes.' She grinned and cried at the same time. 'Yes, I will!' As Nick picked her up in a tight bear hug, the crowd cheered and clapped. When Nick kissed her, it was like their first kiss, only better. It was a kiss of apology, of promise...a kiss to seal a pact to love one another for always.

Pulling apart, Nick gazed down at Poppy. 'I couldn't let you fall in love with Paris without being there to see it.'

'You know me so well.' She sighed in pure happiness. 'Let's experience it together.'

As they walked hand in hand back to the elevators, Leah sidled up beside Poppy. 'See, I told you that you find true love up here.' She kissed Poppy's cheek and gave a conspirator's wink at Nick.

A Hometown Boy

Astler Plain was a town that once you had left it, you never really went back again. Generations of long-standing families married other generations of long-standing families and that was cycle. In the dry blistering bush of country Australia, life was laid back and enjoyed. Nothing happened in Astler Plain that someone else did not find out about. No one gossiped, of course. Instead, they simply *cared* about what happened to the people of their town. Information was relayed in over the fence conversations, accidental meetings in the corner shop and long telephone discussions.

Occasionally, someone would venture to the big smoke, but they usually returned saying they couldn't cope with the impersonal city people and all the rushing about everyone did.

However, on one occasion, a local boy did leave their town and made good. He was the small town's highly regarded home-grown boy, Kane Daniels. The darling of the town, their one claim to fame. Teenaged girls loved him. The highflyer who appeared on the TV talk shows and in magazines, the one who dated beautiful women and partied hard.

The one who had broken his mother's heart.

There was no applause for him this day, his first day back home since leaving as a fresh-faced youth. No fanfare, no honorary dinner given by the mayor, no homecoming at all.

On this scorching, lifeless day, Kane shrugged off his black leather jacket and stared around Main Street, shaking his head at how nothing in the town had changed. But then, in one small way it had. For within a few hours, his Mum, the much-admired Beryl Daniels would be buried in the graveyard of the old church. While living, she had longed for him to return home, and now he had, to attend her funeral. He ignored the pang of guilt that often flared whenever he thought of his mother.

'Why, is that you, Kane?' A woman paused nearby. She was of retirement age, with light grey hair, intelligent eyes and a thin figure of someone who was very active.

'Yes, I am.' He leaned against his dark blue BMW and crossed his arms. Allowing her the time to fully recognise him. For a moment he wondered if he should have brought his personal assistant but dismissed the thought. Signing a few autographs in this backwater wouldn't lead to much.

'There was talk that you wouldn't come back,' she told him, adjusting her basket on her arm. Her stance was one of disapproval.

'I think I would attend my own mother's funeral, don't you?' he snapped. That's all he needed, some gossiping old hag selling her story to the newspapers about his lack of love for his mother.

The older woman shrugged. 'You don't remember me, do you?'

Kane squinted at her in the bright harsh light of midday, even though he had expensive sunglasses on. 'No, sorry.'

'I taught you for a year before you left for Sydney. I'm Miss Worthington.'

'Really? I cannot remember you.' He glanced away, bored.

'Well, you were hardly the best in class. Good day.' Miss Worthington gave him a false smile and walked away.

Kane frowned. His mobile phone rang, and he looked at it distastefully before turning it off. Would they never leave him alone? For once he wanted a few hours of peace to talk to his brother, meet his dad and not have to worry about work.

Hot and thirsty, he walked across the wide road, amazed at the lack of traffic and people. There were few cars parked along Main Street and hardly a soul to be seen. He had forgotten that nearly everyone stayed indoors and out of the heat of midday. Shopping was done in the mornings and visiting was kept for afternoon when the sun was setting, and the heat lifted a little.

Entering the pub, Kane relished the cool interior. A poster showed that the pub had celebrated its centenary last year and the decor reflected bygone times with dark timber fittings and subdued lighting. There was no fancy artwork or the bright colours of modern clubs here. The large bar room was covered in testaments to a town proud of its history. Glass cabinets displayed cricket trophies and silver rugby cups. Framed photos of winning horses and jockeys from the local horse racing carnivals, plus a hundred more pictures and memorabilia adorned the walls.

Kane studied some of the photos while waiting for someone to serve him. He nodded to an old man sitting at the bar cradling a beer.

A pretty young woman came out of a door at the end of the bar and Kane flashed the wide smile he used whenever he needed someone's sole attention. As usual he got it.

She smiled. 'What can I get you?'

'A rum and coke, thanks.' He liked the sound of her voice, soft and deep, rather sexy, actually.

Leaning an elbow on the polished surface of the high bar, Kane placed his money down. Suddenly, he noticed a familiar face in a photo that stood on a shelf behind the woman. Peering hard, he could just make out his brother's face, but not the writing beneath.

'Can you tell me what it says under the picture there?' Kane asked her.

'It says that your brother,' the old man answered before the barmaid could speak, 'scored a hundred and fifty-two runs to help his team win the grand final in the district cricket.'

'Really?' Kane was impressed. He had known nothing about it. He had no idea Blake could play grade cricket, or any other sport. It had been a long time since they fought over their backyard kid's games.

'Over there...' The old man pointed over his shoulder to the display cabinet. 'Are four championship cups with your brother's name on them, as there is on the dart's banner above your head. His name is at the top of the snooker board as well!'

'I'm impressed!' Kane snorted and pulled a face. 'Obviously, he spends a lot of time in this pub!' His sarcasm hit its mark as the old man bristled.

'He's a fine sportsman! He doesn't spend his time poncing around with make up on his face!'

Kane felt the warm flush creep up his cheeks. 'So, you know who I am then?'

'Your mother was proud of you.' The old man shrugged as if that meant nothing, and then sighed. 'Bless the poor woman. At least you came home for her funeral.'

'Did people think I wouldn't?' Stung, Kane gave him a cutting glare.

'You've not come home before.'

'I don't have to explain myself to you.' Kane glanced from the old fellow to the cute woman behind the bar, who was smiling softly at him in sympathy. The kindness in her hazel eyes touched him.

'No doubt your brother will be glad to see you.' The old geezer mumbled. 'Blake had to deal with it all, as usual. He's a good lad. Your dad couldn't do without him.'

Kane gulped down his drink and then strode out of the bar. He had no wish to stay and hear more of his brother's achievements. What did it matter if Blake was the town's sport hero, or his dad's favourite? Had any of them made the enormous amount of money that he had? Gone were the days of doing chores for his parents to earn a few cents for an ice cream. The whole lot of them would be truly shocked if they knew how much money he spent in one night at the casino whenever he was in Las Vegas. Had *they* shaken the hand of royalty at movie premieres, or seen the world?

No. None of them had risen to the glory of stardom as he had. Christ, most hadn't ever left this little dust-filled town!

Outside, the heat hit him full on and he cursed as sweat broke out on his forehead. He hated to sweat! He walked back across the road, taking his car keys out of his trouser pocket.

Coming out of the hairdressers opposite, a tall willowy woman with long black hair stopped and stared at him.

'Hayley?' Kane called, grinning. His mood lightened instantly. Good-looking women always put him in a better mood.

She stepped to the edge of the road. She wore a soft lemon coloured summer dress and looked cool and confident. 'Hello, Kane.'

He winked. 'You look great, sweetheart.'

'Thank you.' Though, she didn't return the compliment, he realised.

Kane tossed his head and did his best to act nonchalant and not the gawky teenager he abruptly felt like. He could not believe how beautiful she had become.

She had always been pretty when they were younger, but with maturity she was a stunner. He recalled the times they had gone out together. She had been so full of life and spirit. So many times, they had kissed and rolled about in the tall grasses down by the creek at the end of town. She had been his girl for the last year before he had left for Sydney. God, she had made him hot for her and teenage hormones had done the rest.

He had never thought to write to her though and he frowned at that. Life had become too busy once he arrived in the city. Back then, he had to work hard to be noticed, to be given work that would eventually take him to the dizzy heights of Hollywood. The teenage girls of his past were quickly forgotten in the quest to be a star.

'How are you?' she asked.

'Good. Good. And you?'

'Fine. I am sorry about your mum. She was a wonderful woman and I miss her. She was well loved and respected by everyone.'

Puzzled, his eyes widened. 'Were you two friends?'

'Yes, of course.'

'I didn't know.'

Hayley's deep blue eyes smouldered. 'There are a lot of things you don't know about what has been happening here.'

'I've been away for a long time.'

'So, you have.'

He grinned, wanting his charm to knock her over and into his arms. 'Did you miss me?'

'At first, yes, but it was so long ago, wasn't it?' She shrugged. 'No letters from you soon had me forgetting all about you.'

He swallowed and tried another tack to win her over. 'Have you travelled at all? I have been filming in India for the last few months, and before that I was in France for a year.'

'And they don't have any form of communication there?' Hayley raised her eyebrows.

He was taken aback by her attitude. What was wrong with everyone in this bloody town? 'What's it to you?'

Hayley gave a snort. 'I can't recall how many times I sat and listened to your mother say how much she longed to just receive a postcard from you, let alone a phone call!'

'That is none of your business!' Kane protested, instantly defensive.

'No, it isn't. See you.' She turned away from him and walked down the street only to turn into a shop and out of sight.

Kane sighed and unlocked his car. Out of habit he turned his phone back on again and saw he had eight missed calls, he cared less.

Starting the engine, he sat back in the seat discontented. The reception he'd received since his arrival had not been at all what he thought it would be like. There had been no hand shaking, no backslapping. Old friends didn't line the street saying they enjoyed his movies or asked for his autograph. He always thought that his homecoming would be so different from this.

He drove down Main Street, turned right into First Street and continued on until the bitumen road became dirt. Dust clouds rose about him. He swore under his breath. 'Damn! The car will have a coat of dust an inch thick!'

At least he was cool with the air conditioning on.

Soon, he slowed down and turned into a gravel driveway. There it was, his old home. He had not seen it for fifteen years.

Kane cut the engine and stared at the old, white-painted house with its tin roof and wide front veranda. The same flowering bushes grew along the front wall, planted some thirty years ago by his mother. At the side of the house was the old shed and garage and beyond that, the corrugated water tank and stand of fruit trees.

Memories flooded back. Days of sweltering heat that he and his brother had hardly been aware of as they swam, kicked balls, climbed trees, rode bikes and fought and laughed. Everything looked smaller, older. Yet, a warm embrace of love filled his heart. Home. His real home. The home none of his movie star friends knew about.

But no Mum. No one to reach for him with love in their eyes.

The sight and sound of his car brought a strange sandy brown dog out from behind the shed. It came to the car and cocked its leg to pee on the wheel. Kane frowned at it. The old dog they had as kids had been small and white.

An elderly white-haired man came out of the house. Dad. He hadn't seen his dad in twelve years, since they last met in Sydney. Kane blinked in surprise. His father was now an elderly man. When had that happened? Where was the tall, well-built man of his youth?

His father stood staring at the dark blue BMW, obviously wondering who could possibly be behind its black-tinted windows.

Kane opened the car door and got out. He stood tall, but uncertain of his father's response after all these years. 'Hello, Dad.' It felt strange saying those words. He hadn't said them for a while. His heart thumped.

'Kane?'

'Yes, Dad.'

'How did you know?'

'Blake got an email to me, through my agent.'

'A what?'

'An email, by computer.'

'Whatever.' Harold Daniels dismissed what he didn't know with ease. Kane smiled sadly. Nothing ever changed.

His father scowled in the harsh sunlight. 'I was on my way to the shed. I thought I would fix the mower.'

Kane nodded and followed him into the tin shed where the heat was so acute, he couldn't breathe. He loosened two top buttons of his silk shirt and groaned as sweat beaded once more on his forehead and back. His father turned the mower upside down and with a spanner he began to tighten its nuts and bolts.

'Dad, maybe you shouldn't do this in your good suit?' Kane said.

'It'll be right.'

'Shall I go inside and make us a drink?'

'There's a beer in that fridge over there, if you want one.' His father pointed to an ancient fridge in the corner.

Kane opened the fridge door and smiled at the rows of beer cans. 'Do you want one?'

'No, your mother wouldn't like it. I was never allowed to drink before going out. She thought it to be bad manners.'

Kane stared at his father's bent head in amazement at the mention of his mother. Closing the door, he stared up at a large cobweb suspended from the ceiling. A lump of emotion clogged his throat. 'Did...did she suffer much? Blake told me in the e-mail, that it was breast cancer.'

'I don't want to talk about it.'

'I just wanted to know that's all.'

'Well, if you'd been here, you would've known, wouldn't you?'

'If I had known she was ill, I would have come home. But no one thought to let me know.' Kane walked to the door. Swift anger and frustration ate away at him. An inner voice tried to speak about his own neglect, but he shied away from its damning accusations.

'For fifteen years your mother has looked down that drive waiting for you to come home. You didn't have to stay long, just a few days, that's all she wanted. But you didn't. You broke her heart, and I'll not be forgiving you in a hurry.'

Kane spun to stare at his father. 'I'm sorry! I didn't think-'

'No, you didn't think, that's your problem.'

Kane desperately tried not to feel hurt by his dad's words. If his dad had ranted and raved at him, he could have handled it, but the soft tone, the uncaring way he spoke hurt more than anything he had ever experienced.

'Maybe, I shouldn't stay here then?'

His dad didn't look up. 'Maybe you shouldn't.'

He left the shed and walked back to his car. The ache in his heart was a new pain to him. His phone rang again, and the dog began barking near his legs. Kane swore at the phone and then at the dog, before turning the phone off once more. He went to open the car door, when he saw an old Ford utility come down the drive. He waited until it stopped beside him.

Instantly, Blake leapt out of his vehicle and ran around to hug his brother. 'Kane!' Tears ran freely down his brother's face.

Kane clasped Blake hard, glad at last of someone being pleased to see him. 'How are you?' He gazed at his strong handsome brother, surprised by the likeable man he saw.

'Okay. Are you staying for a few days?' Blake stood back and wiped his cheeks.

'I don't know.' Kane shrugged, embarrassed by his brother's emotions.

'Come inside and have a drink.'

'No, I won't, thanks. Dad's not too keen on me, I'm afraid.'

Blake looked from him to their father, who had just come to the shed door to watch them. 'We'll go into town then.'

'How long have we got until the service?' Kane inquired.

'An hour and a half. It's at three o'clock.'

'How about we go for a drive, and you can show me the old places we used to go to?'

Blake nodded. 'Okay, sure.'

They went in Kane's car, because of the air conditioning.

Blake marvelled at the power the sleek car had. 'I've never been in a BMW before.' He grinned like a boy as Kane put it through its paces on the empty dirt tracks around town.

Eventually, they stopped by the thin creek, at the end of town, and got out to stand under the huge willow tree, which overhung the trickling water.

'You've been gone too many years, Kane. Not that I blame you. This town is nothing much to come back to, but Mum missed you, and so did I.' Blake bent to pick up a pebble.

'I know.' Kane finally admitted, more to himself than Blake.

'I would've liked you to have been here for my wedding.'

'I'm sorry, but I was in the middle of making a movie in Spain.' Kane shot Blake a quick look, because it wasn't really the truth. He had been in Spain but sailing around on a yacht impressing rich movie producers and bedding models, not making a picture. 'So, where is the lovely misses, then?' he joked, trying to lighten the conversation.

'Hayley is at her shop. She owns the hairdresser shop in Main Street.'

'Hayley? Hayley Christopher?' Kane was flabbergasted.

'Why, yes. Didn't Mum write you?' Blake was bemused.

'Er...um, yes, I think so.' Kane urgently combed his memory for what information he had received about his brother's wedding last year. He couldn't believe the sudden hurt he felt about his brother marrying the one girl he had really liked! He had even thought about asking her out for a meal after the funeral service and making amends with her. He groaned. His brother had got the best girl in town.

'I'm so glad we were able to tell mum before she died that Hayley was pregnant.' Blake's voice cracked with emotion. 'Mum was so pleased.'

'Hayley's pregnant? She didn't look it when I saw her when I arrived.' Kane accused. This was all so absurd. He couldn't take it in.

'Did you see her?' Blake smiled. 'When I told her that I had sent your agent an e-mail, she said you wouldn't turn up.'

'Did she?' Kane was suddenly angry. Hurt and rejection filled him. It was a sod awful day.

'Boy, it was a horrible time. I had just said good-bye to Mum for the last time, and afterwards all I wanted to do was get in contact with you. Sam Flanders, you remember him, the accountant? Anyway, he was the first person I saw, and I was in a bit of a mess. So, he took me to his office and said he would send your agent an e-mail from his laptop. He wrote it and everything, because I don't know much about computers and the Internet. There's not much call for those as a mechanic.' Blake gave a wry smile.

'It's all a bit of a nightmare.' Kane mumbled. 'I never thought I would come home to this.'

'I thought you would never come home, period!' Blake scoffed.

Kane threw a pebble into the creek. He had left town to find fame and fortune and for all these years he had thought himself happy. But looking at his brother now, he knew he lived a half-life, a plastic life full of plastic people and possessions. 'Your life is good, isn't it?' He confirmed, knowing the truth already.

'Yeah, it is. So, is yours, isn't it? All that money, gorgeous women and partying.'

'I thought it was but coming back here makes me think differently.'

Blake gave him a strange look. 'But you have everything!'

'Yes, I do, and that's the problem. I've seen the world, met famous people and made more money than is decent. There's nothing left for me to do.' Kane stared out into the distance. His statement shocked him. When had he started to think like this?

'Well, it's more than anyone else around here has done.'

'You don't understand. I am surrounded by people, but no one interests me. I fill my apartment with women, but no one stays. That is my life.'

'I'm finding it hard to feel sorry for you,' Blake admitted, with a shy smile.

Kane went back to the car. He didn't comment as Blake joined him and together, they sat in silence, deep in thought, as they stared out of the windscreen at the creek and surrounding dry grassy fields.

After a while, Kane started the engine and they drove back into town. Kane dropped Blake off at the hairdressers and told him he would see him at the service. He then drove to the Church and parked the car under some shady trees.

No one had yet arrived, and he walked over to the graveyard to kill time. He felt numb in mind and sick at heart. The one true family he had were either gone or strangers to him. He had been too busy living his frenzied and adoring life to stop and realise what he was missing.

He was ashamed for ignoring his family and even more so about his mother. The feeling of guilt was new to him, and he didn't like it. As an actor, he was used to playing with diverse emotions, but this was different. He wasn't a character in a scene this time, he was just a troubled and lonely man and the thought depressed him.

Kane abruptly stopped, for there in front of him, was the dirt mound of his mother's own grave. The dark cavernous hole yawned before him, as if mocking him. No matter how famous or how rich he was, one day he too, would have one dug for him.

Who would mourn Kane Daniels?

The sight choked him. He stumbled backwards. Groping blindly, he turned to get away from the scene. He had to get out of there, but when he rounded the corner of the church, he saw the funeral director arrive with his mother's coffin covered in flowers in the back of the hearse.

Kane staggered. He had loved her, his dear old Mum.

His feet had a will of their own and before he was aware of it, he was running. Running from the churchyard, from the sight of his mother's coffin and from the hole in the ground into which she would soon be lowered.

He kept on running, even when the sweat began to trickle down his back. He ran through the bush, across fields, stumbled through a creek and on and on, until he couldn't breathe and there was a stitch in his side.

At last, when he could run no more, he collapsed onto the ground under a large eucalyptus tree. He lay gasping, holding his sides and moaning. His pain was too great. He sobbed out his grief, his loneliness, his heartbreak.

For how long he laid there, he didn't know or cared. Through tear-drenched eyes, he watched the sun slowly set behind the gum trees and was thankful for the coolness of the twilight evening. Native birds called out; sounds he'd not heard since he was a youth. They reminded him of long hot summers with Blake, of eating his mum's lamingtons after school. They reminded him of a life when he had been happy and carefree.

He felt empty, numb. Not knowing what to do or where to go.

'Hello there,' a soft voice came from behind him. 'Are you all right?'

Kane spun around and scrambled to his feet. 'Er...I'm sorry...' He swayed, dazed, not knowing why he was sorry. With his sleeve, he wiped the moisture from his eyes.

He felt sore, physically and emotionally. Drained.

'Please, it's okay.' The young woman raised her hands to show him no harm. 'Are you hurt? Lost?'

Kane looked around and realised he didn't know where he was. The thought alarmed him at first and he turned to look at the woman more closely for some clue. She was not very tall, just over five feet. She had long dark blonde hair and soft brown eyes. She was petite, but well proportioned. She wore a long dress of different shades of purple and jewelled sandals that suited the gypsy air about her.

Even in his misery, Kane liked the look of her.

'I live over there, through those trees.' She pointed to the west of where they stood. 'Would you like to come and have a drink?' she invited, with a smile.

'Um...I don't know.' For once in his life, he was speechless.

'My name is Shelly Sunderland.'

'I'm Kane Daniels.' He waited for the expected reaction when she realised who he was but was there was none forthcoming, and he was glad. He didn't want an idolising puppet around him at this moment. He wanted someone real.

'Call me, Shelly. Can I call you Kane?'

'Yes.' He gave her another quick look and took a deep breath. He seemed rooted to the spot. He couldn't go forward or back. He experienced a moment's panic until she stepped closer and softly touched his arm.

'It's okay.'

He nodded.

They walked on with just the noise of the birds flying overhead and the breeze rustling the leaves high in the trees. Kane was pleasantly surprised when they came to her house. Built of stone and nestled in amongst gum and wattle trees, the cottage looked quaint. Geese and ducks roamed the wild vegetable garden, and a cat stretched its legs from its comfy position on the stone step.

Kane followed her onto the cool verandah and sat on the cane chair she had offered, before she went inside to get the drinks.

He sucked in a deep breath and slowly exhaled. He felt naked. Stripped of everything that made him who he was. What the hell was happening to him?

Shelly returned with the drinks tray and set it down on a small timber table. 'I hope you like iced tea with lemon?'

'Yes, I do. Thank you.'

She lit scented candles and they sat quietly listening to the sounds of the crickets chirping in the darkening twilight while sipping their drinks. It was a comfortable silence between them until Shelly reached behind her chair and picked up her guitar. She began to softly play.

Her sweet tunes soothed Kane and he relaxed his stiff shoulders, as the tension gradually left him. He liked the sound of her voice and for once in his life, he was content to just sit and listen.

'That was nice,' he said, when she finally put down her guitar.

'Thanks. Do you play?'

'No, unfortunately.' He smiled briefly.

'Music is good for the soul. It lets the mind and body flow in harmony.'

'For me that would be handy.' Kane joked ruefully, feeling a little better now.

They were silent for a moment, then headlights coming through the trees had them turning to watch. The car drove along the dirt road some distance away and then it turned into the drive and headed for the cottage.

'They must be looking for you. I never get visitors.' Shelly said.

'Most likely.' Kane found himself wishing they hadn't. He didn't want to return to the reality of his life just yet. It had been so good to just sit here with someone who was a complete stranger. Shelly didn't want to know all about him, she had only asked his name and nothing more. She didn't inflict her thoughts and opinions on him. She was just happy to share her songs and help him relax, she wanted no more and that was another first for him.

The car stopped close to the verandah and Blake got out and came to them. 'Kane? Are you okay? I've been looking for you.'

'He's fine now,' Shelley said, holding her hand out to Blake. 'We've not been introduced before, but I've seen you in town. I'm Shelley.'

'Blake.' He shook her hand. 'Thanks for taking care of him.' Blake turned put his hand on Kane's shoulder. 'Are you all right?'

'Yes. Sorry. I just couldn't face it.' Kane shrugged, ashamed of his cowardice. He was amazed at himself for such behaviour, but he'd had no control over it. He had walked on a knife's edge for so long and didn't even know it until today. His whole world had imploded on him.

Blake nodded. 'I understand. It was a bit hard. Do you want to come back with me and pick up your car?'

'I suppose I should.' He looked from Blake to Shelly. For some reason he felt less than pleased to leave her.

As if sensing his indecision, she smiled. 'You could always come back, if you have nowhere to sleep. This cottage only has one bedroom, but there is a caravan out the back that I use when I travel around the country. It's comfortable.'

Kane took another deep breath as though cleansing his mind and soul. 'Yes, I would like that.'

'I leave tomorrow to travel to the east coast. Maybe you could stay here, and house sit for me? All it will cost you is your food,' she explained. She didn't know that money was not a problem for him.

'You're going away?' He didn't like the thought.

'For a few weeks, but I always come back. It gives the town's gossips something to talk about. They love the fact that they have their very own hippy!' She laughed.

Blake nodded and grinned. 'That's true.'

Shelly collected their empty glasses. 'I live a simple life here. The electricity is from a generator, but only for the fridge and the one light bulb in the kitchen. You get hot water by the wood stove and that is also the only way to cook. There is a well-stocked pantry of chutneys and pickles and a large vegetable garden too. You will have to chop wood and feed the animals, but if you need a rest from the world than this is the best place. You will not be disturbed.'

'I am seriously considering this!' Kane scratched his head, dazed at the way things had changed for him. He urgently needed a rest, some time out from the craziness that he once craved more than anything.

'It might be just what you need, Brother.' Blake patted him on the back. 'And Mum would like to know you are near, if only for a while.'

Kane nodded; tears sprung to his eyes. He looked at his brother and realised with a desperate longing that he wanted to spend time with him and get to know him properly. Maybe, even talk to his dad again.

'Thank you, Shelly. I will accept.' He smiled at her, accepting the pain from the loss of his mother and the neglect she had suffered because of him.

It abruptly became clear to him, that maybe, just maybe he could live here away from the world and just chill out for a while. He would read a few quality movie scripts, but that was all in the way of work. Instead, he would take care of this cottage, the garden and animals. He would have responsibilities and be responsible. He might even get the chance to get to know his family again, and, who knows, maybe find himself.

What did he stand for?

What were his principles? He didn't know, but perhaps he now had the chance to find out.

Shelly gave him a long look, one full of promise. 'I'll make us something to eat for when you get back.'

As they drove down the dirt road, Kane kept thinking of the choice he'd just made, and of Shelly. 'Do you know much about her, Shelly?'

Blake shrugged on shoulder. 'Not much. She's been living in that cottage for a few years and doesn't mix with people much, but she seems nice when anyone does talk to her at the shops or wherever. She sang at the local fete last year and was a hit. I like her and she's stunning.'

'Do you think I'm weird to stay with her?' Maybe he'd been too hasty in agreeing?

'Seriously Kane, you need some time to relax. You're a mess. Look at what happened today. We're lucky Shelly found you. You could have got lost in the bush.' Blake turned onto the tarred road and headed into town.

'I know. Stupid of me to run like that.'

'Shelly is leaving, she said, so you'll have the place to yourself. Have a break from your crazy world.'

Kane let out a long breath. 'I'm going to.' He just didn't like the thought of Shelly not being at the cottage too.

When Kane pulled up in front of the cottage a short time later, he cut the engine and climbed out. Lights in the cottage window gave a welcome and he grabbed his luggage out from the car and went up onto the verandah.

Shelly greeted him at the door and took his laptop case from him. 'Just in time. Everything is ready.'

'Thanks. I hope you didn't put yourself out too much?'

'Not at all. Just a simple meal for two. It's nice to cook for someone else.' She showed him where to dump his luggage in the front room and then led the way into the kitchen at the back which was painted bright yellow and any containers that held water had flowers stuffed into them.

A pine tale was set for two on bright red placemats, with different sized candles lit in the middle. A breadbasket sat to one side along with a bowl of mixed salad. The chairs didn't match but each had a coloured comfy cushion and, on the bench, Shelly had a bottle of wine breathing.

The smell of chicken frying made Kane's mouth water. 'Is there anything I can do to help?'

She smiled over her shoulder. 'Pour some wine?'

'Gladly.' He filled two glasses while she plated up the meal and then they sat at the table. It surprised how at ease he felt in her company, not only that, but also the realisation he didn't feel the need to make small talk.

'Please, eat.' She encouraged him, while loading up her own plate with salad.

They ate and drank in silence for a short time, the only sound was soft music coming from the stereo.

In the candlelight, Kane studied Shelly, subtly watching her eat. She had delicate hands, small and nimble fingers. When she lifted her glass to her lips, he caught her gaze and felt the irritable pull of sexual attraction. Damn, he didn't want that now, not that complication.

He cleared his throat. 'So, when do you leave?'

'The day after tomorrow.' She reclined back in the chair. 'It's flexible.'

'You're amazing to let a stranger live in your house while you're away.'

'Your family is known in the town and are good people. I doubt you'll do any damage or hold wild parties.'

'No, no parties, I can guarantee that.' The thought made him shudder. He'd partied enough to last him many years.

'And I have nothing worth stealing.' She gave him a simple smile. 'Besides, I believe in karma. You do good things for others, and it comes back around.'

'Karma...' he said doubtfully. What did he believe in?

'And if you find living here isn't to your liking, just leave the key under one of the hen boxes and tell old Mrs Lambert that you're leaving. She'll see to the animals. She lives up the road, first house you come to on the right before town.'

'I won't be leaving. I need this rest.' He sipped the last of his wine.

'Well, there's plenty of jobs around the place should you become bored.' Picking up his plate, she paused halfway to the kitchen. 'Who knows, I might come home to find you so happy here you'll never want to leave.'

'My agent and manager might have something to say about that.' He grinned, clearing the table for her.

'You could always make a film out here, you know.'

Shocked, he stared at her. 'You know who I am?'

'Of course. I do manage to read the odd magazine and see one or two movies now and then.' A teasing glint lit her eyes.

'I just want to be normal, for a while.'

She filled the sink with hot soapy water. 'You just wanted to be home for a while, Kane. That is what's normal.'

'I've behaved badly. I'm desperately ashamed of what I've done, especially to my mum.'

'Then make her proud now. Make it up to your family. Be a better man.'

'I'm going to try.' And he was going to. He knew he'd toppled over a precipice. He'd fallen and landed with a thump that knocked some sense into him. He gave Shelly a brief smile, still amazed at her kindness, her generosity. She was beautiful inside and out and he wanted to keep her in his life. 'I will be a better man, Shelly.'

'Then start by drying the dishes.' She laughed.

He grinned and grabbed a tea towel.

Let it Snow

Hannah applied the brakes, slowing the corner as it rounded a sharp bend. Thick forest edged both sides of the dirt lane, the tall trees walling her in. She held her breath, trying to keep the claustrophobia at bay.

The rutted track swept around another turn, always climbing higher. The SatNav had long given up on trying to redirect her back to another route, closer to civilisation. She'd turned it off at the bottom of the mountain and without a decent radio signal the car had become eerily silent.

Without warning, not even a simple sign, the road stopped and in front of her was the timber lodge; her destination – the one place where there wasn't a scrap of evidence of Christmas.

Leaving the car, she stared at the lodge, ignoring for a moment the biting cold wind. Perched on an open grassy plateau, the building faced the elements but also gave a commanding view of the valley below. In summer it would be glorious, but on a freezing winter's day, with the sullen grey clouds seemingly just above her head, the lodge looked cold and uninviting.

But then what had she expected?

Hiring this place for a month to write her book had been impulsive, not to say a tad irresponsible perhaps. She'd used up all her allocated holidays from work to escape here. Little did her boss know that she wasn't going back. After her month staying here, she was using the rest of her savings to travel, to explore the world. She'd become a backpacker, stay in hostels, live cheap and easy.

The wind whipped her hair into her eyes and penetrated the jeans and jacket she wore. Hurrying back to the car, she grabbed her bag and headed to the covered porch. The key turned smoothly in the door, and she stepped in gingerly, not knowing what she'd find. However, she relaxed her shoulders in relief as she surveyed the open plan layout. The kitchen on her left was separated from the main room by an island worktop. Large leather sofas with throw rugs and cushions looked cosy on either side of the wide fireplace. A pine dining table and chairs were placed in front of the floor to ceiling windows, which over-looked the valley. The view was spectacular, the mountain range with its deep wooded valley went on for miles.

Remembering the instructions from Sally, her work colleague whom she had rented this from, she returned to the door and studied the panel on the wall next to it. With a flick of a few switches, she turned on the heating and electricity. The microwave beeped into life and the oven clock flashed the wrong time in neon green.

Climbing the spiral iron staircase, she inspected the two bedrooms and little bathroom before claiming the double room with its tiny ensuite as hers.

After several trips out to the car, she filled the kitchen with boxes of groceries, her suitcase, laptop and a bag of books. Out of breath and hungry, she finally closed the door and locked it. Done. She had shut out the world.

She'd been told that there was phone signal here, for at this height the phone companies used the mountain range to build their towers, and with a smile she realised Sally had been telling the truth. Full bars on her phone! She could use her own Wi-Fi hotspot and have the internet. Out of habit she checked for messages, and seeing none, felt instantly let down.

Nothing from Edward.

Her heart lurched at the thought of him.

A radio sat on the kitchen windowsill and Hannah turned it on to drown out the silence and her own thoughts. Popular music kept her company as she unpacked the food she'd brought. For some reason in amongst the food basics of bread, rice, butter, soup and whatnot, a large amount of chocolates had squirreled its way in, plus, and here Hannah grinned like a naughty child, a large bottle of vodka and the required bottles of Cointreau and cranberry juice, and a few limes! Who needed people to have a party? And not a single Christmas thing in sight!

Sleety rain splattering against the windows made her jump. The sudden downfall obscured the valley, the low clouds seemed to be within reaching distance from the edge of the plateau.

Popping the kettle on, Hannah made a cheese melt and put it under the grill. She kept staring at the fireplace, all set ready for a match to light it. She loved an open fire. Yes, they were messy but, on a cold wet winter's afternoon, there was nothing better than sitting in front of one. Finding some matches in a drawer, she lit the paper bundles under the kindling and watched as the fire caught and grew. She found it rather hypnotic and wonderfully soothing.

The rest of the afternoon was spent listening to music while unpacking her clothes and toiletries and pretending she didn't care that Edward hadn't texted her. Stuff him.

With a sigh she flopped down on the sofa. The lodge didn't possess a television, but she could have watched something on her laptop, but she couldn't be bothered starting it up. Outside the snow drifted gently, enclosing her in a white world of her own.

Her phone beeped and Hannah nearly broke her ankle trying to get to it as fast as she could. Heart thumping, she looked at the screen. A message from her mother. Not Edward.

Fighting back the disappointment, she texted back that she was fine, and the lodge was lovely.

Dejected, she grabbed the bag of assorted chocolates and sat back on the sofa, ignoring the response from her mother, who at this moment was cruising the Med with her new boyfriend as her Christmas treat. How was it that her mother had a better social and love life than she did?

The chocolate bar made her feel better, as at the same time, one of her favourite dancing songs came on the radio.

She grabbed a pen and notebook from her bag and started to make a list.

Edward has gone. She underlined this.

Left job.

Have enough money to live on for a few months.

Need to finish writing my book.

Travel.

Write a travel blog?

She tapped her pen by the side of her cheek, thinking of each one on the list. On paper it didn't look so bad.

Thanks to her careful saving over the last year for their trips, she had money in the bank.

Leaving her job had been long overdue. She hadn't enjoyed it for years, and although working for her local council paid moderately well, and there was a chance for promotion, it just didn't excite her. She wanted to travel and write, and this could be the perfect opportunity it. Her women's fiction novel was nearly finished, another few weeks and she should have it done, and could start sending it out to agents and publishers. Her next goal was to write a travel book on all the places she would visit. Here, her thoughts returned to Edward.

The travel book had been his idea.

Together, he said, together they would travel the world and write about it. She'd been sold instantly and started saving money for their big adventure. For a whole year they planned and saved, studying maps and researching the best places to go that would interest people enough to buy their book. She's even started to blog about it.

Suddenly, four weeks ago as they had decorated their flat for Christmas, Edward dropped the bombshell that he'd been offered a promotion at his university, and he wanted to take it. Stunned, she had calmly asked him about their travel plans. He had replied that they could put it off for a few years.

She wasn't proud of her reaction, she'd lost her temper and they'd argued.

From that night their relationship seemed to have imploded.

She wanted to travel now, before marriage and babies and mortgages. He could always teach later.

Edward returned the argument saying that they'd been stupid and naive to think they could travel and make it pay in a book deal. It wasn't what people did in the real world.

In one smooth blow, he shattered her dreams. The following few days were fraught with awkward silences and snappy comments. Their once great relationship dissolved rapidly, scaring Hannah at how fragile it must have been to not withstand this disagreement.

Then, hoping to make up, Hannah went to the university to see Edward and found him in a café sitting very close to another woman, who happen to hug him as Hannah watched from the doorway. Edward looked up at her and the guilt on his face said it all.

She had gone to her mother's, and Edward had gone on a friend's pre-booked stag weekend in Amsterdam. Polite texts dwindled to nothing at all. Edward's last message said he needed to think about his future and was going to stay with his brother in Paris for a while.

Heart-broken, Hannah had searched for a place to go, not wanting to be in her empty flat or at her mother's house filled with Christmas hope, especially with her mother all loved up and off cruising.

Sally offered her this lodge deep in the Welsh mountains. Within two days she had rented it, packed her car and left the flat.

And now here she was. Tomorrow was Christmas day. In the past she had always loved Christmas, the whole shebang of it, the shopping, the wrapping of presents, the eating and drinking, the social parties, the family get-togethers and the wishing for a white Christmas and never getting one – until this one! She enjoyed it all.

The thought of doing Christmas without Edward... well... She couldn't do it. Not this year.

Sighing, Hannah threw another log on the fire, then opened a bottle of wine and more chocolate. Her aim was to drink enough so she could sleep through tomorrow. After that, she'd start her new life...

~ ~ ~

Banging woke her the next morning. She lay for a moment on the sofa, listening. Opening her eyes, she groaned in pain as brightness seemed to shatter her retinas. She was cold and the white light dazzled her.

Snow.

Drifted up against the windows was a foot deep of snow. Looking beyond, the whole mountain range was now a brilliant white. She smiled, despite her thumping head, at the magnificence of it. She loved snow.

The banging on the front door came again.

For a moment she stilled, afraid. No one knew she was here except Sally and her mother. She was alone in the middle of nowhere and someone was knocking on the door. On Christmas Day. In the snow!

Shivering, she slowly pushed back the throws she'd covered herself in during her night of binge drinking, for the bottle of wine had led to cosmopolitans naturally... The evidence was revoltingly scattered around the kitchen and on the floor by the sofa. The dead fire in the grate added to the misery.

Staring at the empty wrappers she must have also eaten her own body weight in chocolate. Had she engulfed her entire supply? That upset her more than the raging hangover which was threatening to split her head open.

'Hello!' The male voice shouted through the door, making her jump.

She unlocked the door and inched it open.

'Thank God. I thought something had happened to you!' Edward? Here? Not in Paris?

She stared at him as though he was an apparition. 'What are you doing here?'

'Can I come in, please?' He raised his eyebrows in question. 'I've lost the feeling in my feet.'

Opening the door wider, she winced at the harshness of the white world beyond the door.

'Did I wake you up?' He glanced around at the state of the room.

'Yes.' She shut the door.

'Looks like you had a good night.' Edward stood in the middle of the room appearing so handsome, so damn sexy. Shaved and wearing jeans and a black jumper, her traitorous heart slammed in her chest as she drank in the sight of him.

She was so thankful to see him yet sad at the same time. Tears welled in her eyes. 'How did you know where I was?'

'Your mum told me. After she ripped shreds off me for being a complete idiot.'

'You are an idiot.'

He smiled, a soft sad smile. 'I know. I'm sorry.'

Hannah smoothed down her hair, which she knew would be a fright. Her stomach churned. She desperately wanted to clean her teeth, shower and have a cup of coffee. She also desperately wanted to run into Edward's arms and beg him to love her again. But she couldn't do any of that and so stood like a statue waiting for him to talk.

'Look, I know you are angry with me. I didn't handle any of this the right way. I guess I panicked.'

'Panicked about what?'

He sat on the sofa, his hands dangling between his knees. 'It was getting closer to us packing up and leaving everyone and everything to go travelling. I was throwing away a good job, selling my car, storing away our things, and it suddenly hit me what a huge thing we were doing. It scared the crap out of me.'

'Why didn't you talk to me about it, instead of just pushing me away?'

'I don't know. Maybe because I knew how much you wanted it.'

'I didn't want it so much that I was willing to lose you over it.'

'Well, anyway I've been thinking a lot about it all, and I realised that you mean more to me than anything in the world. So, if you'll forgive and take me back, then I'll take a year off and we'll go travelling.'

'No.' She shook her head and instantly regretted it as it pounded. 'No. I don't want you to go, not when your heart isn't in it.'

'But it is. I do want to do it. I was just worried about the consequences. I've talked to the people at my uni and they will give me a year off. That makes me feel so much better that I've got a job to come home to, does that make sense?'

'Of course, it does. What about the woman I saw you with in the café?'

'She's a friend, honestly. She's just found out she's pregnant and it's changed all her plans. We were having a pity party when you saw us.' He came to stand before her. 'I love you. I've missed you so much. I don't want to be without you.'

Her whole body seemed to melt at his words. 'I love you too.'

'Will you forgive me?'

She nodded, emotion clogging her throat. When he kissed her, the world righted itself and she was whole again.

Edward, his blue eyes showing her his love, knelt on one knee and produced a black box which he opened to show her the diamond ring. 'Will you marry me, Hannah?'

'Yes.' She hugged him tight as outside fresh snow fell.

'You've got your wish. We finally have a white Christmas,' he murmured against her lips.

'I've received more than one wish.' She smiled.

He looked out of the window. 'If the weather keeps up like this, we might be snowed in.'

'Oh, then let it snow forever!'

Comfort for the Night

The rain fell incessantly. Thick grey clouds hung low over the desolate French village. Broken buildings lay as though drunk along the edge of the High Street. Trees no longer held leaves, their limbs shattered and gone by constant shelling.

Private Shortland crept along the hedge, his fellow men in front and behind him, following the Captain's orders to take the village. Reports were that the enemy had long evacuated the area, but no one was completely sure. So, the weary unit slowly advanced onwards in the rain, alert and strained with tension.

Shortland wiped the raindrops from his eyes. Water dripped off his helmet brim. They'd marched through three days of inclement weather, and he was fed up with being cold and wet and tired. His stomach rumbled, sounding loud in the eerie quiet of the village road. Every muscle ached, he didn't know for how much longer her could go on. His pack on his back grew heavier with each step he took.

Movement to the side of the hedge made him jump. He swung his rifle around to aim but stopped from pulling the trigger as a white and ginger cat sat beneath the dripping leaves of the hawthorn. Its dark eyes looked at Shortland quizzically, before it decided to keep pace with him as they stalked up the road.

Glancing at his companion, Shortland kept a vigil on the road ahead, but every now and then checked to see if the cat stayed with him. He was surprised that the animal was out in such weather, but the sight of it, clean white and bright ginger amongst all the grey and misery of the war-torn surroundings brought a lightness to his heart.

A silent signal went up as the captain deployed his men to fan out into the nearby buildings to check for any hidden enemy. Shortland forgot the cat as he hurried to break cover from the hedge and ran to an old barn on his left. With two other men, they burst into the barn, its large door was broken and hanging by one hinge. The soldiers quickly searched the wide-open space, stepping into the shadows, as well as climbing the wooden ladder to the loft above to poke at the stored hay. Nothing. No enemy.

Breathing a sigh of relief, Shortland went to the barn door and heard from other soldiers outside that the Captain had ordered for them to stay the night in the village, to make themselves comfortable as possible and bed down for the night.

'I reckon we could light a fire in here, and dry out real proper like,' Simmons, a young private spoke softly, hopefully, his face pale with cold.

Nodding, they agreed and started breaking up an old wooden wheelbarrow for firewood.

Shortland went into one of the dark corners, it smelt fusty and a little damp, but largely the broken straw bales were dry enough to use. 'If we bring over some of these bales, we can make beds that'll be far comfier than laying on the dirt floor.'

'Let's get this fire lit. I'm freezing,' Kilpatrick, the other private said, shaking off his sodden kit.

Together the three men stacked the wood in a triangle on top of a small bundle of twisted hay. It ignited quickly and the tended to it for a few minutes until the wood caught and a good fire was burning.

The barn door squeaked opened, and the Captain stepped in. 'Everything all right lads?'

'Sound as can be, sir,' said Shortland with a salute.

'I want someone on watch at all times. This barn is the first building coming up that road. I noticed there's an opening up in that loft, obviously where the hay was brought in and out. It's the perfect look out. Take it in shifts to keep watch and rest up the best you can. We leave at 06.00 hours. Muster in the street just up near the church. Good night.' The Captain left to a quiet chorus of good night.

The three of them looked at each other. Shortland sighed tiredly and glanced at his watch. 'It's 17.05. I'll take first watch until 2200 hours.' He stared longingly at the small fire that sent out the first warmth they'd had in three days.

He took his rations out of his pack and left it by the fire to dry out.

After climbing the ladder in near darkness, he crawled over the strewn straw to the square opening fronting the street. Looking out, he noted the empty street going down to his right and the village buildings on his left. The odd soldier was still walking about, but as the winter's night had fallen, many had found somewhere to escape the cold.

Shivering, his bones aching, he started to pile loose straw closer to the opening. Intent on his task, he didn't realise he wasn't alone until the white and ginger cat slid up against his leg, frightening him.

'Hey fellow, you can't do that to me. I'll take you for the enemy if you do that, and you'll get a bullet for your troubles.'

A soft meow was his answer, and Shortland gently stroked his silky ears.

'Do you want to share my bed and help keep watch with me?' Shortland continued to make a straw bed, but with the night air chilling him, he pushed up more straw to create sides around his body for extra warmth.

Settling down into the hollow, Shortland could easily see down the street, but had the edge of the opening as a back rest and the straw bed to keep him comfortable. Opening his can of bully beef, he gazed out at the dark night, hoping the enemy would stay away and let them rest.

He thought of home in England. Of his mother and father, his younger sister. His missed his mother's cooking and his father's nightly reading from the newspaper, he even missed his sister when she used to annoy him so much. How were they coping during the war? Did they miss him as much as he missed them?

And what of Gilly, his sweet girlfriend. Would she be missing him? Her letters still came regularly, and he was thankful.

From his pocket, he pulled out a slightly battered picture of Gilly, taken at a fair shortly before the war started. He traced her pretty, smiling face with a finger and felt so very lonely. One day they would be together again and have a little place of their own. The thought made him smile. He just hoped it would be soon.

With another meow, the cat joined him, laying on his lap and purring as Shortland stroked his back while he ate.

'Are you all alone, fellow?' Shortland whispered. 'Shall we keep each other company?'

The cat licked his fingers, meowing at the can of beef.

'Oh, you want my food, is that it?' Chuckling, he scooped out a portion of meat and gave it to his new friend.

The warmth of the cat helped to stop Shortland's shivering and the cat's contented purring, eased the tension from his shoulders. Although exhausted, he was feeling better than he had in a long time.

He smiled down at the cat, all soft fur and warmth, and, for a few hours, he could forget the nonsense of war, the cold and the loneliness and simply enjoy the silent companionship they shared. For now, it was enough.

Fran's Fancies

Francesca snipped the stem of another red rose and gently pushed it into the square foam of the bouquet. She stood back and admired the finished arrangement of red and white roses with delicate gypsophila and fern. She deftly folded and tucked the white cardboard box around the foam square and added the red bow as a final touch.

She looked up from her work bench as Tess her assistant came into the back room.

'Can I go on my break now?' Tess asked, all pink dyed hair and piercings. She was, at times, rather scary to look at, but Francesca had managed to see beyond the rebellious teenage garb and tapped into her natural artistic talent.

'Yes, of course. I'm done here.' Francesca placed the bouquet into the fridge and went through to the front of the shop, as Tess scurried out the back entrance to where her boyfriend waited to have a stolen half an hour together. Stolen because Tess's parents didn't approve of the equally pierced and dyed boyfriend and therefore Tess, as most teenagers do, had completely gone ahead and ignored their wishes.

Saturdays were usually the busiest days in her shop, *Fran's Fancies*. Setting up as a florist had been her mother's idea. Something to keep her busy after her last relationship had finally come to its inevitable end two years ago. Since then, she had focused all her energy on becoming a successful florist. Her hard work had paid off. *Fran's Fancies* received lovely reviews online from satisfied customers. She was making good money, easily meeting the monthly repayments of the loan her mother gave her to set up the business.

Out of habit, Francesca glanced up at the antique clock on the wall. She silently scolded herself for doing so. What did it matter if one of her regular customers was early or late this Saturday? What did it matter that he was drop dead gorgeous? She absentmindedly tidied the front counter, her thoughts on guy who came to buy a bouquet of flowers every Saturday afternoon. Tall and lean, his physique was athletic, and Francesca fully expected him to be in the local football team, or something sports-like. This guy – and she wished she knew his name - was the complete package. To go with his great body, he had the most delicious light brown eyes, the colour of rich toffee and a smile that made her heart do double time.

She really had to get a grip of herself. Salivating over a good-looking customer was really rather silly, and unprofessional. Especially when he obviously was very much taken with whoever it was, he bought flowers for each week. No man bought flowers every week unless it was for someone very special – like a new girlfriend, or a wife who has just given birth, or someone he had cheated on...

Sighing, she tidied the stand of small occasion cards. Perhaps it was time she started dating again, now the shop was running well? Maybe she should join one of those dating websites her sister kept telling her to go on? She definitely should go out more. Her weekend, or more correctly, her Sundays, were spent cleaning her flat and doing all the little jobs she didn't get time to do due to her being at the shop six days a week.

'I'm back,' Tess announced coming through from the back room. 'It's starting to rain. There are some really dark clouds.'

'Raining?' Francesca stared out through the large front windows to the footpath where she had arranged a summer flower display in an old wooden wheelbarrow and wicker baskets. 'I'd best bring that lot inside then.'

The phone rang at the same time thunder cracked overhead. 'Tess, get the phone, I'll grab the stuff outside.'

What had been the odd spot of rain landing on the warm pavements suddenly turned torrential. Caught out, Francesca hurriedly brought in the nearest baskets, worried that the rain was so heavy the flowers would be damaged beyond selling.

'Damn it!' The old wheelbarrow was difficult to shift when empty, but full of pots of flowers and with rain teeming down, she struggled to move it.

'Can I give you a hand?' Without waiting for an answer, the gorgeous customer she fantasised about took the handles out of her grasp and wheeled it inside for her.

Flustered, Francesca quickly retrieved the other baskets and followed him in. 'Thank you so much.'

'That's quite all right.' He smiled his megawatt smile, despite being wet through.

'I have a fresh towel, let me get it for you.' She darted into the back and in record time grabbed a towel, agonised over her own appearance in the mirror, and returned to him.

'Thanks.' He dried his face and arms. His white t-shirt clung to him. 'I had to park my car a few streets away. I was hoping to make it back in time before the heavens opened, but it came down so fast.'

Francesca dragged her eyes away from his movements. His jeans weren't as wet as his t-shirt, but his dark hair was dripping. Thunder clapped again making her jump. She looked up at him and found him staring back at her.

'Shall I make us a coffee?' Tess asked loudly over the noise of the downpour.

Francesca turned to the guy. 'Would you like a drink until the rain eases?'

'OK, yes, thank you. I don't fancy going back out in that just yet.' He turned to Tess. 'A coffee would be great, please, milk no sugar.'

Alone with him, Francesca was tongued-tied. She smiled nervously as silence stretched between them. Here, she had her chance to speak to him properly and she couldn't get her words out.

'I might as well get my flowers sorted while we wait?' He grinned.

'Absolutely.' She took the towel from him. 'What would you like this week?'

'You know I come in every week?' He seemed surprised that she had noticed.

'Of course. You're one of my regulars.'

'Oh right. Um…well…what's your favourite flower?'

'Mine? They all are my favourites, but if I had to choose it would be the freesia. I adore their scent.'

'I'll have a bunch of those then, please.' He thanked Tess as she brought him a cup of coffee.

'I have some lovely yellow and white ones.' She went amongst the displays along the wall. 'Your special lady is very spoilt.'

'Yes, she is.' He thrust his hands in his jean pockets, looking a little bashful. 'What time do you close today?'

'Three o'clock on a Saturday.'

'It must keep you busy running a shop.'

'Very. I have no time for a life, so it's a good job I'm not married and don't have kids.' Now why did she say that? She'd love to have both those things.

'You're single?'

'I am.' She wrapped the flowers in soft white tissue paper and then clear cellophane. 'Ten pounds, please.'

He handed over the money and sipped his coffee. 'It's not easy running your own business.'

'No, it isn't. It's time consuming and rewarding at the same time.' She gazed up at him, for he was much taller than her and she was five foot six.

He nodded, taking another sip of coffee. 'I'm Hayden, by the way.'

'Francesca, and this is my assistant, Tess.' She looked around, but Tess had remained in the back room. 'Do you work around here?'

'I work from home. I run an online IT consultancy business.'

'Oh, so you know how hard it is, too, having a business.'

'Yes. It takes confidence that's for sure.'

The phone rang and she answered it. After writing down the customer's request in the diary, she hung up and watched him as he stood staring out of the window drinking his coffee. He wouldn't be out of place at a male model shoot. Again, she thought and envied the woman in his life.

'The rain is easing. I should go…'

She gave him a small smile, not really wanting him to leave. 'See you next week?'

'Probably, yes.' Hayden picked up the flowers. 'Thank you for the coffee.'

'And thank you for helping me.'

He hesitated a moment then left the shop, as large drips plopped from the building's eves.

'Wow, he is hot.' Tess came to stand beside her. 'Seriously.'

'I know.' Francesca let out a long breath. She missed having a man in her life. She missed the quirks, the deep laughter, the arms to hold her. It was time. Time to get back in the dating game.

'You go home, Tess,' she said suddenly. 'It's nearly closing time and the storm will have sent everyone in town home. I think, for once, I'll close a little bit early, make the deliveries and take an extra hour off.'

'Really? Cool. Thanks.' Tess collected her bag from the back room. 'I'll see you on Monday morning.'

'Yes, bye.' With Tess gone, the shop seemed very quiet. The storm clouds were moving away but the street out the front was deserted.

Francesca took out the money from the till, bolted the front door, turned the sign over to CLOSED and turned off the shop lights.

In the gloom she went through to the back room and took out of the fridge the two bouquets she had to deliver and put them in her little van parked outside. She then went through the process of last-minute tidying, placing the money in her bag and locking up.

Heading out to the van, she stopped in surprise as Hayden stood near the back entrance to the road. 'Hello. Is something wrong?'

'No. I just thought I'd give you these.' He handed her the freesia bouquet.

'Oh, but I thought...'

'I bought them for you.' Again, he gave her his megawatt smile.

'Me? Why?' She gaped like a fish and promptly shut her mouth.

'Every week for the last six weeks I have come to buy flowers. The first time I saw you I thought you looked really great and kept thinking about you. Since then, I have been coming each week in the hope I'd have the courage to speak to you, ask your name, and maybe, hopefully, ask you out for a drink or something...' He gave her a helpless look. 'I'm a bit rubbish at chatting women up it seems.' He laughed at himself.

'Yes, you are.' She chuckled, her heart all warm and gooey at his admission. He liked her! She felt as giddy as a young girl on her first date!

'So? Fancy doing something?'

'You *are* single, aren't you?'

'I am. I'm not the type to mess women about.'

'Then yes. Yes, I would like to meet up with you, thank you.'

'Tonight?' He raised his eyebrows, a hopeful expression on his face.

How on earth could anyone resist him? Francesca found it difficult to breathe. 'Yes, I'm free tonight.'

'Great. How about I pick you up at eight o'clock, or you can meet me if you prefer?'

'I think I feel safe enough for you to pick me up.' She took her phone out of her bag. 'Let's swap numbers. I'll text you my address.'

They each added the other's details into their phones and Francesca felt a sense of achievement. She had a hot guy's number. In fact, for the first time in a long time a man had shown interest in her. It felt like a hundred years since she last felt attractive and desirable. She couldn't stop smiling.

'So, I'll pick you up at eight.' He waited for her to open the van's door. 'Have a think about where you want to go and text me.'

'Ok.' She hesitated, not really wanting to leave him, but needed to know the answer to one question. 'By the way, who do you buy all those flowers for?'

He laughed self-consciously. 'My grandmother.'

The Right Man

M olly lifted her face to the hot breeze that whistled through the trees and rustled the leaves. This particular walk took her along an avenue of large oaks made old by time and gnarled by weather. Soft, sweet green grasses and rioting wildflowers bordered the lane. Molly's lightweight skirt swished gently around her knees. In the shade of the avenue, she took off her wide straw hat with its long red ribbon and smiled in pleasure at the serenity of the area.

The peace and quiet along this walk soothed Molly's taut nerves. She promised herself she would come here more often. Indeed, she wished she had found this walk two weeks ago when she first arrived in this small country town, after fleeing her home and the pain there. Instead, she'd trolled along the town's few streets window-shopping, or sitting in the park watching other people picnic.

Now, as she sauntered, she smiled at nothing, and ran her fingers through her newly washed and still slightly damp curls. The sun peeked through the overhead branches, sprinkling the lane with dapple shade. Molly hummed, stopping every now and then to pluck a wildflower, which she twirled in her fingers.

Abruptly, a startling cry rent the air, it halted her mid stride. She looked around amongst the thick tree trunks but saw nothing to cause alarm. Feeling silly, she began to walk once more. When the cry came again, she picked up her pace a bit.

A lanky, black dog ran out in front of her and crossed to the other side of the lane. It disappeared for a moment in the long grass, and then re-emerged, scooting back the way it had come, barking wildly.

Cautious but intrigued, Molly followed the excited dog. The eerie cry came again as Molly left the lane, made her way through the short undergrowth and past the trees lining the avenue. A landscape of waist-high wheat fields opened before her, but it was the guy standing at the edge of the nearest field that caught her attention.

He stood tall and lithe. His hair, a deeper shade than the wheat around him, lifted in the breeze. The dog jumped madly around his jean-clad legs, despite the man's attempts to calm him. It was obviously a puppy, regardless of its size, and it had the behaviour of such. Molly remained unnoticed from her position by the hedge and the man continued to hold his left arm straight out from his body. The position puzzled her until she saw that his hand and forearm were covered by a padded, brown leather glove. Much to the man's annoyance, the dog carried on its silly antics, while above in silhouette to the pale blue sky, a dark brown bird circled and screeched to add to the confusion.

Mesmerised, she watched as the bird angled its way towards the frantic black dog. The man tried to ward the bird off, not in fright, but to stop it and the dog from hurting each other. The action was fast and furious with the man attempting to control both pets.

Molly's mouth lifted slightly at the corners. It was quite funny to watch.

'Hey you! Can you give me a hand?' His deep voice came across the field to her.

She hesitated for a moment before treading carefully towards him. The whirling bird screeched again just above her head and Molly felt an instinctive urge to duck.

'It's all right. It won't hurt you. Can you see the dog's lead anywhere?' he called above the noise and pointed in the general direction of where she stood.

Molly searched in the thick grass edging the field. A short distance away the lead lay curled like a thin snake. She picked it up and dangled it for the man to see. Before she could say anything, a single pounce from the dog knocked her onto her bottom. It barked directly into her ear, making her head ring.

'You bloody animal, Blackie!' The man growled, kneeling beside her within seconds. 'Are you okay?' He helped Molly to her feet while trying to push the enthusiastic pup away.

'I'm fine.' She dusted off her skirt, feeling rather foolish. She looked up at him and paused. Her stomach clenched. Awareness robbed her of breath. His hazel eyes were warm with concern, his handsome face chiselled like those male models in magazines. For an instant, Molly couldn't function as she stared at one of the most gorgeous men she'd ever seen.

'I'm really sorry.' He took the lead from her grasp and quickly attached it to the pup's red, studded collar. 'I'll just put him in the car.'

Within a few moments, he had guided the pup to the other side of the field where Molly could see a work truck parked in another lane.

Dithering, she didn't know what to do. Should she simply walk away or wait to talk more with this mouth-watering hunk with the Greek-god looks? Either option seemed delusional. She was no match for handsome men but walking away seemed rude.

'He's only a man, Molly,' she whispered, summoning her courage. 'I can talk to a good-looking man, of course I can.'

When he returned, minus the pup, he carried a wire cage and gave her a wry grin. 'I apologise for this madness. Thank you for helping me. Blackie is an escape artist. He managed to slip his lead and then proceeded to run off with it while I was busy with my bird.'

'I-I wasn't much help.' She swallowed, conscious of wanting to stare at him, to really look him over at her leisure, but she doubted he'd enjoy being peered at like some exhibit in a museum.

He held out his hand. 'Yes, you were. Thanks. My name is Sebastian Lord.' His smile revealed straight white teeth and a slight dimple in his left cheek that left her tingling with a delicious ache of awareness.

'I'm Molly. Molly Daniels. Pleased to meet you.' She shook his hand, blushing while shivers of pleasure ran through her at the contact. Her reaction to him so immediate and strong. She couldn't take her eyes off him, and she blushed deeper, hoping that he didn't notice. This is so crazy!

'Nice to meet you, Molly.'

Her smile wavered under his lingering appraisal. His eyes locked with hers and she looked away, dropping her hand as though he'd burnt it. To cover her embarrassment, she stared up at the sky. 'Is that your bird, the one with the awful cry?'

'Yes.' Sebastian scanned the trees. 'He's taken an exception to Blackie, but Blackie thinks everyone is his playmate. I want them to become used to each other, but I think it's wishful thinking on my part.' When he gave Molly a boyish grin her knees wobbled in response. Just being near him, listening to his deep voice made her feel like an overexcited child full of sugar.

Sebastian straightened his arm and held it shoulder high. From the avenue of trees, the bird gave a screech, and in a slow arc, it flew to land on Sebastian's gloved forearm. With shiny ebony eyes, the bird stared keenly at Molly as though reading her thoughts.

'He...he's lovely,' she murmured and took a step back.

'Yes, but very temperamental. He can be worse than any woman I've known,' Sebastian joked.

She raised her eyebrows. 'Then you mustn't keep company with the right women.'

He laughed, and Molly liked the sound of it. A strong confident laugh. She wanted to sigh in contentment at the pleasant sound.

'You could be right.' He stroked the falcon's head, his long fingers gentle. 'Do you live close by? I haven't seen you around here before.'

'No, I'm just visiting.' She watched his stroking action. He had nice hands, big hands made for holding a woman, and he wore no ring. Heavens, she had to stop all this fantasising, or she'd go insane.

'My home is just over that hill there.' He pointed to a large hill to the east of them and then unconsciously ran his fingers through his fair hair as the breeze blew it. Molly itched to do it for him. She knew his hair would be soft and silky.

'May I offer you a cup of coffee?'

She gazed up into his eyes, acknowledging his friendliness. For a second, she was tempted, sorely tempted, but then common sense prevailed. He was too good-looking, and her reaction to him frightened her in its intensity. It had been so long since she'd last felt the gut-wrenching pull of attraction as she felt with this stranger. He's dangerous. Men like him chewed up and spat out women like her for breakfast. 'No, thank you.'

'Please. It's the least I can do.' His eyes, a warm blend of honey brown and green, lit with something she couldn't name, and the strength left her legs.

'No, really, I must get go.' Molly stepped back, needing to put distance between them. She didn't want to be attracted to another man yet. It was too soon. Although it had been many, many months since she'd felt any attraction to her husband, her now ex-husband, she couldn't allow emotion to rule her again.

What about sex then, Molly? Mind-blowing sex like the kind you've never had before. The devil within her that rarely showed its head suddenly spoke out. You've never had great sex, Molly, just safe, simple sex with your husband, who then went and left you for a nineteen-year-old.

'I owe you one then.' Sebastian smiled so endearingly that she had to return his smile and force herself not to step closer to him. Unexpectedly, she longed to be held, to be loved, and instinct told her that this man would know exactly how to hold and love a woman. His languid movements seemed effortless, as though he had all the time in the world to do just as he pleased. She liked that and was even a little jealous that he appeared so smooth, so at ease when inside she quivered like a strung bow.

'Sure.' However, she knew full well they wouldn't meet again and, although this disappointed her, she knew it would be better this way. Now wasn't the time to think of other men. Her signature on the divorce papers was hardly dry.

'Maybe we can meet for coffee tomorrow?' Sebastian said, putting the bird back in its cage. 'There's a little café in town—'

'No, sorry, I can't.' Molly backed away from his magnetism, from the peril of wanting something she could never have. She and men didn't work. None of her relationships had worked. She wanted a home, children, a dog—the whole picket-fence syndrome. Men wanted fast cars, fast women, and no responsibilities.

'Molly?'

She hesitated, staring at him, wanting to get to know him, but already separating herself from any involvement that would end with her in pain again. 'Yes?'

His gaze held hers in silent communication. 'It was a pleasure to meet you.'

—————

Later that afternoon, as the heat sapped her energy, Molly sat in her room at Wayland Cottage—the local bed-and-breakfast. The ceiling fan spun slowly, doing nothing but wafting the hot air around the room. On her lap lay a historical novel that last night had engrossed her, but now lost her attention. Sebastian Lord filled her mind. Thinking of the morning's encounter annoyed her. She wanted nothing to do with men, not now, not ever. The time had come for her to stand on her own two feet.

She sighed at her own stupidity. That kind of thinking wouldn't help her. If she wanted children, which she did, desperately, then at some point a man would have to be involved. At thirty-three years old, she couldn't wait forever for the past to stop hurting. Yet, the thought of entering another relationship seemed too exhausting. Tired of behaving differently to suit others, she wanted time to be herself.

A knock on the door preceded Mrs. Henley, her hostess, who brought in a tea tray. Mrs Henley, a widow of greying hair and ample waist, stayed for a moment or two, but Molly's lack of worthwhile responses to her questions soon had her taking her leave.

With another deep sigh, Molly gazed out the window at the street beyond the rose garden. Her thoughts drifted again to Sebastian. She had inadvertently memorised everything about him. His sun-bleached hair, the wideness of his shoulders under his blue T-shirt, the clenching muscles of his arms, the way his worn jeans moulded to his hips, bum, and thighs...

Her body, which had been sexually dormant for so long, sprang to life at her wayward thoughts. Molly groaned. Great, that's all she needed—to be sexually frustrated as well as mixed up and at loose ends. Could her life get any more miserable?

Besides, what was she thinking? Everyone knew that hot guys, the ones who didn't look out of place in magazine shoots, were arrogant arses and usually up-themselves. Did she need that hassle? Hadn't Mike, the husband from Hell, taught her that much?

Though, to be fair, Sebastian didn't seem that way. He seemed sweet and a lover of animals. Weren't they tender-hearted?

She shook her head. It did no good to think of him. They wouldn't cross paths again—unless he was some loser with attitude, since they were the types of men she usually fell for. The types who needed someone to pick up their dirty underwear, loan them money, and usually, it wasn't a girlfriend or wife they required but a mother!

A black flash shot past the gate to the cottage and jolted Molly out of her reverie.

No.

It couldn't be!

Blackie?

Opening the window outwards, she leaned out to get a better view, and searched the street for Sebastian Lord.

Nothing.

She stepped back, furious at herself for thinking of the man immediately. If the black flash had been a dog, and it could've been a large cat, then the chances of it being Blackie were slim. Who knew how many black dogs lived in the town anyway?

Abruptly, the dog reappeared near the cottage path and promptly lifted its leg to pee on the garden gate. Molly closed her eyes. What were the chances of there being two such lanky pups in this small town wearing red, studded collars?

'Blackie!' Molly called, then felt foolish as the silly pup looked at her before dashing off into the street. The dog was definitely Blackie. She recognised the dopey look he gave her.

'Damn dog. It'll get run over at this rate.' She stormed from her room and into the hallway.

Molly opened the front door to a scream of car tires. With her heart in her mouth, she broke into a run.

'Blackie!' She skidded to a halt on the edge of the street. The dog stood on the opposite side, unharmed.

She waited for the road to clear of cars before crossing. Amazingly, Blackie stayed still as she gripped his collar.

'You bad boy!' She dragged him to the safety of the cottage's garden and closed the gate. 'How am I going to get you home?'

Molly fumed at the situation. She had no wish to meet with Sebastian again. She didn't like the way her skin tingled when he gazed at her, or the way her heart skipped a beat at the sound of his deep voice. Her holiday was a chance to find herself again, not to indulge in fantasies of model-type men. She'd had enough of living in a fantasy world, a world in which she thought if she held on and pretended everything in her marriage was wonderful, then in the end, it would be. Everyone knew marriages had to be worked at...

She dismissed those thoughts. Now wasn't the time. 'Mrs. Henley?' she called through the open front door.

'Yes, my dear?' Mrs. Henley came outside, wiping her hands on her ever-present apron.

'This dog has escaped its owner.'

'Oh, dear. He can't stay here. Mr. Braithwaite is allergic to animal fur. We'd better take it to the vet. He's only around the corner.' She untied her apron strings. 'Shall I take him, dear?'

'No, it's all right. I will take him.' Molly puffed, trying to keep a firm grip on Blackie, who was determined to cover Mrs. Henley with slimy, wet licks.

'Turn right at the gate and right again at the corner,' Mrs. Henley instructed.

Molly hung on tight to Blackie. He seemed to want to drag her along behind him as he bounced and jerked on two legs all the way to the vet's rooms.

The waiting room was full of people and their animals. Blackie spied a nearby cat and was doing his best to become acquainted with it.

A harassed secretary glanced up at Molly. 'Yes?'

'I found this dog,' Molly began. 'He—'

'We're not the pound. There is a shelter for strays on the other side of town.'

'No, you see I know the owner. I can give you his name and you can hold the dog until he comes.'

'Look, sorry this is a bad time. We're really busy, and we don't have enough cages for the sick animals, never mind the lost ones. You'll have to take him to the shelter, we're too busy today.'

The phone rang shrilly, and the secretary immediately put the caller on hold. Fumbling under her desk, she was quick to pass Molly a phone directory before reaching over to grab another phone and plonking that on top of the directory. 'I'd really appreciate it if you could ring the owner, if you know him. We're snowed under here, thanks.' She turned away to answer the phone call just as a man and child came to the counter with a parrot in a cage.

Molly muttered something unintelligible, but inside her head she swore like a sailor. She yanked at Blackie's collar, while with her other hand she opened the phone book. Why was it, the busiest places had only one secretary while the empty places had loads of staff sitting around chatting?

'Blackie, you blasted dog!' Sebastian Lord stood in the doorway, and the pup sprang out of Molly's hand to bound up at his chest.

'Did you find him?' His surprise was evident as he struggled with the adoring pup.

'Yes. He was nearly run down in front of the B & B! Can't you control him?' Molly spat, striding from the waiting room. She was angry with the sudden tightening of her stomach at the sight of him. He had showered recently as his hair was damp at the ends where it touched his collar, and he had changed shirts. She didn't want to note all the details about him, didn't want to be interested in a stranger. He was too tall, too attractive, and too damned sexy even in old jeans and a white T-shirt. Molly had the sudden urge to kiss him, to touch him, to run her hands through his hair...

Oh my God!

Amazed by such feelings, such needs, she hurried away. She had learnt nothing from the past it seemed. Steer clear of the male sex. Especially the good-looking ones who made your heart thump just by looking at them. She'd married a man who once turned her knees to jelly just from one smile and look where that got her.

ele

Instinctively, Sebastian followed her out into the car park. 'Molly, look, I'm sorry he's been a pest and I'm sorry you have been troubled by Blackie. It won't happen again, I promise.'

'He's your problem.' Molly's brown eyes flashed hostility, causing him to raise his eyebrows at her tone.

'I'd only parked the car to buy bread and milk. I put the window down a bit for him, but he broke it completely trying to get out. It's a wonder he didn't cut himself.'

'As I said, it's your problem!' Molly walked faster.

'Thank you, anyway.' He kept the pace easily even with Blackie as a hindrance.

She gave him a tight smile and walked away.

Sebastian couldn't help but notice her small bottom under the swishing skirt. Likely the dog would be the death of him, but the pup had brought the lovely Miss Daniels into his world again. 'Can I take you out to dinner as a thank-you?' he called to her retreating back.

First coffee and now dinner!

Why was he asking her out to dinner? This wasn't what he did. Dates, women, and the whole relationship business weren't his thing anymore, hadn't been for many years.

Molly stopped and turned. 'No, thanks.'

He frowned at her refusal. She was as prickly as a thorn, but quite stunning. 'I'm only trying to be friendly.'

'I'm sure you are, but I'm not interested.'

'What can it hurt?' He shrugged with a smile. Normally, he wasn't one to be pushy, and didn't really believe in chemistry and all that nonsense, but something about this woman affected him. He wanted, very much so, to spend time with her. It had been so long since a woman had stirred the latent embers of his interest. Some instinct told him to not let this one go.

'Sorry.' Molly shook her head, and he liked the way her soft dark curls bounced.

'Do I offend you in some way?'

Her step faltered, and she turned to him with an apology in her eyes. 'No. No, you don't.' She sighed and wiped her hand wearily over her eyes, which intrigued him.

Why was she strung so taut? He could tell by the stiffness of her shoulders that something bothered her. He could sense her fragility and his heart constricted. He sensed she had been hurt before and was perhaps now wary of it happening again.

Sebastian hauled Blackie back from lifting his leg on an electrical post and smiled his best smile, something he hadn't done for a long time. 'I'm sorry about my dog being a nuisance.'

'It's fine, really.' She paused, worry shadowing her delicate face. 'I didn't mean to be so short with you. I'm not normally rude. Sorry.'

'It's okay.' He held out his free hand. 'Thank you again, Molly.'

A second passed before she placed her small hand in his. He wasn't expecting the sensual warmth that jolted up his arm at her touch. His heart thumped against his ribs like a butterfly trapped in a net. The world around him faded and narrowed to focus solely on the petite woman in front of him. For the first time in a long time, he felt alive and ready to enter the world again.

ele

The next morning, Mrs. Henley served Molly breakfast in the dining room. 'My nephew called late last night. He said you found Seb's pup,' she said good-naturedly. 'I didn't even know he had a new dog.'

Molly blinked and lowered her toast. 'You know him? Sebastian Lord?'

'Of course, he's my cousin's boy.'

'Oh, I see.' She tried to blot out his image but, like last night, Sebastian's face hovered before her eyes. She'd lain awake most of the night thinking of him, even fantasising about him making love to her. How crazy was that? But it had been so long since someone had held her, wanted her. She wished she was one of those carefree women who enjoyed one-night stands with total strangers, those who flirted and chatted with any man who took their fancy, who wanted to have sex, and just did it. Before, she had been revolted by the thought, but now she understood it. Desire was very powerful. She acknowledged that Sebastian created a yearning in her, but she didn't know how to handle it. Was she strong enough to resist it? Could she change her nature and simply go with the flow?

'A nicer man you couldn't find.' Mrs. Henley's chatter broke through Molly's thoughts. 'Sad though, what he's been through.'

'Oh?' Molly sat straighter in her chair, her interest roused. She hadn't thought about his past or present. He had simply represented a gorgeous guy who made her skin prickle with awareness.

'Yes, poor thing. He lost his fiancée, Jenni, in a car accident. She was driving because Seb had drunk too much at his thirtieth birthday party held at a local restaurant. She lost control going around a bend. She was going too fast, but Seb blames himself for making her drive in the first place. He wasn't sure if he was over the limit, in fact, he didn't think he was, but to be on the safe side, he didn't drive home. Now he thinks if he had driven, she would still be alive today.'

'That's so sad. When did this happen?' Molly asked quietly. Knowing some of his history made him more real and not some stud-muffin in her fantasies.

'Four years ago. He hasn't moved on, though. He's content to stay at his little hobby farm and see to his animals. He gave up his job as a company adviser in the city and has remained permanently here. He hasn't touched a drop of alcohol since either, not that he was a big drinker. Of course, he wasn't,' she quickly added.

'He-he asked me out for dinner to thank me for finding his dog.'

'Never!' Mrs. Henley's eyes widened before a smile spread across her face. 'He's not been out with a woman since the accident. Oh, that is good news! His mother, Susan, will be so pleased he's showing an interest in women again. We'd given up all hope.'

'I said no,' Molly told her softly.

'Why?' Mrs. Henley looked at her as though Molly had taken leave of her senses. 'He's a good man, Molly. Attractive too, don't you think? Half the women in town want his shoes under their bed, believe me.'

'Er...I don't date.' Molly blushed and rose. 'Shall I help you weed the vegetable garden today?'

Mrs. Henley blinked. 'You don't need to do that, my dear. You're here for a holiday.'

'I enjoy gardening, Mrs. Henley, it's soothing. Besides, I have nothing else to do.' Molly smiled. It would keep her out of the way of bumping into a certain attractive man with smiling eyes.

'How long do you think you'll stay, Molly?'

The question surprised her. 'I'm not sure.' She shrugged. 'I have nothing to go home to really, and I've taken extended leave from my job. Why?'

Mrs. Henley straightened her apron and appeared business-like. 'From our conversations, I know you've not had it easy recently, and I was thinking that if you wanted to stay longer, you'd be welcome to make your home here. You might be able to get a part-time job or something?'

Molly nodded as the idea grew. Who said she had to stick with her plans and leave by the week's end? Her mind whirled with thoughts of living in the peaceful township. Could she obtain work here? She was a primary schoolteacher and majored in music. Did the local school have a vacancy? If not, then could she do something else? She might tutor music or something? That chapter of her life had well and truly closed. Her parents were planning a holiday abroad, and their lives were always so busy, they wouldn't miss her that much. Her flat could be rented out easily and would be a small income too. No one needed her or would miss her.

The prospect of staying appealed to her. She could go for more walks along the avenue...

ele

Molly spent the next week doing odd jobs for Mrs. Henley. Sunny days spent gardening and reading passed the time. She enjoyed being useful to the older lady. Though, come the weekend, Molly was eager to be alone again. She'd seen no one else except for Mrs. Henley and the Braithwaites, a retired couple, who were the only other guests. Their constant chatter and questions about her background, although meant in a kind-hearted way, proved tiring.

'I'm going for a walk, Mrs. Henley,' Molly mentioned after breakfast on Saturday.

'Don't go far. It looks like one of those summer storms, my dear,' Mrs. Henley warned. 'They did say storms for today. We always get them after a run of hot weather. I'd not like you to get caught in it and catch a cold.'

'I don't think I'll be long.'

Molly had intentions of going to browse around the second-hand bookstore. Instead, she found herself walking once more through the cool shade of the avenue. Mrs

Henley's prediction came true. Soon after entering the lane, lightning split the sky, which turned a unique dark purple colour. The avenue harboured no screeching birds or barking dogs today, no Sebastian Lord, only the rumbling thunder in the distance.

Was it possible, no, sensible to feel attracted to a man so soon after Mike? Indeed, she didn't think she would feel that way about anyone ever again. Not after Mike and all the troubles they had gone through the last few years. The love she felt for him had never been all consuming, due to his lack of emotional commitment, but she did try to make them both happy. She hadn't realised until much later that it takes two willing people to make a relationship work. Everyone in her family told her Mike wouldn't settle down long term, but she didn't listen to them. Now, she wished she had. Three years wasted in trying to make a man love and want her. It's time to start living again, time to put the past behind her and move on.

As the first drops of rain splattered the dry, hard road, a blast of a horn startled her, and she spun on her heels to face a suave silver sports car. The driver let down his window and stuck his head out.

Sebastian Lord.

'Can I offer you a lift or don't you do that either?' His tone held a sarcastic note, but his grin took away the sting. 'I actually thought you had left town. Have you been avoiding me intentionally?'

'How big is the local school?'

Sebastian frowned. 'I... I don't know. Big enough, I suppose. It's not something I know much about.' His puzzlement deepened. 'Why?'

'I want to try for a position there,' Molly told him, rain dripping into her eyes.

'Get in the car, Molly. You'll catch your death out there.'

She hesitated only a moment, and then hopped into the front passenger seat, as thunder roared overhead.

He faced her with a smile. 'Thinking of staying here, are you?'

'I might be.' She stared out the rain splattered windscreen. Could she? She'd thought of nothing else all week, but sitting next to Sebastian, his tall frame lounging in the seat so close to her she could nearly touch him, the idea became very appealing.

'Are you running away from something or someone?'

Blinking in surprise at his question, she glanced at him and then away. 'No, the someone has already run away from me.' She waited for the hurt to come as it always did, but found, thankfully, that this time the mention of her broken marriage didn't hurt quite so much.

'You don't have to tell me.'

'What's one more person knowing?' She really didn't care anymore, and it was a comfort to realise that. Maybe life wasn't so bad after all. Perhaps this holiday had done some good. Maybe she'd entered the next stage of grieving. The pain had gone, but in its place lingered a taste of sadness over what could have been.

'Molly, we don't know each other well. Everyone has problems—'

'I'm recently divorced.' She cut into his flow of words with the statement. She still hadn't looked at him properly since entering the car. Couldn't trust herself to not leap into his lap. Heavens, what was wrong with her?

'I'm sorry. It must have been awful for you.'

'It was.'

'I can't believe any man would be so stupid.'

Her laugh was forced, but he went up another notch in her estimation for such a kind remark. 'Well, I don't stack up against a nineteen-year-old who has an enormous amount of money, all thanks to her rich father. As far as my ex-husband is concerned, I'm boring. Whereas, his new piece of fluff has all the talents of a Playboy Pet, plus the money to go with it. She is perfect for him.'

'Then to me he seems rather shallow.'

'Oh, he is. Always has been, but I refused to see it.'

'He might come back.'

'To me?' She looked at him in disbelief. 'No. Never. And even if he did, I wouldn't have him back. I've taken him back too many times after his silly flings, and nothing ever changes. I'm tired of it. Tired of him. Tired of how my life was. We weren't suited. I want children, a happy home life, stability. He wants a good time with no responsibilities.' She didn't add that she wanted someone to love her deeply, passionately, which seemed more the guise of romance movies rather than real life.

He nodded slowly, weighing her comments. 'So, you're thinking of staying here? Away from your family and friends?'

Molly shrugged. 'My grandmother had a saying. 'It's as good a place as any and better than most.' That's how I feel.' A wry smile lifted the corners of her mouth. 'I lasted a few months of friends being sympathetic, but eventually I had to go. So, I took leave from my job and decided to have a holiday. I picked a name out on the map, packed my car, and drove here.'

His eyes softened. 'But running away won't solve anything.'

'I'm not running away. I just want to do something different. I want to experience new things and meet new people. I want to live somewhere else completely different to where I come from.'

'And where was that?'

'Sydney.'

'What about family?'

'My mum and dad will understand. They'll come and visit. They have a full life of their own and like to travel, so they're not around much anyway.'

'The country is nothing like the city. There are not many theatres, night-clubs, or fancy restaurants here.'

'What does that matter?' She raised an eyebrow. 'Besides, I'd prefer a good book and a box of chocolates anytime. I'm very disappointing as a city girl, I'm afraid.'

'Sounds like you have it all planned out?' He smiled and his eyes sparkled at her, warm and inviting.

'I think I might have,' she whispered. She couldn't return his smile; her mouth had gone dry. He looked at her as though he wanted to kiss her, and she desperately wanted him to. Her heart thumped erratically against her ribs, and Molly glanced away again. She needed a clear head and to focus, something she couldn't do when he gazed at her with his gorgeous laughing eyes and little-boy smile.

Sebastian's presence filled the car. His wood-scented cologne filled the interior. Molly glanced back at him and saw he struggled to overcome some inner torment of his own.

He peered out of the windscreen, but not really seeing the rain lashing against it. This lovely woman had managed to burrow under his skin and start the process of his living again. He'd been happy to remain single for the rest of his life. Being in love was too hard sometimes, too risky. Yet, somehow, without him being entirely aware of it, she turned his contented world upside down. For the last week he'd done nothing but think of her day and night. He'd made excuses to go into town to try and catch a glimpse of her near the B & B. Though he'd not actually stopped by the B & B because then that would mean something-mean he wanted out of his current lifestyle and, if he was honest, he'd admit that the thought was scary. He'd spent the week tossing up the idea whether it would be worth entering the real world of emotions again.

Could he take the gamble? Could his heart take the strain of being held by another woman again? Did she want it? This poor woman had been to Hell and back by the sounds of it, so why would she want to enter into another relationship? Perhaps he should stay well clear... Only he liked her, really liked her. She seemed genuine and had mentioned the same things he wanted for himself —a family, a home life, stability. Was she the one for him? The one he'd been waiting for all his life? At one time he'd thought Jenni had been his perfect mate, the one he'd grow old with, and maybe she might have been, yet fate had decided otherwise.

Finally, he sighed, the decision made. 'I will help you, if you need it.'

'Help me?'

Sebastian nodded, his heart turning at how small she looked, how vulnerable. He wanted to gather her into his arms and keep her there for all time. Actually, he wanted to kiss her until neither of them could breathe, and then he would make love to her, leisurely. He knew she would be delicate, smooth, warm, and moist. His groin tightened, his jeans became too tight and restrictive. He mentally shook himself and cleared his throat. 'If you want to move here permanently, then I can help you find somewhere to live and give you hand to find a job and all that.'

She looked at him with wide, brown eyes. 'Really?'

'Sure. I'd like to be your friend. The local school will be closed for the summer holidays, but perhaps we can find you a part-time job until it re-opens?'

'That's awfully kind of you.' She smiled and his heart leapt as a rush of warmth flowed through his veins. He took a deep breath and tried to slow his frantic pulse rate. The last thing he wanted was to scare her off.

ele

'I'm off to the shops, Mrs. Henley,' Molly called from the front door.

'Actually, my dear, could you do a favour for me?'

Molly placed her straw hat on her head. 'Of course.'

'I saw Seb in the supermarket the other day, and he said he had a dozen eggs for me. If you're walking that way, could you pick them up for me? I do prefer to serve fresh eggs when I can, and Seb's hens lay good eggs.'

While Mrs. Henley chatted about the freshness of farm produce and sorted through the kitchen cupboards for a suitable basket, Molly tried to think of a good excuse not to go. For the last few days, she'd struggled to stay calm and respectable in Sebastian's presence as he made inquiries on her behalf for jobs in town. He'd stopped by twice at the B & B with information on different places looking for workers, and each time she wanted to throw herself into his arms, rip his clothes from his body, taste him, touch him. She'd wound herself into a tight knot of burning need, a slave to her own sexual fantasies.

Yesterday, when he called, he'd stared at her with what seemed the same hunger in his eyes, sending signals that turned her bones to water. Try as she might, it was impossible not to think of him all the time; he invaded her thoughts when she least expected it. At night when the heat of the day still lingered, she tossed and turned in bed, her body pulsating with yearning until she was forced to take a cold shower.

And now she would see him again. Perhaps it was inevitable. Perhaps she had to speak with him more, learn more about him to make him just a normal man and not some sex-god she'd been dreaming about. He offered friendship, but she hesitated, because deep down she knew it wouldn't be enough. She wanted him as a lover too, but where would that get her? A dalliance with the local, most eligible bachelor wouldn't be a good start to her time in the town. From now on she wanted all or nothing from a man, someone who wanted the same things she did. So, she had to erase Sebastian Lord from her thoughts. After today's visit, she would keep her distance, which, in turn, would help her keep her sanity.

Within ten minutes she walked toward the avenue of trees where she'd first met him. All was quiet except for the native birdcall. The sun baked the countryside. A shimmering haze enveloped the horizon, and Molly realised she'd been mad to walk. She should have borrowed Mrs. Henley's car. She felt hot and thirsty and a bit sticky with perspiration. What had she been thinking? How could she possibly show up looking like she'd just stepped out of a sauna?

At the end of the avenue, the fields opened out before her. She hesitated when she spotted Sebastian's farm on the rise. Despite the need to see him, or more truthfully to drool over him, she didn't want to turn up looking like a sweaty tramp.

Suddenly the noise of an engine shattered the quiet. From behind a cluster of trees, a tractor appeared and riding high in the seat sat Sebastian, wearing a cowboy hat, jeans, and an unbuttoned pale blue shirt, Blackie at his feet.

Molly's mouth went dry at the sight of Sebastian's chest with its fine sprinkle of fair hair and washboard stomach. Her dreams hadn't done him justice. He was a living, breathing advertisement for what all men should look like. She managed to collect her thoughts enough to wave in response to his hail. 'Hello there!'

He drove closer to the wire fence that separated them and called out over the noise of the engine, 'You out walking again?'

'Actually, I've come to see you.' She held up the basket. 'Eggs.'

'Jump on.' He patted a flat part of the tractor up behind his seat.

After only a moment's hesitation, Molly climbed through the fence and walked over to the tractor. Grinning, she took the hand he offered and hoisted herself onto the machine. Blackie was told to get down, and he jumped clear before running up the field toward the house.

'You okay back there?' Sebastian laughed at her nervous nod. 'Hold onto my shoulders.'

As the tractor jerked forward, Molly quickly clung to his shoulders. The firm feel of them beneath her fingers sent a delicious tingle throughout her body. If she leant forward, she could see straight down his bare chest and the glistening sweat that beaded there. Her insides clenched, and she grew hot and moist at the very core of her body. She closed her eyes in acute pleasure and pain of being near him and wanting him, yet unable to have him.

Again, the reaction to him knocked her for six. Of course, there had been attraction between her and Mike, but never like this, never these mind-numbing, nerve-tingling sensations from a mere glance. Being close to Sebastian made her a little crazy. She wanted to do things that would never normally enter her mind. Thoughts of running her tongue down his taut stomach or—

'Hold on, there's a bit of a bump here.' His call brought her back to the present, and her face grew hotter at what she had been thinking.

Molly swayed as the tractor rumbled down a shallow ditch and up again. She'd never ridden on a tractor before, and the bumping experience made her chuckle. Adrenalin sizzled through her, bringing everything into sharper focus —the smell of the tractor's engine, the scent of crushed grass, the musky deodorant he wore.

The heat of the day paled, the problems of her failed marriage seemed no longer important as Sebastian glanced over his shoulder and winked at her. Who would have thought that the simple act of riding a tractor with a handsome guy would give her such joy?

He drove into the yard and around the back of the old farmhouse into the large barn. Once inside he cut the engine, and the calm, lazy noises of summer regained control again. He climbed down and then held out his hand to help her.

Stepping down beside him, she looked up into his eyes and grinned. 'I enjoyed that.'

'I'm glad.' His gaze dropped to her lips and Molly could only stare and wonder if he could read the desire in her eyes. Surely, he could?

Her whole body came alive, clamouring for his attention, his touch. His hand still held hers, and she didn't want to break the contact. They stood close, only inches apart. His bare chest was so tantalisingly near, and she wanted to feel it beneath her fingertips, to lick, and kiss the bronzed skin. He was like a sickness, and she had no cure. Perhaps she should have wild sex with him to get him out of her system. Mike had done it all through their marriage. It was just sex, he would say. Just sex, it meant nothing...

Could she...?

For once her old timid self stayed in the past, and the new, carefree Molly urged her on.

After what seemed an eternity, he stepped back, a wry smile lingering on his mouth. 'Would you like a cold drink?'

Another cold shower was more appropriate!

Molly nodded and on shaky legs followed him across the yard to the back of the house. He opened the screen door and indicated for her to go through. She took off her hat and stepped into the cool kitchen. A little outdated, but it felt homey and comfortable. Blackie's bed lay by the door, a soft couch was on her immediate left under a large window, and to her right stood a big pine table and chairs. A large fireplace took up the opposite wall.

She turned to Sebastian. 'This is nice.'

He smiled, hung his hat on a hook near the door, and ran his hands through his hair, making it spike up. 'Thanks. It needs doing up badly. I'll get around to it this winter.' He opened the refrigerator door and took out two cans of soda. 'Would you like a cola or ginger-ale?'

'A cola, please.' She put the basket down by her feet.

'Take a seat,' he said, removing two glasses from a high cupboard.

Molly sat at the table, which held a stack of old newspapers and a few financial magazines.

'Do you want something to eat?' He poured her drink into the glass, passed it to her, and then leaned against the sink.

She shook her head. 'No, thank you.'

Alone with him in his house, she became more aware of his size. He was at least six foot, and although lean, his shoulders were wide and powerful, as though he did a lot of manual labour. Her gaze strayed to his muscled tanned arms. 'Do-do you live here alone?'

'Yep, unless you include Blackie.' He grinned and looked out the window above the sink. 'God knows where the blasted animal has got to now.'

'Does the farm keep you busy?'

'Yes. Too busy sometimes.' He turned back towards her. 'I decided last winter to expand. I wanted to try my hand at planting crops and raising a herd of Hereford cattle, but it's all a bit much for one person.'

'Still, you must enjoy it to stay here, and do it?'

'Absolutely.' Sebastian pulled out a chair and sat at the end of the table. 'I used to work in corporate business, but the stress kills people. I didn't want to have an ulcer at thirty-five or a heart attack at forty. So, I decided to change my lifestyle.' His eyes softened as he gazed at her.

She took a sip and studied a few family photos on the mantlepiece, anything to take her mind off wanting Sebastian to sweep her off her feet and into the nearest bedroom. What was wrong with her? It'd only been a year since she last slept with Mike, yet here she was acting as if she was some sex-starved nymphomaniac! Maybe she'd suffered too much sun?

'I was thinking that since you've not managed to acquire a summer job that maybe you could help me around here, if you want. I'd pay you.'

'What?' She shot him a look so fast her neck creaked. 'Sorry. What did you say?'

The wry smile of his was something she was getting used to. He took a sip of his drink and then placed it on the table. 'I need a hand here and you need work.'

Molly stared at him, unable to believe what he just offered. 'Yes, but I don't know anything about farming.'

'I'll teach you what I know, and the rest we can learn together.' His warm smile reached his eyes. It was at that moment her heart seemed to explode in her chest.

She rose and fumbled for the back of the chair. She didn't want to fall in love, not yet. The last time she had done that, it had led to nothing but problems. Was it so wrong of her to want time to pick someone better suited to her? And now look what had happened. The first man to smile at her had also taken her heart. God damn it! She wanted to cry at the injustice of it all.

'Molly?'

She blinked, pushing away her thoughts, and paid attention to the man before her, who looked at her with such caring tenderness.

'I have to go!' She turned to run from the kitchen, but Sebastian shot up from his chair and grabbed her arm.

'What is it?'

'Nothing.'

'Do you feel it too?' he whispered, moving deliciously closer.

Her heart thumped so loudly it banged in her ears. 'No.'

'Liar,' he breathed. His gripped eased and both his hands slowly rubbed her arms, giving her goose bumps. 'You don't know how to handle what you feel, do you?'

She looked up into his eyes, a fatal mistake as they narrowed with want and she lost all use of her limbs. 'I have to go.'

Seb smiled, a slow sexy smile that made her blood run hot. 'From the first moment I saw you, I wanted to kiss you.' His hand slid around to her back and ever so slightly drew her a little closer. 'You didn't feel the same?'

'I can't...' The words died in her throat as he lowered his head, and all willpower fled as she reached up, threaded her fingers through his hair, and their lips met. The spark, the aching, the burning need gripped her body. His tongue caressed her lips before it flicked into her mouth and then his kisses trailed her neck to the soft skin under her ears. She arched into him, wanting to give him better access. When he brought his mouth back to hers, she grasped at him hungrily, not able to get enough of him.

'Molly...God. Molly...' His deep voice murmured her name over and over like a chant. Sebastian's hands cupped her bottom, dragging her against him. His hardness, the manliness of him sent fire along her veins.

Without being aware of it, he'd shuffled them both to the couch, and it knocked Molly behind the knees. She was grateful to sink onto it, bringing Sebastian with her. Taking his weight on one elbow, he kissed the soft flesh where the top button of her blouse had come undone. Then slowly unfastened the next button with his free hand and kissed that spot too.

Molly squirmed, impatient with desire. She ran her fingernails gently down his bare chest and delighted in his small shudder. Her hands paused at the top of his jeans, but it was as though she'd been possessed, because nothing could stop her now. The old Molly would be horrified by her impulsive actions, yet she hoped and prayed that the old Molly would understand that she had started a new life, become a new person, and sampling the delights of this man was a great way to celebrate that new beginning.

'Molly?'

She gazed up into his eyes, darkened with desire, and smiled. 'Mmm?'

Sebastian kissed the tip of her nose, softly, almost reverently. 'I'll do whatever you want. I'll stop right now if you'd like.'

Molly tucked her fingers inside his jeans and popped the button stud free. Ever so slowly she unzipped him and laid her palm on his underpants against his erection. 'I want you inside me, filling me, taking me to another world,' she said, her voice low.

He groaned deep in his chest, and as if she'd opened the floodgates of his lust, he gathered her tight against him and kissed her thoroughly until she no longer thought but only felt.

She pulled at his briefs, releasing him into her hands. He was so hard, yet silky, like hot velvet. She stroked him as he undid her blouse and eased it off, all the while kissing, licking, tasting whatever skin he revealed. Her lacy bra soon joined her blouse on the floor, and she thought she would orgasm when he cradled both breasts in his calloused hands and alternatively nibbled and sucked her nipples.

'Seb!' She arched into him. 'It's been a long time since…oh God…'

'I know, sweetheart, it has for me too.' He panted, kissing her. 'I want to go slow and savour you, but…'

Molly smiled, threaded her fingers through his hair. 'Can we go slow later?'

Seb chuckled, unzipped her jeans, and pulled them off. He sat back on his knees between her legs and traced the pattern on her lacy panties. Then carefully, he nudged her legs open a bit more and bent to kiss her very centre. He sucked at the material, and the sensation was so erotic,

Molly bucked against him. Seb slipped his fingers under the bikini panties and found her moist and ready for him.

'Take them off,' she whispered hoarsely.

With a lazy smile he did as she asked and then stood and disappeared into the hallway. Gone only for a minute, he returned wearing a condom. 'I didn't think I had any. I found this in the back of a drawer thankfully.'

She bit her lip, grinning, goggling at his proud erection. She reached out and stroked him until he groaned and re-joined her on the couch.

'Do you want to go to the bedroom?'

Molly shook her head. 'No, here is just fine.'

Sebastian gathered her close again, and she sighed contentedly, liking the feel of his arms around. She felt safe, secure, but when his hand cupped her breast and his thumb worked its magic on her nipple, the yearning returned, and she adjusted her position so that she lay under him fully, with him between her legs.

He hesitated, poised above her. 'Are you sure?'

'Absolutely.' To show she meant it, she lifted her hips to him and guided him into her. He filled her, expanded her until she gasped, but the feeling was wonderful, pure, and intoxicating.

Seb hugged her close, kissing her as he edged himself deeper within. 'Molly. God, you're beautiful.'

Raking her nails gently down his back, she rejoiced as he shivered, and his movements became quicker. His tongue stroked hers with each of his thrusts. She opened her legs wider to accommodate him better, wanting everything he had to give.

Suddenly, he withdrew entirely, and she stared at him, then ever so slowly he inched into her again, deeper, further, until she gripped his backside in urgency. Her senses narrowed on this one moment. Seb kissed her and rocked into her hard, and she shattered into a thousand stars.

'Seb...'

With one more desperate lunge, he exploded into her, shuddering from the enormity of his release. Chests heaving, they lingered on the clouds, stunned by the experience and the connection they shared.

Seb sucked in a breath and withdrew from her, his smile tender, though anxious. She touched his cheek. 'Thank you. It was perfect.'

'It was?' Relief shadowed his eyes. 'You don't regret it?' He sounded hopeful and excited.

'Not a bit.'

He sighed and climbed off the couch. 'I'll be right back.'

While he was in the bathroom, Molly dressed and tidied her hair, which she knew would resemble a bird's nest. She was sipping her drink when he returned dressed in another pair of jeans and a T-shirt.

'Would you like some coffee?'

'No thanks.' Molly watched him pick up his discarded clothes and fling them into the laundry room off the kitchen.

He turned back to her and grinned. 'Will you stay a while?'

Letting out a breath she didn't know she held, she nodded. He wanted her stay. In one stride he stood before her, pulling her into a solid embrace, and she once more melted against him. They kissed tenderly, sharing their new-found knowledge about each other.

'I'll cook us dinner.' Seb gradually eased away and went to the fridge and cupboards, searching for ingredients.

'Did you want to have a shower?'

'Yes, I would like that, but-but only if you join me.' Her boldness surprised even her. The old Molly, the shy woman who kept her emotions hidden, knowing they would be rejected by her selfish husband, had gone, fled. The change alarmed her a little, yet she felt invigorated, alive in a way she never had before.

Sebastian took her hand and kissed the palm. 'I think a shower would be wonderful, and while you're scrubbing my back, you might think about working here with me.'

She smiled at his cheekiness. 'Perhaps I will even agree, as you soap my toes.'

'Toes?' He pretended to look horrified and, laughing, they walked along the hallway to the bathroom.

ele

Molly could never remember laughing so much in her life. For over six weeks now, she had spent her days with Sebastian on the farm, working beside him, talking, learning about him, and making love. They'd gone for dinner in town, had picnics down by the river, lunches with Mrs. Henley and Seb's mother. They spent hot, lazy nights watching movies or listening to music as the ceiling fans did their best to cool them.

She'd fallen hard for him, how could she not? He was warm, generous, funny, caring, tender—all the things she had looked for in her husband and found missing. With one look from his gorgeous eyes, Molly's bones liquefied. Sometimes when the hot weather had him stripping down to just his jeans, she would stare longingly at his bronzed body, beaded with sweat, and would simply take the initiative and seduce him wherever they were—the barn, the fields, the kitchen, the car. Condoms had become a nuisance, and she'd visited a local doctor and gone on the pill, so that their lovemaking could be as spontaneous as they liked.

Under his guidance and secure in his attention, she learnt new ways in the art of lovemaking. Her marriage bed had always been a place of quick actions, her husband happy to have his pleasure and then fall asleep, not caring if she was satisfied or not. However, Seb wanted her to climax, took special consideration that she always did, whether it be with penetration, his fingers, or tongue. She was in awe of him, her new-found sexuality, and the way they fitted so well together.

Only, she did wonder where all of this was leading. Was it simply a holiday romance? She really must start organising a real life soon, a proper job at the local school, hopefully, and find herself a home. She had left a good job, family, goldfish... Yet, none of it seemed worth returning to. Her belongings were packed in boxes at her parents' home, untouched since she dumped them there when she left to go on this holiday. So, what was her future? It was too soon to think that Seb featured into it. She'd like to think he did, but, in all honesty, she had to be sensible. Despite having lots in common with him, she wanted someone who wanted the same things she did. She'd wasted enough years on clinging to fragile hope.

'Hey, sweetheart, remember me?' Seb laughed, waving his handsaw at her.

Molly gazed up at him on the ladder, while he cut dead branches off the apple tree. He wore jean cut-offs, a white T-shirt, and brown boots and looked as sexy as hell from her position. How had she managed to have wild sex with such a man?

'Who are you again?' She grinned.

'Do I need to come down and remind you?' he threatened light-heartedly.

'Maybe you do, my memory seems to have deserted me.'

Laughing, he slowly climbed down, threw the saw onto the ground, and advanced towards where she sat against another tree, crunching on a freshly plucked apple.

She held up her hand to warn him off. 'Don't come any closer. You're hot, sticky, and filthy.'

'You don't want to play dirty?' His eyes narrowed with passion that never ebbed.

'Ah, remember I am the hired help. You can't take advantage of me. I have rights.' She chuckled as he fell onto the grass beside her.

'Perhaps those rights need defining?' He ran his fingers ever so lightly up her bare calf, making her skin come alive. 'What if one of your perks was that your employer had to beg you to make love with him?'

She shivered in anticipation when his fingers roamed over her thigh and under the cuff of her shorts. 'And if I refused it?' she whispered.

'You don't want me to beg?' His eyes widened in mock innocence as he edged one finger under the elastic of her bikini panties.

He had the power to suspend her breath. 'Begging is good...' She opened her legs a little wider, allowing him to get another finger under her panties.

Seb moved closer and took a bite of her apple. 'You're as juicy as this apple, my girl.'

Her gaze lingered on his lips where juice glistened. Gently she licked it off and at the same time his finger probed deep within her, making her squirm with want.

'I have a present for you,' he murmured against her mouth.

'I bet you do,' she teased, not really listening as his finger worked a special magic.

He nibbled her ear. 'You know the project I was working on this morning while you were doing the accounts?'

'The project in the barn?' She unzipped his jeans and pushed him over onto his back so she could take him into her mouth. Oral sex had never been something she did until Seb did it to her. She liked giving him the same pleasure he gave her.

'God...Molly...' Seb threaded his fingers through her hair as she sucked on him. 'I-I was trying to talk...'

She raised her head and gave him a devilish smile. 'Talk away. I'm listening.'

He closed his eyes briefly as she played with his erect penis, and then abruptly he jumped to his feet, tucked himself back into his jeans, and took her hand to help her up. 'I'll show you.'

Giggling at his obvious discomfort, she followed him out of the orchard's shade and up the slope to the barn.

Heat blazed the district. It was one of the hottest summers on record and inside the barn it was like an oven, but Seb guided her past the farming equipment, then out to the back under the small awning.

Molly stopped and stared, before bursting into laughter. Seb had bought a child's paddling pool and filled it with water and bubbles.

'We can pretend it's a spa at some flash resort in the Bahamas.' He grinned.

'It's fantastic!'

'Not at all stupid?' He frowned and scratched his head, looking apprehensive, as if she'd think less of him.

Molly placed her hand against his cheek. 'Whatever you do for me, big or small, is wonderful and appreciated. I'm a simple woman with simple needs. I don't need expensive presents, just honesty and tenderness.'

He kissed her hand. 'You'll have that from me, always.'

Sudden tears clogged her throat, and she tried to lighten the atmosphere. 'What's in the cooler?' She pointed at the large blue chest beside the pool.

Seb opened it and took a bottle of wine. 'I've also got cheese, dips, crackers, and fruit. Everything we need for an afternoon of relaxation.'

'I don't have my swimming costume.'

He shrugged and replaced the wine. 'You won't need it. We're secluded around the back here. Blackie usually barks if anyone comes up the driveway.' He stepped closer and kissed her. 'Are you hot?'

She nodded. He made her even hotter as he blazed a trail of kisses down her neck, his hands cupping her bottom and pulling her tight against him. Slowly, he unzipped her shorts and wiggled them down to her ankles. Next, he took off her top, and she stood there in her underwear, aching for him to make love to her.

Taking her hand, he helped her step over the side of the little pool, and then he quickly shrugged off his own clothes. Naked, he joined her in the pool, and they sank to their knees in the water.

Molly ran her hands over his upper body and bent to lick his nipples, nibbling them with her teeth. 'Lay down,' she whispered, savouring the feel of him. Seb did as she asked, the shallow water gently lapping over his body like a gentle caress.

'Are you going to feed me grapes too?' He winked and fondled her breasts through the wet bra.

She teased his penis with her tongue, which effectively stopped him from speaking, and instead he groaned deep in his chest. Playfully, she licked and kissed his skin along his flat stomach before taking off her panties.

'Molly…' Seb grasped her waist and brought her up to him to kiss her thoroughly and as he did so, she straddled him and rubbed herself against him. The water swished around them, helping to heighten the sensations that throbbed through Molly's body. She shifted her weight onto her knees and then guided his penis into her, throwing her head back as he filled and stretched her so wonderfully. They moved in rhythm, and she let the storm build inside.

Seb sat up, wrapping her legs around his waist, and sucked on her nipples. Such deep penetration sent her closer to heaven, and while he greedily assaulted her breasts, she gripped handfuls of his hair, urging him into her harder, faster. Then as though her body knew it could take no more, the tightness blasted, rocking her mind, searing her soul.

'Hell, Molly,' Seb panted, hot against her mouth. With one final thrust, he too found completion.

She rested her forehead on his shoulder, breathing heavy and loving the feeling of having him inside her. She tightened her embrace and smiled inwardly as he cradled her even closer.

'What are we to do?' he murmured. His fingertips made circles on her back.

Molly raised her head and frowned in puzzlement. 'About what?'

'You and me.' He smiled with boyish innocence.

Frightened a little by the idea of them no longer being together, Molly eased off him and moved away a bit. 'I don't understand.'

'Are you happy here?' He drew his knees up to his chest and rested his arms on them. 'Do you want to stay and make a life here?'

'Yes, I do.'

'With me?'

She swallowed and felt very vulnerable both inside and out. She wished she had clothing to cover herself. 'That depends on your feelings and on what you want.'

His gazed didn't waver. 'I want you.'

'But for how long?' She attempted to smile, to make light of the subject, but couldn't. 'I mean do you simply want to take each day as it comes and make no plans or…' The words dried in her throat as Seb got up and opened the cooler.

'Fancy something to eat?'

Molly stared at him. She was baring her heart, and he was thinking about his stomach.

Seb offered her a plate of crackers and dip. 'Try the avocado and bacon dip.'

'No, thanks.' She backed away, feeling stupid and exposed.

'Go on, try it, it's excellent.' Smiling, Seb took a cracker, scooped it into the dip, and handed it to her. 'Here, taste it.'

Tears welled, and Molly fought the urge to shout at him. How could he be so blasé? He'd started an important conversation and now acted as if they'd been talking about the weather. She glared at the offending cracker and dip, ready to tell him to stick it where the sun don't shine when suddenly she spotted something poking out of it.

Chuckling, Seb put the plate down on the grass beside the pool and examined the dip more closely. With finger and thumb he plucked the object from the gooey mess and held it up.

A ring.

Molly sat on her bottom with a thump, sending the water cascading over the side of the pool. Her hands shook as she stared from the sticky ring to Seb.

Swishing the ring in the water, Seb then held it up again to reveal its beauty. A single diamond, cut in the shape of a hexagon, on a gold band. A large single diamond.

Suddenly, the green in his hazel eyes darkened. 'You don't have to take it. I know it hasn't been a long time since we met. But I wanted to get you something. I felt I needed to…to express some of what I feel about you.' His wry smile appeared. 'You don't have to call it an engagement ring if you don't want to, or if you don't feel ready for such a step. We can call it a friendship ring if you'd like.'

Her mind whirled, went numb, and then whirled again. An engagement ring!

At her silence, his expression changed to one of doubt. 'You don't have to accept it, of course.' His face lost all colour. 'I'm not normally so impulsive.' Seb swore and turned away. 'Sorry. I shouldn't have bought it. God knows what I was thinking. You must think me as someone desperate and sad.'

'All I know is that I love you,' she said, smiling through her tears.

He paused and looked back at her. 'Really?'

'Yes, really.'

'It's not just some rebound reaction from your divorce?'

She swallowed, hearing the uncertainty in his voice. 'I mourned my marriage long before we divorced. I'd been alone for so long even when Mike slept in the bed next to me. This is no rebound, Seb. I love you for you, for what you make me feel, for helping me to become the person I've always wanted to be. I love you for the person you are.'

Molly was unable to say anything more because he crushed her to him in a hug so tight, she couldn't breathe. He rained kisses over her face, murmuring her name and how much he loved her too. She laughed, feeling light-headed on love and happiness. Could this be true? Could this wonderful man love her? After the heartache of her failed marriage, she seriously doubted she'd find someone to love again or someone who would love her as she wanted to be loved. Yet, here she was, being held in the strong arms of a gorgeous, sexy guy; the kind who never went out with little homebodies like her. For so long she had felt alone, even when surrounded by people, but not anymore. Sebastian was the man of her dreams—the one for her.

Seb threaded his fingers through hers and gazed adoringly into her eyes. 'Will you marry me one day? Take a chance on another man, another marriage, and perhaps children?'

Heart full to bursting, Molly blinked back tears of happiness and grinned. 'Oh, I think I might be convinced to do so...'

What He Taught Her

Rob Heely replaced the phone on its cradle and reclined in his swivel chair. The leather creaked, the only sound in the room. He'd done it. After years of working hard, saving money, and living with a determined focus to be successful, he'd finally succeeded.

Staring out of the window, he smiled. The magnificent view of the crystal-clear ocean lapping the white sand, as the palm trees swayed with the gentle, warm breeze was lost on him. Instead, images of a different paradise flickered in his mind. A beautiful resort built from his plans and ideas, owned and operated by him. It would be eco-friendly, classically smart with clean lines, soft décor, and be fully equipped with modern conveniences. It'd also be ideally tucked away from the world where people could relax, de-stress from life and, for a brief time, enjoy being pampered.

Energy zinged through his body. He stood and prowled the office as happiness burst inside him. That had been the most important phone call of his life. Now, not only did he have the bank's support, he'd also been given the green light to start looking for a suitable site.

Carl. Jonathan. He needed to ring his investors. He checked his watch. It was the middle of the night, London time. Despite the great news, he doubted they'd appreciate being woken up.

He couldn't stop grinning. He wanted to shout the news, shake hands, crack open a bottle of champagne! The little red lights on the phone switch lit up, but he ignored the demands of his time, for now, anyway. Outside his door, the staff walked, talked, and got on with their jobs—

exactly what he should have been doing, but he couldn't sit still, too buoyant to continue with office work.

Grabbing a stack of papers, he'd already signed, he left his office and walked down the corridor to his secretary's desk. Finding it empty, he placed the documents on her in-tray, and continued to the hotel's main reception area. Stacey and Claire, the two elegant receptionists on duty, were busy at the front counter checking out guests.

A minibus from the wharf had spilled out its human cargo and smiling couples shuffled through the glass doors, holding hats and sunglasses. A small group of pensioners walked in, clutching bags and scanning the area for assistance. Beyond them a family entered, the father ushering in four small children while the mother read a check-in print out. In the midst of dealing with guest departures, Stacey and Claire were going be swamped with new arrivals. Rob stepped into the noise and crowd with his usual friendly smile. 'Welcome, everyone. I'm Rob Heely, the resort's manager.'

He focused on the older visitors, indicating for them to relax on the sofas done in colours of ochre and dark sand. 'Please, take a seat. Stacey and Claire won't be long and will soon have you shown to your rooms.' He plucked attractions leaflets from a stand and passed them around to give them something to take their mind off the short wait.

Rob turned as two male staff, dressed in the resort uniform of white shorts and navy-blue collared shirts, wheeled a couple of luggage trolleys through the glass doors. He was about to speak to them when he noticed a tall woman standing behind the family party.

Compared to the casual clothes everyone else was wearing she looked out of place. She wore a dark business suit, sheer stocking and heels.

He frowned, momentarily distracted by the thought that there must be a conference scheduled this week and he'd forgotten about it. But no, he had checked the events board only yesterday at the staff meeting. She stood ramrod straight. One of the kids knocked into her and she lifted her chin with annoyance and offered the apologetic father a brittle smile. The family shuffled forward to the counter so Claire could check them in. The woman stayed put, keeping her distance from the unruly mass of children. Her shoulders slumped and she set her thin laptop case at her feet as though its slight weight was really too much for her. Rob wasn't the least bit surprised. She was rod thin. A strong wind could probably blow her over.

Skirting a young couple who were both chatting away on their phones, he kept his gaze on the woman. Unlike everyone else, she didn't seem happy to be on holiday.

In fact, she looked downright miserable though it didn't diminish her fragile beauty, or stylishness.

She appeared remote, untouchable and judging by her Gucci handbag, he could safely assume she was wealthy.

He waited in the lobby until she had been checked in and left the reception before casually strolling up to the desk. While Claire and Stacey continued to handle check ins he tapped away on the keyboard until he found her on the computer system.

Why did she intrigue him? The resort accommodated thousands of guests each year so why did this willowy woman with the sad eyes claim his interest?

She was alone. Why had she booked the beach cottage, which had enough rooms to cater to a family of five?

ele

Cassandra Kearns smiled her thanks to the resort employee who set her suitcases in the spacious beach house's living room. Once he'd left the room, she sank into the nearest wide cane chair's green cushions and closed her eyes.

She'd done it.

She'd come to the other side of the world, alone. Could Hamilton Island, a little speck on the east coast of Australia, be further away from New York, from her ex-husband?

No one would find her here. She'd left no details of her destination with anyone but her daughter, Chrystal. Her secretary had her cell for any emergencies, which Cassandra knew wouldn't arise because she had spent hours clearing her desk of any potential problems. Apart from Chrystal and two older male cousins on her mother's side, whom she hardly ever saw, she had no other family to worry about. She could relax.

Two weeks in Australia.

A rare smile dawned on her face. The beach house was hers for two glorious uninterrupted weeks of solitude and leisure. She took survey of the elegantly styled room, decorated with soft hues and odd touches of dazzling bright colours such as rust-orange, fuchsia and lime green.

Beyond the sliding glass doors, a magnificent vista of a cloudless sky and a sparkling sapphire ocean beckoned her. She slipped off her sandals and stepped lightly across the cool polished floorboards and out onto the deck, which wrapped around the full length of the house. Standing between two large comfy cane chairs, she stared out at the view. A slight sea breeze lifted her hair from her forehead, cooling her.

In front of the deck, a lush lawn, complete with a couple of sun loungers, swept down between the strands of tall palm trees to the pristine sand at the water's edge. Her own private beach. Heaven.

Her spirits lifting, she walked back indoors. From the sitting room, she explored the kitchenette, dining area, the spacious blue bathroom that included a round spa bath, the clean spare bedrooms with its bunks and single bed, and then lastly the main bedroom. Her smile widened at the sight of the enormous king size poster bed, complete with white linen hangings and a white and gold damask cover. Her bed faced out toward the deck and the view ocean beyond delighted her. I could get used to the idea of waking up to that view every morning.

'Hello?'

Cassandra jumped. She hurried from the bedroom into the sitting room. In the doorway, she stopped and stared at the man standing on the deck. He had his back to her and seemed to be peering over the railing, looking for someone.

Straightening her shoulders and lifting her chin—a gesture that had earned her Oscar's, her ex-husband's, scornful nickname, 'Ice Queen'—and stepped forward. 'May I help you?'

He spun around and smiled. 'Hello there.'

Cassandra froze. The man was simply gorgeous, breathtaking in fact. He wore white shorts and a green print shirt that accentuated his deep tan and bright teeth. She blinked, trying to capture her dazed mind. She was a mature woman, a lawyer, for God's sake, not some adolescent girl.

'I'm Rob Heely.' He grinned and held out his hand. He didn't enter the sitting room but stayed on the deck, forcing her to go to him.

'Hello. I'm Ms. Kearns.' She remained where she was. 'Can I help you?'

He dropped his hand to his side. 'Actually, I'm here to help you, Ms. Kearns.'

His Australian accent wasn't too harsh, softer than a few others she'd heard before, not that she'd spent much time in the company of many Australians apart from the odd business associate back home.

'Help me? I don't understand.' She folded her arms, resisting the urge to smooth down her black skirt.

His megawatt smile made her heart thump a little faster. 'We are very hands on here. We like to make sure our guests are comfortable. It's my job to cater to all your needs.'

The blood drained from her face. 'There must be some mistake. When I booked this accommodation, I asked for complete privacy.' She glanced to the kitchenette on right. 'They said this cottage could be used as self-catering.'

'It is, absolutely.' He bowed his head, and she was keenly aware of how his sun-kissed hair, the shade of wet sand with lighter blond streaks, fell over his eyes. 'However, I am here for you, too. Kind of like a personal assistant.' He flashed his white teeth again, depriving her of the power to think. 'I can organise a massage, boat trips, a round of golf, tennis, snorkelling, a table in the restaurant, anything that takes your fancy.'

She swallowed and played with the plain gold chain around her neck. She didn't want to do any of that. Peace and quiet was all she asked for. Was that too much? The whole point of coming here was to escape her frenzied life. 'Thank you, but that won't be necessary. I don't want someone waiting on me.'

Rob took two steps closer to the sliding doors. He had fine features, a strong square jaw and startling deep blue eyes. The bridge of his nose wasn't completely straight, like it might have been broken a time or two. He was, as Chrystal would say, gorgeous eye candy. 'Ms. Kearns?'

'Yes?' She blinked and tried to concentrate on his words and not the buff, well defined body his loose shirt seemed to be teasing her with. Lord, she had to get a grip on herself. She was off men for good. Perhaps it was jetlag? Something had to be responsible for her keen observations of his attributes.

'Near the kitchen door is a wall phone. Press one to get reception, press two for me.' His smile faded. Instead, he gazed at her intently, his eyes, such magnificent blue eyes, seemed to know her most intimate thoughts and her cheeks warmed.

Lord, was she having one of those hot flashes? Was she old enough, or was menopause hitting her early?

'I'm sure I won't need anything. Thank you. I am quite capable of taking care of myself, but I appreciate your concern.' She gave a sharp nod, dismissing him. She'd spoken in the cold tone she used in court, one that defied argument. The poor fellow was probably up for staff person of the month or something and was pulling out all stops.

Rob bowed like a gentleman, surprising her. 'As you wish, Ms. Kearns.' He went to turn away but stopped. Again, his gaze held hers. 'I wish you a pleasant night.'

She shivered at his whispered parting and watched him descend the small flight of wooden stairs down to the path leading to the main hub of the resort.

When he was lost from sight, she turned back to the ocean. Slivers of gold danced on it and coral pink streaked the sky. It was a beautiful place, and if the 'hired help' was as attractive as Rob then what would that hurt? Perhaps her decision to be 'off men' was a little harsh. Looking at hot men wasn't a hardship, and after all, she was single now and on holiday.

Cassandra stretched her neck, kneading the knot of strain. The sitting room dimmed in the twilight, and she switched on two lamps. Instantly, the room warmed, the soft crash of the waves on the beach and the insects in the bushes tickled the hem of the seductive quiet. A yawn escaped her. She needed a long soak in the bath and then bed.

Running the hot water into the bath, she poured in a liberal amount of the perfumed salts the resort had supplied and undressed. She caught sight of herself in the full-length mirror as she removed her bra. She counted her ribs. Extra weight had never been her problem, but the stress of divorcing Oscar had reduced her to waif thin. She looked ugly. Her breast had shrunk two sizes and her hips bones were grotesque knobs under her pale skin.

What had happened to her?

She'd been a celebrated New York beauty at one time. Not now though. No wonder Oscar had affairs. Angry at her self-pity, she slipped into the water, determined to relax.

Tomorrow would be the start of her holiday.

Tomorrow she would have fun. Unfortunately, she had the sneaking suspicion she had totally forgotten what fun was

———ele———

'Ms. Kearns!'

Cassandra looked up from her map of the island and frowned. Rob jogged toward her, wearing only navy shorts and running shoes. His bare chest was smooth and sleekly muscled. He was no boy, but a man in his prime. The width of his shoulders hinted at a subdued power. He wasn't a muscle-bound Mr Universe, thankfully, he just looked very fit and healthy. He was a walking advertisement for what a man should look like.

Despite herself, her pulsed raced. Her body seemed to overthrow her better sense. There was a surging in her veins, an awareness of him as a male and herself as female —a primal awareness.

Damn it! Physical attraction wasn't called for or needed right now, if ever again.

'Want to join me?' he slowed to a stop. Even though the sun was only just peeking above the horizon, the tropical heat simmered. Sweat gleamed on his tanned skin and she had the sudden urge to touch it.

Alarmed, she took a step back. Her frown deepened. 'Er, no thank you. I'm on my way back to the beach house.'

'The jet lag kicked in, did it? Got you out of bed before dawn?' He stretched his legs on a thick log at the edge of the path.

'Yes, something like that.' Nothing would make her admit that she only slept five hours a night every night. Her dedication to her work had her walking on the treadmill at six and after a shower and a quick coffee she was in the office before eight. 'Well, enjoy your day.' She nodded and turned back the way she'd come. So much for her morning walk. Maybe she should have gone somewhere really remote, like the deserts of Mongolia.

'How about breakfast?'

She spun back to him. 'Pardon?'

'Breakfast. You know the food you eat after you've woken up and have before lunch?' He grinned and tilted his head totally cocksure and secure within himself. The gesture melted her bones with a breath-taking burst of desire. A confident man always got her attention.

'I-I don't eat breakfast.'

'Really?' his blue eyes widened in horror. 'That's insane. Breakfast is the most important meal of the day.'

'Not for me.' In fact, eating meals was always way down on her list of things to do. There was never enough time. 'Yes, it shows.' He performed a few more causal stretches.

She stared at him. 'That is rather rude.'

'Nah, just truthful.' His gaze roamed over her as though he was summing up goods at a market. 'You are in desperate need of a good feed.'

'A good feed?'

He pulled his arms back over his head, his chest thrust toward her. 'Do you have an eating disorder?'

Cassandra gasped. 'No!' She glared at him. 'Are all Australians as rude as you?'

'I'm not being rude.' Rob shrugged, finished his stretches and jogged in place. 'I'm making conversation. Don't Americans like straightforward conversation?'

'Of course, but you were being personal.'

'I was?' He looked unconcerned and jogged a circle around her. Suddenly, he stopped and smiled. 'I like you. A lot of Americans we get here can be a bit…'

'Loud?' She glared.

'That's one way of putting it.' He laughed.

'We aren't all like that, you know.' Why am I even talking to this guy?

'I know. Some are wonderful. We see all kinds here. I could tell you some stories.' He winked and she couldn't help but to relax a bit. He was harmless, she supposed.

'I'm sure you could, but I have to go.'

'Oh, have you signed up for any of the aerobics classes, or the scuba diving lessons? Maybe you're going deep sea fishing?' His mouth curled wryly, teasing her, they both knew she had no intentions of doing any such thing.

'Goodbye.' She stepped away, annoyed that he, a man she barely knew, could read her so easily. No one had been able to do that before.

'What's your name?'

She glanced back at him. 'I told you yesterday. Ms. Kearns.'

'No, your first name,' he said softly.

She hesitated. 'Cassandra.'

'Cassie.' He smiled. 'I like that. It suits you.'

'No one calls me Cassie.'

'I will.' He jogged backwards from her a few paces. 'I'll collect you for breakfast in fifteen minutes.' He turned and trotted away down the path.

She lifted her hand to call him back, but he was already lost in the lushness of the rainforest around them. Frowning, she walked back to the beach house.

Breakfast with Rob. How crazy. Why would he want to have breakfast with her, or she with him? They were strangers. Besides, she wanted to be alone, not spend time chatting about nothing with a man she didn't even know.

On the deck, she paused and tapped her fingernails on the railing. When he arrives, she'd just tell him to go. Simple.

A moment later she ran into the bedroom and changed her brown slacks for a long flowing lemon skirt and white sleeveless top. A few touches of makeup and a quick brush of her hair, which she then promptly gathered up and secured with a clip and she was done.

Taking a deep breath, she frowned at her reflection. What was she doing? Who was she trying to impress, for God's sake? Some resort employee? He was at least ten years younger than her. She was probably some kind of bet between him and his friends. She paused. No, he didn't seem that kind of guy and she was usually a good judge of character.

When she returned to the sitting room, she found Rob standing on the deck, wearing khaki dress shorts and a dark blue shirt. Attraction hit her like a bullet and a blush crept up her neck.

'Already then?' His blue eyes, a lighter colour than the sea behind him, were alight with some inner joy.

She hung back, anxious. 'If this is just part of your resort policy then it's wasted on me.'

'Resort policy?'

'Yes. The kind that makes sure guests are entertained, not left to mope or something. The type that has the young males dancing with old women, and all that.'

He laughed deeply, infectiously. 'What mad idea is that?'

'It happens.' She defended, though she sounded stupid even to her own ears. Had she lost her mind crossing the ocean from America to Australia?

'Not here, Cassie. We just like to make friends.' He made it seem like wanting to make friends was the most natural thing in the world.

However, he didn't know that she didn't make friends. She could count on one hand the number of friends she had, and she didn't consider any of them a close. She had associates, acquaintances, not a best friend. She lifted her chin, ready to argue, defy him and his carefree ways. 'Honestly, there's no need for you to escort me to breakfast.'

'I want to, really. Listen you need to eat, and I want to eat, so why not do it together?' He shrugged in that lazy way he had which suggested he didn't care one way or the other.

'I don't know…'

'Come on, Cassie, you're on holiday. You can do anything on holiday.' A challenging glint lit his eyes. "You can even eat with a stranger…"

Never one to shy away from a challenge, she joined him on the deck and took a deep breath. 'Breakfast it is then.' Heavens, she felt as if she had given the man her soul, not simply accepted a breakfast invitation! What was wrong with her? It crossed her mind that she might need to see a doctor or a psychiatrist.

They talked all the way to the main restaurant, which was around the curve of the beach and sheltered from sight by the natural vegetation and some well-placed palm groves. Cassandra listened to Rob as told her the history of the resort and of the island. His pleasant voice relaxed her, and she enjoyed their short walk. She encouraged him to keep talking as they sat at a small table for two on the restaurant's timber deck.

She was a good listener, that's part of the reason why she was an excellent lawyer. Besides, she preferred listening to Rob than talk about herself, which would bore him within ten minutes. She had nothing fascinating to tell him. She was a divorced lawyer from New York and mother of a grown-up daughter. Boring with a capital B. Ho-bloody-ray for her.

Hungry guests filled the area, but for once Cassandra was uninterested in her surroundings as she listened to Rob. He was a natural entertainer and throughout breakfast he regaled her with funny stories of the different, and some very strange, visitors to the island.

It'd been a long time since someone had made Cassandra laugh, or even kept her interest for more than five minutes outside of work, and she was surprised how easily the time slid away. She glanced at her slim gold watch, surprised to discover they'd sat there for two hours.

'That's a nice watch.' Rob sipped his second glass of orange juice.

She hid a smile. 'Nice? I should hope so. It cost a fortune.'

He ran his fingertip around the rim of his glass of juice. 'Just because an item is expensive doesn't mean it is good. Something can be ugly whether it is worth or lot or nothing at all.'

'True.' She looked away, embarrassed. Once all she had cared about was money, position and having the best of everything. Well, she had all that and where had it got her? She was forty-one years old and alone.

'How about a swim?' Rob stood and circled around the table to hold her chair as she rose.

'A swim?'

'Yes. You know, that activity you do in water?' He grinned, the teasing back in his voice.

Like a spell had been broken, she became prim again, rejecting any further friendship. 'No, thank you.'

'You can't swim?'

'I can swim very well actually.' She thought of the countless hours and laps she'd dedicated to her apartment complex's indoor pool.

'We can snorkel in front of your beach house. There's a small reef on the right.' He escorted her down the steps to the path. 'You go and change, and I'll get some gear. I'll be ten minutes.'

'I don't know…'

'It'll be fun, I promise.'

'Really, I…'

'Don't you like having fun?'

Cassie blinked. Fun? That word again. What was it exactly? It'd been so long since she had simply had fun. Her life didn't cater to fun.

Rob lightly touched her arm. 'Give me ten minutes. You'll enjoy it I promise.'

He disappeared around the back of the restaurant, and she started back toward her accommodation. She rubbed her arm where he had touched it. Snorkelling? She didn't much care for it, but for some reason she couldn't say no to Rob.

Where had her decisiveness gone? All she had to do was say no and stick to it, mean it. That wasn't so hard, was it? She swore softly under her breath, denying the truth that crept up on her. Having Rob for company allowed her to pretend she wasn't here in paradise by herself...

ello

Rob jogged to the equipment sheds behind the main buildings, where all the paraphernalia for active guests was stored. His phone rang in his pocket, and he answered the call while collecting snorkels and flippers. He'd officially taken the day off from work, but being a live-in manager meant he was still an easy target for the staff when things became heated or difficult.

Having dealt with that mini crisis and telling James, the assistant manager, where the file he required was, he grabbed the gear and hurried over to his own apartment.

Overlooking the water, the spacious apartment was the best perk of the job. The rooms were white, decorated with ocean inspired splashes of colour—-blues, greens, turquoise and sand. He ripped off his shirt and paused. He glanced around and tried to see it through another's eyes— Cassie's eyes. She was a sophisticated woman. Would she like this place?

He gazed at the newspapers, bills and work documents littering the black granite kitchen bench tops. An empty orange juice carton adorned the sink. The fruit in the bowl were over ripe.

The lounge room fared no better. He'd left his running shoes near the sofa, his tennis racket leaned against a wall, and the suit he'd collected from the laundry still lay over the dinning chair...

What the hell was he stressing about? The apartment was fine, lived in, a home, his home. Who was he trying to impress? Why had this Cassie chick suddenly become the sole focus of his attention? Yes, she was an attractive woman, in a controlled kind of way, which normally wouldn't have caught his interest, but for some reason, since the first moment he saw her, he had thought of nothing else.

He changed into his old favourite board shorts and wondered if he'd been without a woman for too long. His last sexual encounter had been months ago...

Yes, that was it.

He was frustrated. Simple.

Chuckling at himself, he seized the snorkelling gear and his keys. As he walked along the pathways through the resort, he kept himself in check. Cassie would be a pleasant diversion for a few days. He deserved some pleasurable entertainment after weeks of demanding work, both as a manager and the long hours he'd spent planning and organising his future.

After changing into her dark chocolate conservative one-piece swimming costume, Cassandra grabbed a towel and waited on the balcony for Rob. The scent of tropical flowers was heavy in the air. The crash of the waves and the odd call of a bird was the only sound as the heat rose. The relaxed atmosphere renewed her spirits, or was it the idea of spending a few hours with Rob that gave her morale such a boost? She smiled briefly.

On the chair inside, her laptop and phone sat silently, as though they accused her of neglect. She fought the urge to check her messages and emails. Chrystal had made her promise not to work while she was away, and well, a promise was a promise, but even still, it was dreadfully tempting to see what was happening back home. Was her office in an uproar without her?

She hadn't taken a holiday in seven years and even then, it was only for a week when her mother died. Perhaps she should just check her messages. Cassie took one step, but Rob appeared out from the trees, a smile playing on his lips. 'All set? I've left the gear down on the sand.' Shirtless, his coloured surfing shorts clung to his thighs. 'You're a stunner in that swimsuit.'

'Thank you.' She blushed. Why did his presence send her heart racing? She'd seen half naked good-looking men before. In fact, the gym in her office building was often a hive of shirtless men. So, why did this one young man have the ability to make her light-headed with want?

He looked like an old surfie with his sun-bleached hair, a total opposite of the sleek suit-wearing men she normally mingled with. Rob was the kind of guy she'd never looked twice at. If she'd seen him at home, she'd have had him pegged as a loser within a nano-second. He'd have been placed in her mental folder as a person with no drive, no power, too casual, too lazy, too carefree...

'How old are you?' she blurted out. He studied her with a lazy heated gaze, and she wished she had pulled a dress or wrap over her costume. She felt exposed and hardly decent.

Rob, halfway up the stairs, halted. 'Why do you want to know that?'

'I'm interested.' She held her towel in front of her of her body.

'I'm thirty-five.'

She blanched. Thirty-eight would have sounded better. 'Six years younger than me.'

'Is that a problem? Am I too young to go snorkelling with you?' His eyes widened with mock innocence. 'Must I be over fifty to get in the water?'

Despite herself, Cassandra laughed and went down to meet him. 'Is doing this stuff safe? I mean I'm not going to be eaten by a great white shark or anything, am I?'

'I promise it won't be a shark that eats you.' Rob murmured and took her hand in a protective manner. She jumped at the contact, but he ignored her reaction and guided her across the grass down to the beach, talking all the time.

Physical contact was something she didn't do. She wasn't a 'huggy' type of person and refused to be over familiar even with her own family. However, and as crazy as it seemed, his hand holding hers felt right. And that's when the fear set in.

'You okay?' Rob dropped her hand and collected the snorkelling gear from the white sand. 'You've gone a bit pale. Don't tell me you're frightened of the ocean, are you?'

She gave herself a mental shake. She was a New York lawyer for God's sake, she could do anything! 'Of course not.'

'Good. There's nothing to be scared of. I'll be with you the whole time.'

She smiled and accepted the goggles. Little did he know being with him was the only thing that scared her, but she'd rather die than admit that to a soul.

With patience and skill, Rob made sure she felt secure, and her equipment was on and functioning correctly before he took her hand and led her out pass the small breaking waves and into the turquoise water that spilled over the shallow reef.

'Ready?'

She looked around at the vast expanse of water and tried not to be nervous. 'As I'll ever be, I guess.'

Rob raised his eyebrows, his face full of excitement. 'This is fun, so relax. Do you know how to relax?'

She gave him a cool stare. 'Don't play smart.'

'With you? Never.' He chuckled. 'Let's go.'

She nodded and started to swim, her face in the water. It took a moment for her to focus and concentrate, but then she saw them. Beautiful fish of all colours and sizes swam through the pale coral. Rob stayed within her vision, gently swimming before her around the reef, pointing out different things they came across, a bright starfish, an octopus, and schools of tiny baitfish.

Breathing through the snorkel, which had been difficult at first, became easier and more regulated as she grew comfortable using it. Cassie became absorbed in this underwater delight. The ocean was warm and caressing as she gently floated on the surface. The wonder of the ocean, which was divulging its secrets to her, gave her a feeling of peace. With the sun warming her back, she swam slowly, wishing she had a camera to capture the beauty beneath her.

At last, they swam back to the shore and Cassie grinned like a silly girl, but she couldn't help it. On the beach, she grabbed her towel and hugged it to her chest. 'Thank you, Rob. That was magical. A wonderful experience.'

'I'm glad you enjoyed it.' He grinned, drying his chest.

Cassie glanced away in an attempt not to stare at his well-developed six-pack. 'How lucky you are to do this sort of thing every day.'

'Unfortunately, I can't do it every day, because I have to work, but once a week isn't so bad.'

'Am I taking you away from your work now?'

'No, not at all. As of today, I'm actually on holidays.'

'You stay here for your holidays?'

'Not usually, no. I return to the mainland and visit my parents in Brisbane, but they've gone to my uncle's place in Sydney and so I decided to stay here.' He gave her an intense look. 'Everything I wanted is right here.'

She found it hard to swallow all of a sudden and looked away. 'I'd like to bring my daughter Chrystal here. She would love to do all everything this resort offers. She's very sporty.'

'Is she as beautiful as her mother?'

She jerked back and stared at him, a blush heating her face. 'Chrystal is far more stunning than I ever dreamed of being.'

His eyes narrowed and darkened. 'I doubt that.'

Taking a step back, Cassie's grip on the towel tightened. 'I'd best be getting back. Thank you, again.'

'Will you have dinner with me?'

The warmth left her face, and her breathing became rapid. 'No. No, I don't think so.'

'No?'

'No, sorry.'

'Why? Don't you like me?'

He scowled as if such a thing was impossible and suddenly, she wanted to laugh.

'Yes, I like you.'

'Well then?'

'It-it wouldn't be right. I'm—'

'It wouldn't be right for whom?' Rob stepped closer and she read the desire in his eyes. The pit of her stomach quivered.

'Right for you? For me?' he whispered.

'Both. I'm not the kind of woman who...who...'

'Has dinner?' he prompted, teasing her again.

Her laugh was strained. 'Naturally I have dinner.'

'Good. I'll pick you up at seven o'clock.' He gathered up the equipment and turned away.

She raised a hand to stop him. 'Rob, really, I don't think —'

His tossed her a seductive look over his shoulder. 'Cassie. Stop putting up walls. You're on holiday. Relax. I'll see you at seven.'

ele

Taking a deep breath, Cassandra twisted in front of the mirror and critically eyed her dress. The pale gold satin shimmered over her body. Chrystal had bought it for her and packed it, knowing full well she'd never wear such a thing, but Chrystal insisted on packing for 'emergencies'. How such a dress could be considered an emergency Cassandra had no idea.

Still, it had come in handy because she had packed nothing else worth wearing on a dinner date. Though of course, when she'd been packing for this holiday, the idea of having dinner with a man had been so way off scale it was laughable.

Yet, here she was, fluffing her hair, applying make-up and praying she looked presentable, even a little sexy. She didn't want people to think she was his older sister or something.

Leaning towards the mirror, she studied her wrinkles. She had a few, mainly frown lines; a natural side effect of her heavy scheduled and stressed lifestyle. Well, she had a few wrinkles, so what? It didn't matter. She didn't care what Rob thought of her.

Liar.

She frowned. Disgusted at herself for allowing a man to get under her skin again, she snatched up her purse off the bed and stormed into the sitting room. She'd have dinner with Rob and that would be it. Tomorrow would be a new day and she'd spend it by herself reading a book or...or... something!

A low whistle destroyed the frustrated silence and she spun toward the door. Rob leaned against the doorframe, looking splendid. The top two buttons of his crisp white shirt were undone, and the tailored black trousers accented his lean legs. Desire flared in her, pinning her to the spot.

'You look magnificent,' he said softy as stalked toward her.

'Thank you.' Her eyes drank in every inch of him. He moved with an easy grace like a jaguar. His soft cologne filled her senses with images and scents of spice and moonlit exotic beaches, and she forgot to breathe.

'Shall we go?' He stepped aside so she could pass, and he closed the glass sliding door. 'The resort has wonderful chefs. I hope you're hungry.'

'Yes.' She waited for him at the bottom of the stairs, alarmed by the rapid beat of her pulse. Her body yearned for his touch, and she stiffened in order to stop from reaching out to him.

They walked in silence for a while, the air warm on their skin. The golden glow of sunset had given way to a deepening dusk, which seemed to throb with the sounds of insects and the tropical scent of rainforest.

As they neared the main buildings, music echoed over the waves crashing onto the sand. Strung lanterns replaced the twilight, shedding bronze circles of light along the path. A large bonfire blazed down on the beach and an open barbeque was in progress.

'Are we eating down there?'

'No, I have booked us a table at the restaurant.'

'Is that a private party?' She gazed at the young couples eating slices of pork straight from the pig on the spit. With the ocean as a backdrop and the large fire shadowing their bodies in copper and gold there was a sense of excitement, of anticipation in the air.

'No, it's for the guests.' Rob stopped and watched her.

She smiled a little uncertainly. Never in her life had she wanted to break the mould. She thrived on organisation and routine, but for some strange reason tonight she wanted to be different. She didn't want to eat at a fancy restaurant, listen to soft piano music or be served by silent efficient waiters.

'Would you prefer to go down there? We can, if you want.'

'No. You've booked a table and—'

'And it doesn't matter.' He grinned, leaned closer and whispered, 'We can do whatever we want.'

'I'm not dressed for the beach.' She glanced down at the slinky dress and heels.

'Take them off.' Rob shrugged, took her hand, and pulled her along behind him. 'I did mean your shoes, but if you want to go further that's fine by me.'

On the edge of the sand, he bent and took her ankle, placing her foot on his knee. With deft fingers he slowly slid her shoes off her feet. Cassandra's insides melted at the sensual gesture. His head was bent, and she wanted to run her fingers through his hair, but Rob straightened and with his usual cheeky smile, he took her hand, and they ran lightly across the sand.

Serving tables had been set up near the spit. Glasses and bottles of wine, beer and spirits covered one table, while plates and utensils were set up on the other with bowls of salads and side dishes. Rob asked one of the waiters, all dressed casually in black shorts and red shirts, to pour two glasses of wine. He handed one to Cassandra. Pop music came from a stereo placed under one of the tables and on the other side of the fire blankets were spread out with colourful cushions scattered across them. Couples sat, balancing glasses and plates piled with food.

Rob pressed his palm against the small of her back and guided her to the spit. They talked with Steve, one of the chefs, who basted the pig. The aroma of roasting meat together with scent of salt air gave the scene a tribal feel. It was fully dark now and as Steve handed her a plate of juicy pork slices, Rob added some salad to it.

'Shall we sit over there?' She indicated to a blanket furthest from the group of people

'Yep. Good idea.'

With laughter and dexterity, they managed to sit on the blanket amongst the pillows without spilling their food or drinks. For a while they ate and just listened to the sound of the waves, the chatter of the other people and the crackle of the fire as it devoured large logs.

Meat juices ran down her chin and Cassandra chuckled 'I need a napkin.'

'I've got some...' Rob hunted around the blanket and came up with a handful of napkins, but in the process knocked over her wine glass. Thankfully, it soaked the sand. 'Oh, shit. Sorry. I'll get you another.' He jumped up and went back to the tables.

Watching him grin and talk with the servers, Cassandra wondered what it was about Rob she liked so much. He was very easy going, had none of the strung-up tension most men she knew possessed. However, that could be because she was only around men at work, lawyers like herself, who strove for excellence in a job that was mentally taxing and demanded long hours. If Rob was stressed in his position as resort manager, he didn't show it. In fact, he seemed to thrive on life.

'Here we are. A full glass and the bottle.' He flashed the bottle at her and then dug it into the sand to hold it upright.

'Thank you.' She took the white wine from him and enjoyed a long sip while she eyed him over the rim of her glass. 'Tell me about yourself.'

Leaning on his elbow amongst the cushions, Rob picked up his fork. 'What do you want to know?'

'Whatever you want to tell me.'

'I was born in Queensland. I am the eldest of three children. My father worked on the railways and my mother was a teacher. They are both retired now. I had a great childhood.' He speared some salad onto his fork and ate it. 'Rather boring, really.'

'Have you ever been married?'

'No.'

'Why?'

'Didn't find the right person. I came close once, but I realised at the last minute that we didn't want the same things.'

'Which were?'

'Lots of things. I wanted to travel for years. She wanted a large white wedding and four kids.' He sipped some wine. 'I actually saw her a few years ago. Sue is her name. She has all that she wanted she told me. I'm happy her dreams came true, but they weren't mine. I'm glad we didn't get married. It would have been the biggest mistake of our lives.'

'Life can be funny sometimes.'

'Life can be what we make it, too, though.' He raised his eyebrows at her, sending her a silent challenge. 'Are we masters of our own destinies?'

She drank her wine. He was hardly ever serious, and she wondered why. 'Fate plays its part, I believe.'

'Perhaps. Eat up.'

She ate some more and stared out over the ocean. He hadn't asked about her life. Was he interested? And why did she care? Maybe she should take a page out of his book and just lighten up a bit. Not everything had to be analysed all the time. She was here to have an enjoyable time. Rob was good company, sexy as hell and for tonight her partner. She didn't need anything more.

'Why that pensive look, Ms. Kearns?' Rob refilled her glass and his own from the bottle.

'I'm not pensive.'

'Would you like to talk about yourself?' He took her hand, his hold strong and comforting. 'I'd like to learn about you.' A wicked glint appeared in his eyes. 'Tell me your darkest secrets.'

'I have none.' She shivered slightly at the intimacy of his gaze and forced herself to pretend that the sexual sparks between them weren't there. 'I'm a lawyer from New York.'

'I know that. Tell me more.'

'My daughter is named Chrystal.'

'I know that, too.'

He played with her fingers, and she found it hard to concentrate.

'I'm divorced...'

'Lord, woman!' He gave her a frustrated look.

'Oh, okay... My mother died several years ago, and my father died when I was a teenager. My mother and I both worked extremely hard so that I could get into Harvard. I was the first person to do so in my family.'

'That must make you proud.' He stroked her thumb.

'It does. We never had the money to...you see, when I was in high school, I worked two jobs, as did my mother.' She flung her hair back impatiently, pushing back memories. 'Well, anyway, it was a difficult journey, especially when I stupidly got pregnant so young...'

'That would have been hard for you. Did you think Harvard was out of reach?'

'Yes, very much so.' She liked the rhythmic caress of his fingers. 'But Oscar's family, Oscar was my husband, Chrystal's father...' Hurt bit her, but amazingly enough the bite wasn't as deep as it had been in the last year.

'Tell me,' Rob murmured, looking down at their joined hands. He turned her hand over to trace the lines on her palm. The gesture was simple, but it filled her with longing.

'Oscar...' She swallowed as Rob's fingertip made circles on her inner wrist. 'Oscar's family is wealthy and didn't want us to marry, but Oscar insisted. We did love each other then.' She quickly drank more wine. 'His parents wanted to control the situation. His father was hoping to get into politics, and he needed us to be the perfect family. We weren't, of course. Oscar and I were determined to do things our way. It caused problems. In the end we lived in a tiny apartment and thankfully Chrystal was born just before summer break, so I had a few months at home with her before I had to go back to school. My mother came and lived with us for a year.'

She hesitated; alarmed she had spoken so much of her past. It was a topic she never discussed with anyone. 'I am so sorry. I never talk like this about myself. It must be the wine.' Embarrassed and thankful the darkness hid her flaming cheeks, she turned away slightly.

Rob's soothing pressure on her fingers increased. 'Don't be sorry. You know it might not have anything to do with the wine, but more the need to talk. My sister always said that talking helped to sort out your head.' He grinned. 'My sister is always sprouting things like that.'

Relaxing, Cassandra gazed down at their joined hands, enjoying the feel of him. 'So, you have a sister?'

'And a brother. I love them to bits. I have two little nieces and a small baby nephew, too.'

'Do you see them much?'

'Every Christmas we all get together, and I also try to get them out here during the slow season when we aren't so busy. My whole family comes, and we have a wonderful time just being at the beach.'

'I didn't think a place such as this had slow season.' She was grateful for the lighter topic. What had possessed her to tell him so much?

The music changed to a faster tempo and some of the couples got up to dance. Rob got them another bottle of wine and refilled her glass. Cassandra studied him as he secured the bottle back in the sand. Had she ever met such a man as him before? Yes, he was attractive, but he had something else that drew not only her attention, but the stares of other women around him.

There was magnetic quality about Rob, a mixture of a devil-may-care attitude and an inner strength of purpose which fascinated her. Desire grew inside her, igniting and she felt a delicious heat in the pit of her stomach. It had been so long since she'd throbbed in need for a man's body.

Reggae thumped out of the speakers. Rob stood and held out his hand. 'Come on, let's dance.'

'Really?' She stared, as he helped her to her feet. 'You dance?'

'Don't you?' He led her closer to the fire.

'I haven't for a long time, and the men I know never dance, at least not to this type of music.'

He didn't answer her as the music was turned up and the Jamaican rhythm of steel drums and a Caribbean voice urged them to let themselves go.

Fired by the wine, the heat of the fire and the music filling her senses, Cassandra was transported to another world, one full of sensual stimulus, of earthy primal urges: to eat, to frolic, to cavort. Nature's way was enormously powerful, and she didn't fight against it.

She raised her arms and swung her hips, dancing as she hadn't done for an awfully long time. Laughing, Rob twirled her under his arm. The flames reflected off her gold shimmering dress. All the guests were dancing now, the music infectious, the atmosphere festive. Everyone seemed to just want to have fun, forget their problems and dance.

Cassandra squealed as Rob lifted her off her feet and spun her around. He stepped aside, grinning as a guy in his twenties came up to her and did a bit of dirty dancing with her, grinding his pelvis against hers, and she threw her head back and laughed. She felt young and completely alive. Within moments he'd gone on to another woman, a young twenty something wearing hardly anything at all. The people around her were happy and it had been forever since she'd felt this way.

The music changed to Salsa and Rob took her in his arms and pulled her against him. Sexual need lit his blue eyes. He hungered for her. Her skin heated, longing for his touch.

Her smile melted away as the length of his body moved as one with hers, their steps not perfect, but instinctive, powerful. His shoulders muscles bunched beneath her hands. She ran her fingers down his back and he tightened his hold even further.

They were locked in a dance as sexy and sensual as actually making love. Rob's eyes never left hers, his mouth only inches from her touch. His hands cupped her hips, guiding them against his own. She shimmied, turned and with her back to him danced in a way she'd never done before. Every provocative movement was a gesture of intimacy, of want, of promise. Through music their bodies touched, sending silent messages to one another. Rob flipped her around to face him again and slipped his thigh between hers. His hands slid down over her bottom and she gasped at the ache throbbing inside her.

The music changed again, back to a pumping beat. Rob slowly released her, and she regained some of her sense and took a step back. Shocked at her wanton behaviour, her smile was perfunctory.

God, she hoped she hadn't humiliated herself. She desperately wanted to sit down. What had gotten into her? She turned away from the bonfire and wandered away from the other dancers. Rob kept pace with her.

'Would you like to go for a walk up the beach?'

'No!' She jumped at the harshness of her refusal. 'I mean no, sorry, thank you. I think it is time I went back to the beach house.' She gathered up her purse and shoes from the blanket, refusing to make eye contact.

'Cassie...'

'Please, Rob. I must go. Thank you for tonight. I had a fun time.' She flashed him a tortured look, silently begging him not to say or do anything else. 'Good night.'

As fast as she could run in the soft sand, she left the beach and headed up to the steps to the path. 'What a mess,' she cried. Not bothering to put her heels back on, she ran, along the shadowy path, away from Rob—wishing she could run away from the feeling he brought out in her too.

—eee—

The sun was high when Cassandra woke. Sluggish and thirsty, she struggled out of bed and plodded into the kitchen. A glass of orange juice made her feel a little better, but what she really needed to help make her feel normal again was a long shower. A slight headache pulsed in her temple. She hadn't drunk so much in years.

Half an hour later, dressed in white shorts and a pink halter top, she felt human again, and decided to go for a walk, but she stopped dead in the sitting room.

Resort staff had set up a massage bed on the deck and a petite Asian woman placed little bottles of oils on a small table. A young man laid out fruit platters on another table.

Sliding open the glass door, Cassandra stepped out. 'Excuse me? What is all this?'

'Good morning, Ms. Kearns. Mr. Healy instructed us to prepare this for you.' The young man smiled, his perfect teeth brightening his suntanned face. 'Aisha is ready to give you a massage, or would you prefer brunch first?'

'Rob...' Cassandra breathed. He had ordered all this for her. Her throat tightened. She couldn't remember the last time someone had gone to so much trouble on her behalf.

The brunch looked spectacular, but the massage bed was even more inviting. 'Thank you.' Cassandra smiled. 'A massage would be wonderful.'

Aisha rubbed and kneaded the scented oils into her back as Cassandra lazily watched the waves crashing onto the beach below the lawn. She couldn't recall ever being so relaxed, so dreamy! She never wanted to leave the bed, but her stomach rumbled and the strawberry finger sandwiches, sliced fruit, cheeses and the glass of iced juice beckoned.

While she ate Aisha cleared up her oils and the young man came back to help her. When they had gone, Cassandra continued eating until she was so full, she could barely move, surprising herself.

She nestled down on the sun lounger, closed her eyes and listened to the ocean. This was what a holiday should be...

She woke with a start. A bird called from where he sat perched on the deck rail a few feet from her. He trilled loudly. Black and white, he was not a kind she'd seen before. She'd have to ask Rob...

The thought of that gorgeous man made her smile.

The sun was setting behind the beach house and she realised with a ping of shock that she'd sleep through the whole afternoon. But the sleep had refreshed her, and the waves rolling beneath the orange sky beckoned her. She went inside and changed into her swimming costume.

Within minutes she was in the ocean, floating on her back over the reef. The descending sun was warm on her face as the waves rocked her body gently. She rolled over and swam for the shore. Would Rob come and see her tonight?

A pang of hunger clenched her stomach as she walked across the sand to the cottage.

Closing the door shut behind her, she made her way to the large bathroom. Had he called earlier and found her asleep? She blushed with embarrassment, hoping he hadn't. Turning on the water, she stripped off her clothes and stepped into the hot spray. Perfumed soap filled her senses as she lathered the foam over her body. The stark whiteness of her skin seemed to have been reduced somewhat in favour for a creamier shade. A few more days in the sun and hopefully she'd be a soft copper colour.

She thought of Rob as she slipped on her lace underwear. She applied light make-up, wondering if thinking about a man 24/7 would send her mad? Was it terrible of her to want to see more of him? What he'd done today was so sweet. How kind it was of him to send her a masseur, as though he knew exactly what she needed without her saying a word. Who said romance was dead?

She paused, clutching her long black skirt in her hands.

Romance?

Was he romancing her?

Was she to be another little fling he had now and then with one of the guests, especially divorced women on their own? Someone as sad as her?

Had she made a huge fool of herself?

Cassandra slowly stepped into the black skirt and zipped it up. Rob was attentive and gorgeous. Someone like him, good-looking, kind, powerful, this very resort's manager couldn't possibly live like a monk. Did she want to be a name in a long list of women?

She took out a shimmery blouse of pale rose silk from the wardrobe. It was her favourite; one she wore to special work-related functions. Tonight, it gave her a sense of herself, something she desperately needed right now.

'Come on, Cassandra,' she told herself in the mirror. 'You can do this.'

Collecting her black heels, she went into the kitchen and poured herself a glass of cold water. Dusk spread a bronze glow across the lawn, turning the sand a deeper gold. She stared at the ocean and wondered what to do.

She found Rob desirable. Could she sleep with him? Yes. Only, would that make things worse?

Could she have a holiday affair? She'd never had an affair in her life. Heck she'd only slept with one man her entire life!

Resting the cool glass against her face, she remembered conversations with other women in the office. So many of them had managed several partners in their lives. They thought her strange having married the first man she met.

She sighed and rinsed the glass in the sink, still uncertain of which route to go. Should she tell Rob thanks, but no thanks? Or throw caution to the wind and have wild passionate sex with a man she'd never see again?

As if fate was playing her hand, Rob climbed up her steps, whistling as he went. He knocked, and Cassandra moved to the sitting room. Upon seeing her, he opened the sliding door.

'Good evening.' He grinned, appraising her openly.

'Hello, Rob.' She smiled, taking in his classy black trousers, midnight blue shirt the colour of which darkened his sapphire blue eyes.

She wanted to kiss his tanned neck, thread her fingers through his light chest hair, taste him...

'Cassie...' the night's breeze carried his whisper. 'Sweetheart, don't look at me like that.' He took her hand and kissed the back of it, his eyes never leaving her face. 'I've come to take you to dinner.'

She stepped closer, wanting him with an urgency that gripped her in a silent heart-stopping hold.

Raising her arms and encircling his neck came as naturally as breathing to her. His lips drifted over hers. She sighed. They were a perfect fit, as she knew they would be.

He captured her waist, pulling her tight against him, as his tongue danced with hers: seeking, exploring, tasting. She curled her fingers into his hair, and she smiled inwardly.

Never in her life had she desired a fair-haired man before. She always went for the dark ones. But then, she'd never kissed an Australian man before either, so perhaps tonight was going to be a night of firsts.

Breaking away, she smiled and stared into his eyes. In the courtroom she had a reputation for being fierce, a fighter, bold. Someone who went for what they wanted, and usually got it. Suddenly she was emboldened to break out of the reserved controlled person she normally was.

Taking his hand, she led him into the bedroom.

'Cassie, wait.' Rob tensed. 'Are you sure?'

She raised her eyebrow. 'You don't want to?'

'God, yes!' He ran his hand through his hair. 'But only if you're sure…'

'I've never been more sure.' She gave him a saucy wink and then laughed at herself. Where had this new woman come from? A week on Australian soil and suddenly she was acting like some man-crazy weirdo.

'We can just go out for dinner, if you want? There's no pressure.'

The concern in his gaze made her sigh wistfully. He was wonderful, inside and out. She cupped his cheek. 'I want to have sex with you. There,' she shrugged, 'I've said it. Are you man enough to handle such honesty?'

He grinned and nibbled the soft skin beneath her ear. 'You want honesty, do you, sweetheart? Here's some honesty for you.' He grabbed her hips and crushed her against him, pressed his erection against her pelvis.

Her eyes widened and she sucked in a gulp of air. White heat pulsed through her like a lightning storm on a summer's evening.

Closing her eyes, she allowed her mind to go blank, and when he kissed her, she kissed him back with a passion she'd never experienced before.

'God, you're beautiful.' Rob panted against her mouth as he cupped her bottom. 'I want to be inside you… I want to kiss every inch of you, taste you…'

'I…I want it too.' No man, or more correctly Oscar, had ever spoken so freely to her about sex. It was shocking, but also enticing. She kissed him hard and pulled up his shirt, yanking it out of his trousers.

Rob walked her backwards toward the bed. He eased down the zipper of her skirt and pushed it over her hips. It dropped to the floor. He bent and lifted her into his arms, kissing her hard and urgently.

His gaze roamed her body as she lay on the bed, dressed only in her panties, bra and her pale rose silk blouse. A tinge of embarrassment coloured her desire and she lifted her arms to cover herself. But he stopped her. He knelt on the bed and slowly undid each button on her blouse, kissing the exposed skin down her stomach. Then, sliding down to the bottom of the bed, he took each of her feet in turn and kissed and caressed the inside of her ankles, all the way up her legs to the hem of her satin panties.

She closed her eyes as he kissed inside her thighs and then her poky hip bones that she was so ashamed of. A shiver went through her as he kissed a path up to her breasts, stopping on the way to lick a circle around her belly button. Since her weight loss during the divorce, her bra was a little too big for her, and again she felt unattractive.

As if reading her thoughts, Rob raised his head. 'After this, we're going to have the largest dinner you've ever had, Ms. Kearns. You're skin and bones, but you do look a little better than you did on your first day.'

Cassandra squirmed, blushing furiously. 'Was I so bad?'

'You looked like a small breeze would blow you away.' Rob, a cheeky smile lifting his lips, rose above her and took her tightly in his arms. 'I've got two weeks.'

'Two weeks for what?'

'To give you your life back.'

Tears pricked her eyes, and she wrapped her arms around him. No one had cared for her in such a long time. It was a wonderful feeling to be treasured, if only for a little while.

'I don't know what Oscar did to you, or why you always look so sad, but I'm determined to change that.' He placed traced the shape of her lips with his fingertip, and ran his hand down her throat, along her collarbone. 'And I promise you'll love every minute of it.'

'Rob…'

'Shh…Let me make love to you, Cassie.'

Closing her eyes to hide the tears that had gathered there, she breathed deeply and gave in to the magic of his fingers, his mouth. He unclipped her bra and suckled her nipples. She arched into him, wanting him to take her away to another world—knowing he would.

Her panties slipped away as did Rob's clothes. He rolled onto his back taking her with him. 'Touch me, Cassie.'

She hesitated. She'd had spent the majority of her adult life with Oscar and had very few ideas of what men really wanted. Her and her ex-husband's lovemaking had never been wild or spontaneous, but smooth and simple, in their early years it had been gentle and caring. Later, when they'd both become so busy, sex had been relegated to odd occasions. Only, she hadn't known the world's best kept secret; her husband had been having an affair for eight years.

'Cassie, look at me.'

Startled out of her memories, she stared at him.

'It's a small issue, I know, but I normally prefer the woman I'm sleeping with to actually focus on me.' He lifted one shoulder, the teasing glint in his eyes again. 'Wherever you are, can you come back?'

'I'm so sorry.'

He leaned back a little. 'Do you want me to go?' He kissed her shoulder. 'It's your call.'

'No...stay.'

'Sure?'

'Yes. It's just been a long time for me. I'm out of practice.'

'Then let me be your teacher.' Rob rolled her onto her back and nestled himself between her legs, his penis rubbing against her very core. He kissed her hungrily, demanding her to respond and feel his passion. 'Touch me, Cassie.'

She reached down and held his penis, carefully stroking it. 'Like this?'

He smiled wryly. 'That's not bad at all.' He suckled one nipple and then the other and she stroked him harder, feeling his urgency.

'Rob...' she panted, wanting him inside her.

'I'm right here, darling.' He inched his way inside, making small thrusts to open her gently, all the while kissing her lips. 'You're so beautiful, Cassie.'

His voice washed over her, liquefying her body, mind and soul. She opened her legs wider and lifted her hips to take the full length of him. Gripping his backside, she rose to meet his thrusts. Her climax rose as he moved quicker, deeper. She held him hard against her as her body drove towards the ultimate fulfilment. A moan escaped her and with one final plunge she went still as her body exploded.

It had been such a long time. She savoured every moment of her release, as well as the descent back down from her sexual peak.

'Okay?' Rob kissed the tip of her nose.

She paused, he pulsed inside her and his shoulders were strained. He hadn't had his release. He pulled out of her, and she blinked in astonishment. 'What's the matter?'

'Nothing, gorgeous,' he whispered, kissing her beneath her ear. He knelt up on the bed, his penis glistening with her juices. 'You need it more than once I think.'

'More?'

He kissed her thoroughly, his hands caressing her body. She sighed against him, loving the feel of his hands touching her, of the way he murmured sweet endearments she could barely hear. He shifted lower on the bed, cupped her thighs and sank down, sucking her clit until she was a raging torment of sensations.

'God, Rob!' She bucked beneath his tongue, her hands in his hair. He was taking her upwards again, lifting her into a vortex of sexual feelings. She wanted him inside her again, needing him there.

'Wait, sweetheart,' he whispered against her lips as he gathered her in his arms and thrust inside her. Together they rose, meeting each other with every desperate thrust until her mind shattered and he shuddered into her, gasping into her hair.

She lay beneath him, and an overwhelming sense of happiness invaded her. He looked down at her and she grinned, loving him for giving her such pleasure. 'Thank you.'

'Thank you.' He kissed her sweetly and laughed. 'I'm starving. Are you?'

'Actually, I think I am.' It was true. She was starving for the first time in a really long while. 'Let's go have dinner and then come back.'

'Your wish is my command.'

—ᵉᵉᵉ—

Cassie swept her arms through the water and kicked out behind her. Early morning swims were idyllic. The pink tropical sky forecasted another sweltering day and she wondered absentmindedly what she and Rob would do today.

She grinned and splashed the water. Nine days. Nine fantastic sex-on-tap days with Rob. How was it possible to have so much fun? She felt young and beautiful again. Her skin had tanned, and she'd put on a little bit of weight, which was hardly surprising considering she did nothing but laze about with Rob eating and making love.

Her skin tingled at the thought of how much sex she'd had in nine days. Rob made love to her with a spontaneity that shocked her. This holiday had been one of many firsts, but she never would have believed 'sex firsts' would have played such a big part.

They'd made love on the beach in the moonlight, in the bushes when they went for a walk, in the shower, on the table, on the floor of the sitting room, in a golf buggy that took guests around the resort, and last night in the public spa at three in the morning he'd delved deep inside her, making her cry out into the deserted pool area.

She grinned as she swam, her skin tingling with remnants of the pleasure Rob had given her. Aside from the great sex, Rob had encouraged her opinions on his new venture. The building of his own resort was especially important to him, and she'd been delighted when he asked for her ideas. He'd shown her the plans of the resort on the small island in the pacific. Together they had searched the internet for furnishing and equipment. She'd helped him make lists and contact builders. They had worked on his budget, and just yesterday started writing down advertising ideas.

Turning over to float on her back, she imagined living on a beautiful island with Rob. It would be so far removed from her old life. She closed her eyes against the sun and let her mind wander at how lovely that would be. To be involved in his plans to operate one of the best boutique resorts in the southern hemisphere...

Large hands grabbed her waist and she nearly jumped out of her skin. Rob stifled her scream with a kiss. 'You could have given me a heart attack.' She slapped his bare chest. 'I was miles away.'

'Good morning, sweetheart.' He hugged her to him, and she wrapped her legs around his waist and laid her arms on his shoulders.

'Can you touch the bottom?'

'Yes.' He shook his head, clearing the water from his eyes. 'You should have woken me.'

She laughed. 'You were sound asleep.'

'Well, what do you expect when you keep a man awake all night?'

'Me?' Cassie tightened her hold with her legs and played with his wet hair. She kissed him playfully, amazed at how open and free she was with him.

Why had she not lived like this before?

And why on earth did she ever let her work consume her life?

'You know...its rather erotic making out in the ocean.' Rob's hand slipped down between their bodies to the crotch of her swimsuit. He nudged the material aside and inched his fingers inside her. She gasped and nearly fell under water.

'Rob...' She threaded her fingers through his wet hair, gripping tight.

'Hmm?' Distracted, he shifted her weight and suddenly his penis was inside her, hard and throbbing.

'Rob!'

'What?' He wriggled his eyebrows at her.

'I-I-you…' She gasped again as the sensation of him and water caressing her body sent her mind spinning. 'Oh God…'

'That's right, sweetheart,' he murmured, bringing her to another climax. 'Take all of me…'

─ell─

Two days later, Cassie was applying the last touches of her make-up when she heard the door slide open. 'I'm nearly ready,' she called, screwing the lid back on her lipstick. She turned to find a bright red Hibiscus flower poking around the bedroom door.

Rob's head followed the flower. 'Hi, pretty lady.'

'Is that for me?' She took the flower and gazed at it.

'Well, I was going to give it to the housemaid I passed on the path, but she might have got the wrong idea.' He winked.

'Likely she would.' Cassie reached over to kiss him. 'Where as I…'

Rob pulled her into his arms. 'Whereas you know exactly what I have in mind.' He nibbled her ear.

'Did I get dressed for nothing?' She giggled, winding her arms around his neck and arching into him.

'What a question.' His fingers found the zipper of her white linen trousers. 'I only have to see you, or think about you, and I'm hard.'

She blushed, still not used to his forthright expressions. 'Stop it. This is our second last night together. We have to make it extra special.'

The amusement died in his gaze. 'Don't remind me that you're leaving.'

She flattened her hands against his chest, her heart restricting at the thought of saying goodbye to this wonderful man. 'Sorry. We promised not to speak of it until tomorrow, didn't we?'

'That's right. Tonight, is for living in the moment. Tomorrow night is for goodbye sex.' He laughed, but seeing her stricken face, bent his head and kissed her softly, delicately. 'I'm sorry. I'm an idiot.'

'Yes, you are.' She slapped at his arm but was always surprised by the layering of loving he gave her, knowing instinctively when she needed a gentle touch or faster, harder urgent love.

'Hello!' someone called from the deck.

They both jumped and stared at each other in puzzlement.

'Room service?' Rob whispered. 'Or housemaid?'

'I didn't request for either.' Cassie stepped out of his embrace and straightened her clothes. She smiled and walked into the sitting room and gaped in surprise to see her daughter standing on the veranda. 'Chrystal?'

'Mom!' Chrystal opened the sliding door and ran to hug her. 'Surprise!'

Cassie hugged her back. 'What are you doing here? Is something wrong?'

Chrystal, looking tired and jet lagged, shook her head. 'No, nothing is wrong. I just thought I'd come out here and spend a couple of days with you and then we can journey home together.'

'Oh.' Cassie's mind whirled.

'I thought you might be going a bit crazy by now with loneliness and needed some company.' Chrystal looked around the room. 'It's nice here.'

'Yes, it is.' She swallowed nervously as Rob entered the room. She glanced back at Chrystal, who was busy staring at him. 'Chrystal, this is Rob, a friend.'

Rob held out his hand. 'G'day. Your mother has told me much about you.'

Chrystal shook it, her mouth gaping open. 'She has?'

'All good, so don't worry.' He smiled and Cassie nearly collapsed as Rob hooked his arm around her waist. 'We were just going out to dinner. Care to join us?'

She took a sideways step, embarrassed by his display of possession. 'I'll have to cancel, Rob, I'm sorry.'

'No need to cancel. I'm sure your daughter would enjoy a delicious meal after her trip.'

'I think it's best if we didn't.' The last thing she wanted was to sit through a meal with Chrystal at this moment. Knowing her daughter, Chrystal would be bursting with questions. She could make things awkward for Rob. 'I'll talk to you tomorrow, perhaps.'

'Perhaps?' His expression changed, turned serious for the first time in days, and she hated herself for disappointing him.

'I…you see…' Her brain wouldn't for the words she wanted to say. She gave him a helpless look.

He nodded and bowed his head. 'Of course. Good night, Cassie. Nice to have met you, Chrystal.'

He left the beach house without looking back and Cassie's heart somersaulted in her chest.

'Jesus Christ, Mom!' Chrystal collapsed in the nearest chair. 'My God, he's amazing!'

'Chrystal, please.' Cassie felt the sudden need for a chair, and a stiff drink.

'This is unbelievable.'

Annoyed, Cassie stiffened. 'What is so unbelievable?'

'Well, first that you've found such a hot guy and secondly, you've obviously become rather intimate since he came out of your bedroom and thirdly, he calls you Cassie! No one calls you that. You'd kill anyone who called you Cassie.' Chrystal scrambled to her feet and put her hands to her chin as if in prayer. 'I can't believe it.'

'What is so wrong with me having some company? I'm on holiday.' Cassie went into the kitchenette and filled a glass with cold water from the fridge. The moment Chrystal walked into the room the reserve, the controlled emotions, the solitude of the old Cassandra came flooding back and she hated it. She didn't want to be as she once was, where work was the only thing she had in her life. Oscar had rejected her. Chrystal had her own life. So, what did she have? Work.

And it was no longer enough.

Eleven days with Rob had shown her another life, one filled with laughter, love, lightness and joy.

She couldn't go back to the old Cassandra. Never again.

'Mom.' Chrystal stood beside her and rested her head on her shoulder. 'I'm sorry.'

'Don't worry about it.' Cassie walked away. She looked out the door to the darkening night. The crickets and frogs chirped in the ferns near the path. The scent of the tropical flowers, which the night air seemed to accentuate, hung heavy in the air. And she desperately wanted to be in Rob's arms.

'I'll go home Mom.' Chrystal looked close to tears. 'I shouldn't have come.'

'Don't be silly. You just arrived.'

'I thought you might be lonely, that's all.'

'That was very thoughtful of you, darling.' She managed a tight smile.

'I'm happy you weren't alone, Mom. Dad treated you terribly. You needed to…'

'Spread my wings?'

'More like have wild sex with some hot stud.' Chrystal grinned, full of amusement.

'And I have.' Cassie tried to keep a straight face, but they both burst out laughing and hugged each other. They fell onto the sofa giggling like a pair of teenagers.

'Tell me all about it,' Chrystal begged. 'Every gory detail.'

'You really want to hear about it?'

'Not the sex part, obviously, but everything else. How did you meet? He must be something pretty good to make you smile and laugh like this. I've never seen you so happy. Look at you. You're tanned and glowing. I want to know what spell this magic man has cast over you.'

'I've never felt so different. Sometimes, when I'm with him, I can't remember who I once was. Rob has this ability to make me feel…oh, I don't know how to say it, but I feel kind of light, free.'

'In love?' Chrystal, all trace of tiredness gone, pulled her legs up under her and waited expectantly.

'I don't know if it's love. It can't be, can it? It's only been a short time.'

Chrystal frowned, her honey-coloured hair falling over her shoulders. 'Do we need a time frame, Mom? I don't think so.'

'Rob's younger than me.' She worried her bottom lip with her teeth.

'So? Who cares?'

'I care.'

'Why? What differences does it make to anything?' Chrystal took Cassie's hand and squeezed it. 'If he makes you happy for just one minute, then I will adore him forever. You need to be loved, Mom. You work too hard and have no life. It's not healthy. I want you to be happy and if this Rob is the one who makes you so, then that's great.'

'All I know is that I like being with him.' She shrugged self-consciously.

'I'm dying to know all about it.' Chrystal sighed wistfully.

Cassie frowned and studied her fingernail polish. 'I don't know where to begin.'

'From the start!'

~ele~

Cassie walked along the sand; the waves rushed in, tickled her feet and then receded. The ocean breeze was cooler today as wind-whipped clouds played hide and seek with the sun. She tugged her pink cardigan closer. The long skirt of her white sun dress flapped wildly against her legs making it difficult to walk.

She'd spent the morning looking for Rob but hadn't been successful. No one had seen him at the resort, and he hadn't answered his door. She'd left Chrystal sunbathing on the lawn in front of the beach house and gone for a walk to clear her head.

Tomorrow evening she would leave the island and make her way home.

Tomorrow she'd leave Rob.

She bowed her head as her heart constricted. A holiday fling had never been on her agenda. She hadn't needed another thing to be burdened with, another loss.

Yet, after having spent the night discussing Rob with Chrystal, she'd come to understand one thing; what she felt for Rob wasn't just a holiday romance. The thought of leaving him made her sick. She loved him. It was a simple as that.

Whether he felt the same about her, she didn't know. He showed her all the signs that her cared for her, but was it deep enough for something long term? He loved her body, and he behaved so sweetly towards her when they did things together. However, they never discussed the future. The topic of what would happen between them when she returned home seemed taboo.

She looked up from watching the water seep from the sand and noticed a jogger running toward her. Rob. Her stomach clenched. She stopped and waited for him to reach her. Clad in only black shorts, his taut body glistened with sweat. Her pulse raced. Her very core ached with want. She didn't only want and need this man physically, but mentally as well. Rob brought out the best in her. He challenged her to do things she wouldn't try otherwise. He showed her what it was to live a full and contented life, where the goal was to work to live, not live to work. They could talk about any subject and laugh at the same things.

And she knew she couldn't exist without him and be happy.

'Hello.' He slowed to a stop beside her, his blue eyes narrowed with wariness.

She flashed him a hesitant smile. 'Hi. Have you run a long way?'

'Not far enough yet.' His lips curled in a self-depreciating smile. 'You're still in my head.'

'I'm sorry about last night.'

'Don't be. I can see now how hard it must have been for you.'

'I go home tomorrow.'

'Yes.'

'We've missed our chance to have our last special night together.'

'It couldn't be helped. You didn't know Chrystal would turn up like that.'

Silence dragged out between them, the only sound was the crashing of the waves and the cry of a seagull overhead as it glided on the air currents.

'I never expected to meet anyone, you know.' Cassie sighed, feeling frustrated and apprehensive.

'Neither did I. I've been on this island for five years and no one has caught my interest like you have.'

'I'm pleased. I'd hate to think I was just one woman in a line of guests you...entertain.'

He frowned. 'Do you think me so shallow?'

'I'm sorry, no, I don't, not now.'

'But you thought, at the beginning, that I seduced single female guests?'

She shrugged, not meeting his eyes. 'I found it hard to believe you were interested in me, that's all.'

'It was easier for you to think that I chatted up guests regularly rather than believe you are someone special.' He folded his arms across his chest and stared at her. 'I'm not Oscar, Cassie. I'm not a player. I don't cheat or lie.'

'I know.'

'Do you, really?' he huffed, not impressed. 'From what you've told me and how you were when you arrived here, it is obvious he did a job on you. A pathetic bastard like him isn't worth another thought, but he's so entrenched in your head I doubt you'll ever be free of him.'

'Don't say that, please.' The thought horrified her. She wanted to live her life differently now. Rob had shown her how to enjoy each day. She couldn't believe that her old ways were all she had, or ever would have. Like he repeatedly said, there had to be more to life.

'Look, it doesn't matter now anyway. You're going back to New York.' He ran his fingers through his dark blond hair, looking every inch of some Roman god. 'Do you want to stay in touch?'

Cassie tears burned behind her eyes. Why is he being so cold? 'To be honest I don't know what to do.'

'Well, I'll leave it with you then. You have my contact details?'

'Yes.' She bit back her sorrow. How had it ended like this? But then, what had she expected? She didn't know his heart. How stupid was she to make more of it than it was? Why had she fallen for him? Hadn't she learnt from Oscar? To love someone more than they loved you was asking for hurt.

'I'd better go.' He sucked in a deep breath, and she realised he wasn't so unaffected by her leaving as she thought.

'I have to go home, Rob...'

'It crept up on us, didn't?' He gave her a brief smile. 'The day when you would leave.'

'Yes.'

'I hated last night, not being with you.'

'Me too.'

'New plans arrived from my architect. I wanted to show you the changes I had made to the resort. I have news—'

'Changes?' she queried. 'Why? You were happy with what you showed me a few days ago.'

'Well, I had to alter the plans to fit the land to the east. You know where the cliff edge is?'

'Oh, yes.' She sensed his excitement and suddenly her leaving, and heartbreak, was forgotten. 'Was it for safety regulations?'

He nodded. "It's all sorted now. I'm flying out there on Saturday to meet with the builders and the project manager.'

'Oh Rob! That's so great.'

'I was going to tell you last night over dinner.' The joy radiated out from him, gripping her in his enthusiasm. "I wanted to know if you would like to come with me?'

"Go with you?' She stared at him, surprised.

Suddenly, Rob crushed her into his arms, and she held him just as fiercely. 'Oh God,' he whispered into her hair. 'Don't do this to me!'

She cried into his shoulder, gripping his back. 'I don't know what to do.'

'Stay with me.'

'I can't. My home, my work, Chrystal is all in New York.'

'Then I'll go to New York.'

She reared back, stunned. 'You'd leave all this? For me?'

'I'll give it a go. I'll fly between the island and there.' He smiled, flashing his white teeth. 'I can't promise I'll survive in New York, but I'm willing to try. For you.'

'But your life is here.'

'Not for much longer. I'm resigning to concentrate on the building of the resort. Someone must oversee the construction and every stage of getting the project off the ground. I want to be there.' He looked down at her. 'I had hoped you might like to be a part of it, too.'

Her eyes widened. 'Really?'

'You think I would joke about something as important as this?' He kissed the tip of her nose. 'Say you will, Cassie. Chrystal can visit any time she wants to. Say we have a future, please.'

She rubbed her forehead, amazed at the enormity of what was happening. 'It's a big decision.'

Rob pulled back and stared intently into her eyes. 'I love you.'

'Oh Rob.'

'I knew you were special the first time I set on eyes on you. We've not known each other long, but this isn't some fling, Cassie.' He touched his chest where his heart lay. 'I feel it in here. We are meant to be together.' His cheeky smile warmed her heart. 'We can spend the rest of our lives living on a pacific island, growing a brilliant little business together...' He kissed her softly. 'Nights of reclining in bed listening to the waves on the sand...' His kiss deepened. 'Days of sharing ideas, solving problems, laughing, sailing, enjoying life...'

She closed her eyes at the magical words, at the delicate touch of his lips nibbling hers. It was a done deal. How could she possibly leave him forever? 'But what about our age difference?'

'What about it?' He nipped at her bottom lip.

'People might talk...' She arched her neck as his lips lingered down over her jaw and neck.

'Let them. Who cares? It's five years, Cass, it's nothing. Besides, it's no one's business anyway.'

'Don't you want to get married and have children?'

He looked puzzled for a moment. 'I can't marry you when the time comes?'

'Well, yes,' heavens he didn't know what those words meant to her, 'but what about children?'

'They've never been on my list really. Does that make me a bad person?'

'No. It's just that I don't want to deny you something you might want later.'

Rob shrugged into his relaxed easy-going way. 'Let's not worry about something that isn't going to be an issue. As I said, I never thought to have kids anyway. I'll have you, the resort and we'll get a couple of dogs. Perfect.'

'It does sound perfect. You make it sound so easy.'

He silenced her with a long deep kiss, and she curled her toes curl in need. 'It can be, if we want it enough. I'm not saying we won't have some difficulties, but I don't foresee huge problems which will tear us apart, unless, of course, you can never leave New York?'

'I can leave it.' And she knew that was the truth. 'It'll be a wrench at first, but I can always go back and visit.'

'I'll make you happy, Cass, if you're willing to try a new adventure.'

She held him close, loving the feel and smell of him. 'I am very willing.'

'Let's make a deal then.'

'A deal?' she asked softly, rubbing her nose against his. 'What kind of deal?'

'You go to New York tomorrow, while I pack up my life here. We'll live together in your apartment, and I'll commute to the island once the building starts. Then, when you're ready, we'll live on the island. What do you think of that idea? A deal?'

'With a couple of dogs?'

'And the dogs.'

A warm glow spread throughout her whole body. He wanted to build a future with her. He was willing to leave his homeland to live in New York with her until she was ready to move with him to the island. No one had ever sacrificed anything for her before. Tears rose again and spilt over her lashes. She'd finally found the one man her soul had been searching for all her life.

'Hey, don't cry, sweetheart.'

She hugged him tight, never wanting to let him go, ever. 'You have a deal.'

'Are you sure?'

She grinned and kissed him, pressing her body close. 'Trust me, I'm a lawyer.'

Art of Desire

New York

Antonia swore softly under her breath at the sign, 'Elevator out of service.' That meant five flights of stairs with her luggage. Brilliant. She had a fleeting thought of the TV show Big Bang Theory, which also had a non-working elevator, and it made her smile. Would she find her neighbours to be neurotic scientists too?

Hitching her oversized handbag and cabin bag over her shoulders, she bent and grabbed the two suitcase handles, ready to haul them up the stairs. Behind her came the unfamiliar hoot of horns from the busy New York traffic, reminding her that she'd face many difficult things in this new life she'd chosen, and loads of stairs would be just one of them.

'They look heavy. Like a hand with those?'

Antonia blinked at the guy coming across the foyer, the glass door swinging shut behind him. He was tall, with straight brown hair that reached to his collar. Over his shoulder was a tan leather satchel and in one hand he held a laptop case. He wore jeans and a plain white shirt with a black leather jacket that emphasised his wide shoulders. Had a magazine model just walked in? She fully expected him to strike a pose any minute to a flash of cameras. Desire hit her. Hard. The model was rather scrumptious!

'The lift is out of order.' She couldn't stop staring.

'The lift?'

She smiled in return to his lop-sided grin. She nodded to the elevator.

'Oh, the elevator. You're English?'

'No, Australian.'

His grin widened. 'I should have known the accent. I spent a couple of months in Australia a few years ago. It's a great place, though there is a difference in language sometimes.'

'Yes, it is.' She always felt proud when someone admired her country. 'We do have a few sayings and words that are unique to us.'

He glanced at her luggage. 'Just moving in?'

'Yes. I've rented the rooftop apartment.' A thrill of excitement filled her at the prospect of it.

'I'm one floor down.' He held out his hand. 'Ronan Kelly.'

How marvellous! The model lived in her building. She shuffled her bags aside and shook his hand, liking the feel of its warmth and strength. 'Antonia Deakin. Nice to meet you.'

'Come on,' he picked up her suitcases, 'I'll help you. If you take my laptop, I'll take these.'

'Oh, but they're heavy.'

'I'm sure I can manage.' They swapped bags. 'Lead the way.'

Guilty that he carried such weight, she hurried up the narrow staircases. By the time she'd reached the fifth floor her legs were burning. She wouldn't need a gym membership living here, all she needed to do was take the stairs a couple of times a day and she'd be fit enough to run a marathon. As if she would!

'Here we are,' she panted, throwing him a grateful look. 'Thank you so much.' She hated to think of the effort it would have taken carrying them up herself. She rummaged through her full to capacity handbag and found the keys to her new home.

'What do you have in here, bricks?' He heaved the suitcases closer to the door.

'Sorry. I packed a lot.' Antonia unlocked the door and pushed it open. A wave of mustiness hit her. The open plan layout meant the living room and kitchen were together separated only by an island bench. The last rays of the evening sun streamed through the windows over the kitchen at the back.

Placing the bags on the living-room floor, she glanced around the furnished apartment for the first time. It was smaller than she thought, but better than she hoped. Arranging this via the internet had been a gamble, but one she felt had paid off. The brown sofa opposite the electric fireplace wasn't new, but the floorboards were polished to a high shine. A four-chair wooden dining table was to the right of the door near another window and close to the kitchen.

'I've not been up here before.' Ronan said, standing by the door. 'The couple who lived here previously were just moving out when I moved in, and it's been empty since then.'

'How long ago was that?' Antonia moved towards the little kitchen, her eyes taking in as much as she could.

'About three months ago. I think the owner did some painting.'

She looked around at the white walls. They did seem freshly painted and there was a slight smell of paint trapped in the air. 'It's nice.'

'This building is a good place to live.' He nodded, giving the apartment another glance. 'I like it here.'

'I organised to live here a couple of weeks ago.' She inspected the compact and empty fridge before coming back to Ronan. 'Thanks so much for helping me.'

'It wasn't a problem at all.' He gave her a warm smile, picked up his laptop from the floor and turned for the door. 'Welcome to the building, and to New York.'

'Thank you.' She was suitably impressed to find a gorgeous man living in the same building at her, and to have met him on her first day had to be a good omen.

'I'm downstairs if you need help for anything, number ten.'

'Thanks, that's kind of you.'

With a last long look at each other, she closed the door as he stepped lightly down the stairs.

Leaning against the door, she let out a held breath, and then laughed a little. New York might be just what she imagined it to be.

In her bag, her phone jingled with the tune of Land Down Under song. Her cousin, Kay, had insisted on putting it as her ring tone to remind Antonia where she came from, as if she could forget. 'Hello?'

At her mother's abrupt greeting, she sighed. 'Hi, Mum.'

'You've arrived then?'

'Yes, safe and sound. I've just collected the keys and I'm in the apartment.'

'Does it look alright? They haven't ripped you off, have they?'

'No, it's exactly as it looks on the internet. I went to the office and spoke to the person I've been emailing, and she had all the paperwork. Everything is fine.'

'Good. Well, that's something then.'

Antonia waited, knowing her mother hadn't finished. The silence dragged out. 'Anything else, Mum?'

'No. I just wanted to make sure you arrived and got to where you had to be, that's all. I'd hate to think the place wasn't there, or something and you'd paid all that money to some scam.'

'It's not a scam, Mum. I'm in the apartment.' Antonia rolled her eyes. Her mother thought the worst of everything and everyone until proven otherwise. It was a lot of money to spend on a whim, but it was her inheritance and she had been wise by investing most of the money. Surely, she could spend some of it on what would make her happy. After all, hadn't they just witnessed how short life could be?

'Right, well, I'll go then.' Her mother sighed.

'Okay. Thanks for phoning. I'll talk to you in a few days once I'm settled. I'll put photos on Facebook, get Kay to show you them.'

'Yes, alright. That would be good... You can come home anytime you like, remember, if it doesn't all work out as you wanted it to. I'm sure you could get your old job back.'

'Mum, I don't want my old job back. I wasn't happy there.'

'Well, if you hadn't slept with your boss, things might have been different.'

Antonia closed her eyes in frustration. Why did she have to bring that up again? Her relationship with Steve was finished and buried months ago. 'Yes, Mum, you could be right. I've got to go.'

'Oh. Ok. Goodbye then.' The silence of the dead phone was loud in Antonia's ear, but she was used to her mother's short exchanges, unless she was getting her point across. Never one for light-hearted talking, was her Mum, or feelings, for that matter.

She took a deep breath and expelled her mother from her thoughts. There were happier things to think about than her strained relationship with her parent.

Walking through the apartment, Antonia opened cupboards in the kitchen, thankful for the crockery she saw, it would one thing less to buy. The bedroom was large and held a double bed and mattress, but no sheets as she was instructed to bring her own, which she had. Folded blankets and pillows were in the closet, but again she had squashed her own pillow into her second suitcase, along with the sheets and two towels. Aside from the bedside table and lamp, there was a small table in the corner which held a television set. This made her smile, as watching old movies on a cold rainy winter's day was a favourite pastime of hers.

Back into living room she surveyed the space. Behind the dining table were two steps leading up to the double glass French doors. Through these Antonia stepped out onto the roof terrace. This was what had sold her on the apartment, and what had made it so expensive.

Joy burst in her veins. The terrace was such a magical spot. From here she could see two hundred and seventy degrees of the surrounding New York area. She would never get tired of looking out at this view - the blue sky which was fading to an orange pink as the sun set beyond the towering grey glass high rises. She leaned over the edge, staring down to the copper-leaved trees lining the busy city streets below. It all captivated her mind, her imagination, her quest for adventure.

New York. America.

Renting an apartment - chasing her dreams.

Well, she deserved it. The last year had been completely crap. Her father said to her repeatedly as he fought cancer that she had to grab life and strangle every last ounce of happiness out of it. And she planned to. She made a promise to him that she would do exactly what she dreamed of doing.

If only her mother had understood.

ℓℓ

Ronan placed his satchel and laptop bag on the round table in the living room and walked into the kitchen. Opening the fridge, he took out a bottle of water and drank deeply. Resting his backside against the sink, he pondered on what had just happened.

Antonia.

His new neighbour.

His beautiful new neighbour.

His beautiful, *hot* new neighbour.

He drank some more of the cold water, his fingers tapping the edge of the sink. It was just attraction - a simple boy meets girl attraction, that's all it was. He could deal with it. Heck, he might not even see her that much.

Going through to his bedroom he pushed her from his mind. To not think about her cheeky smile would be the best thing, or the way her blue eyes lit up as she gazed around the room, or her pert backside clad in tight jeans...

No!

No thinking of the woman upstairs.

He grabbed a clean towel and headed for the bathroom. Turning on the shower, he stripped and got under the hot spray. Perhaps it should be a cold shower? He laughed at himself. 'Get a grip, man!'

With a determined effort he washed his body and thought about other things, but before he was dried and dressed, he was thinking of places to take her, and how he wanted to taste her kissable lips.

ele

Antonia looked down at the reflection pool where one of the Twin Towers once stood. She'd stood in silence for a few minutes to absorb the site, the quiet atmosphere, despite the other tourists, and to remember the lost lives. It didn't seem real to her, from watching the distressing images on TV to actually being at the spot of such devastation. Innocent people killed, loved ones lost. She thought of her father. He'd have liked to have visited this memorial. He'd been a fire fighter himself. She remembered how he sat in their living room in stunned silence as the towers fell and squeezed her hand.

Tears rose hot behind her eyelashes, and she blinked them away. She missed her father so much. His death had left a hole in her life. Strangely she felt close to him here, and she knew she'd come back often.

Winding through the crowds, she checked her map and then looked around. It was getting late. She'd spent the entire day playing tourist and enjoyed every minute of it. Another day of sightseeing to get it out of her system would allow her to concentrate on touring the art galleries tomorrow. Although she'd been so tempted to visit some of the museums, she avoided them, knowing she'd get distracted. This week was for relaxing and shopping. Work would begin tomorrow.

Now her feet were throbbing, and she was hungry again. The amount of walking she'd done had burned off the pancake breakfast hours ago.

Walking up Broadway, she kept her head down as a sharp breeze blew in her face. It was too far to walk to her apartment, on a nice day she would have done it, but not today. Rains clouds hugged the tops of the skyscrapers and on impulse Antonia stepped to the roadside and signalled a yellow cab to stop.

The cabbie gave her a smile as she told him her address. She liked New York cab drivers, they were either happy to chat with you or leave you alone if you preferred. In the last week she'd had many discussions with them on where she should visit as she got to know the city.

Alighting in front of her building she paid the fare and went inside. Ronan was coming down the stairs and the warm lop-sided smile he gave her made her stomach quiver in response.

'Hello there.' He wore faded jeans that hugged his hips and a navy-blue shirt. He looked amazing.

'Hi, Ronan.' She was very aware of her windblown hair and her crumpled shirt under her jacket. A day playing tourist left her feeling a bit grimy.

'The elevator is out again. Useless it is.'

She looked at the new 'out of service' sign. 'They only fixed it two days ago.'

'I know. It must need replacing entirely.' He stopped at the foot of the staircase. His soft cologne and still damp dark hair from a recent shower sent her senses into overdrive. 'Had a good day?'

'Yes, thanks. I've been seeing more of the sights...' She blushed and didn't know why. She was here to enjoy herself so why should she feel ashamed because she was having a holiday while everyone else was working.

'I've not seen you since your first day. How are you settling in?'

'Oh fine. I love it. I have used this week to buy what I needed for the apartment and see the sights.'

'How long are you staying for?' His hazel eyes were inquisitive.

'The tenancy agreement is for three months, with the option to stay longer if I want.'

'Would you like to have dinner tonight, if you've no plans? My treat.'

The question threw her off balance. She hadn't been expecting it at all. 'Oh, um...ok. That would be lovely, thank you.'

'I'll make reservations at a restaurant I know; they have tasty food. Or would you prefer to go somewhere really fancy? I'm sure I've got a tie I can wear.' Laughter danced in his eyes.

'No, I'm happy to go anywhere. I don't need fancy.'

'Say about seven o'clock then? I'll come up and get you.'

'Wonderful. Thank you.' As nervous as though it was some grand important date with a new boyfriend, Antonia dashed up into the apartment.

The clothes she bought with her were all she had, and she mentally sorted through her meagre wardrobe while she showered. She had a shower; grateful she'd gone for a wax and beauty treatment before leaving Australia. Wrapped in a towel, she picked through her clothes. A long black skirt and a sleeveless gold silk top was the best pick, but it was too cold for the top and she had to make do with a mint-coloured cashmere sweater. Twisting her nose up at the selection in the wardrobe, she vowed to go clothes shopping, proper clothes shopping, not rubbish cheap jeans and t-shirts. She needed so much. What processed her to leave all her good clothes at home? Perhaps because at the time, she'd been grieving for her father and having dinner dates were as far removed from her mind as swimming the length of Sydney Harbour.

Somehow the two hours until seven o'clock went by like five minutes and she was still touching up her make up when the doorbell rang. Slipping on her black heels, she hopped to the door and opened it awkwardly in a half-bent position. 'Hi Ronan, come in.' She straightened and stared as he walked in. Dressed casually in black trousers and a white shirt he looked so hot she wanted to step into his arms and kiss him hard.

'You look really nice.' His kind eyes appraised her with admiration.

'Thank you. I didn't bring many clothes with me. I need to go shopping.' She dragged her gaze from him, but every part of her body seemed to want him. Whenever she glanced at him her stomach clenched in acute awareness of him. It'd been so long since she was attracted to someone. It seemed an age since she was held, desired, physically fulfilled.

'Ready?'

'Yes.' Grabbing her purse, she gave a last quick look in the wall mirror by the door, trying to keep her skittering heart under control. With such thoughts in her head how on earth was she going to last the night?

—ele—

'Should I have picked somewhere quieter?' Ronan asked as they delved into their main course.

'No, I like it.' And she did. The family atmosphere of the Italian restaurant and the enjoyment people were having far outweighed the types of other places where guests were too scared to talk above a whisper in fear of upsetting their neighbouring tables. No, Antonia liked to be comfortable, and this place suited her.

'Do you like it?' Ronan gestured towards her plate of cannelloni.

'It's delicious.'

'This place is a favourite of mine.' He paused in eating his ravioli, his face turning grave. 'I have a confession to make.'

'Oh?'

'I already had made a reservation to eat here tonight with a friend, but they cancelled.'

'So, I'm second choice? Or maybe even third or fourth?'

'No, never that. I had planned to ask you out, or offer to show you the city, but this came up and I thought, why not ask you? It can be difficult to get a reservation here and I didn't want to lose it.'

'Thanks for telling me.' She sipped some wine and looked around, doing her best to ignore the disappointment that she was just someone he decided to bring along to fill an empty seat.

Ronan forked up some more food. 'We've discussed what to see and do in New York, but I want to know about you. Tell me about yourself.'

'What do you want to know?' She threw back. He'd robbed her of the magic of the night, and she wasn't in the mood now to relax. It was silly really, to think like that, but she had expected to be special, that he'd gone to the effort to book the table just for the two of them. Heavens, it must be because it's that time of the month, otherwise something like this wouldn't normally bother her. Yes, she was hormonal, that was the reason for her silly thoughts.

'Are you here to work?'

'As in a paid job? No.'

'There's another type of work?' he grinned, oblivious to her sudden turn in mood, but then they were strangers, how would he know her moods?

She sighed, wondering if she told him the truth, he'd think differently of her. Most people were prejudiced about artist at the best of times, and now she was a self-funded artist it might alienate him. 'I paint. That's why I wanted the rooftop apartment because of the light.'

'You're an artist.' Interest lit his features and she wished he wasn't so damn attractive. Every one of her senses was homed in on him like an eagle on prey.

'And you?' She sipped more wine. 'What do you do?'

'I teach history. And I'm not going to apologise for it.' He laughed.

'Why would you? It's a perfectly sensible job.' God, she must stop with the cold sentences. She wanted to punch herself for being so uptight.

'Well, being sensible sounds very boring and old fashion. I'm not either of those I don't think.' He frowned. 'Do you like history?'

'Some of it, yes. Two years ago, my father and I travelled to England. We visited many castles and manors. We don't have anything like that in Australia, but my father's family were from England.'

'My ancestors originally came from Ireland and were servants to a family who owned a castle. I think it was a trip back there when I was a child that hooked me on history.'

'I've never been to Ireland. I'd love to go one day.'

'I'm due to go back there soon, to visit family. I'm looking forward to it.' He wiped his mouth with his napkin. 'Do you sell many paintings? Are you incredibly famous?'

She cringed, wishing the subject hadn't swung back around to her. 'I'm not famous at all. I'm just starting out really. I used to teach, but I felt I could always do that later. I've sold some pieces in my local town, and won a few competitions, only small-time ones. But they gave me the courage to pack in my job and I thought that since life was so short, I should take my inheritance and try to make my way in the art world.'

'I can imagine that it's a tough industry to get a foothold in.'

'Yes. I need to make contacts and learn my trade, see where I fit, if I do.'

'And you thought New York would be the place to do it?'

'Here and Paris, perhaps London, too. I need inspiration to paint. I'd like a large portfolio eventually, but to begin with I need to have one or two pieces on display, and hope I get some interest.'

He raised his glass to her. 'Here's to your new adventure. I hope it's an enormous success.'

She raised her glass and touched it lightly to his. 'Thank you. Let's hope so.'

They were interrupted but a noisy group of people who entered the restaurant and when seeing Ronan, they whooped and came up to their table laughing and talking.

'Ronan! You dog, what are you doing here?' One guy who looked Ronan's age of about thirty stood with his arm around a scantily clad woman, who wore far too much makeup and very little clothes. Behind them, another loud couple pushed through to say hello. They all talked at once wanting to know who Antonia was and Ronan quickly made introductions.

'You're Australian?' The first guy, she learnt was called Tyler, bent low and swayed a little, clearly worse for drink.

'Yes, I am.' Antonia replied, annoyed by this rude intrusion.

'Do you know Hugh Jackman, the actor, he's Australian?' Tyler laughed as did his companions and Antonia's opinion of them dropped another level.

'No, I don't know Hugh Jackman, sorry.'

'That's not real smart, Tyler.' Ronan's mouth tightened.

The woman leaning into Tyler as though without him she'd fall was called Mel or something, Antonia couldn't remember nor cared, she slipped to one side in her impossibly high heels. 'I lurve Hugh Jackman, don't you?' She picked up Ronan's wine glass to take a sip and promptly spilt wine down the front of her revealing blouse.

Ronan jerked to his feet. 'Tyler take her home for God's sake. You're all a mess.'

'We're having a good time.' Tyler frowned. 'You would be too if you hadn't fought with Kirsten. You shouldn't let her get to you. She's been impossible lately and now we see you've dumped us for this one.'

'I'm quite capable of having a meal with someone else besides you lot.' Ronan grew tense, giving his friend a hard look as he sat back down.

'Kirsten won't like it. Are you two completely over then?'

'Yes, Tyler. Now, if you please...'

Tyler waved him away, his words slurring. 'Kirsten is high maintenance, I give you that, but she's got it all, man. Why do you blow so hot and cold with her?' Tyler glanced from Ronan to Antonia. 'Although, this one is very nice...' His blood-shot eyes roamed over her. Antonia felt slighted by his leering observation of her. 'I suppose it's possible you'd like something new after years of Kirsten.'

'Tyler, enough!' Ronan snapped, while the others giggled like a gaggle of schoolchildren.

'Look, sorry. Don't be mad.' Tyler patted Ronan's shoulder, his eyes wide and Antonia wondered if he had even blinked the whole time he was here. 'Listen,' he continued, 'we're meeting Kirsten here soon. She's running late, like always. Patch it up with her, will you?'

'She's coming here?' Ronan glanced at the front door with a groan. 'I don't want to see her tonight!'

Kirsten? Antonia was sick of hearing her name. Who the hell was she? Did Ronan have a current girlfriend? Was she the person this table reservation was for? And Tyler could go to hell, the rude obnoxious arse.

Antonia reached down for her bag, drew out some money and threw it on the table. 'I think I'll go, Ronan.' She stood up, apologising as her chair bumped into the leg of the other friend, whose name she'd forgotten immediately.

'Antonia, wait.' Ronan stood, too, but was trapped from reaching her side by his friends.

'Thank you for dinner.' She slipped out between tables, hearing Tyler to forget her and fix it with Kirsten.

Antonia walked out into the chilly night air. A couple were just alighting from a cab, and she took it before the driver had the chance to say anything.

On the way back to her apartment she thought over the last couple of hours. Ronan was gorgeous, she admitted that. She felt an attraction to him, there was no denying it. But did she want to get mixed up in another person's life? Did she want to get close to someone else? Relationships were hard work. Did she have the strength to deal with it? Did she even have a chance anyway with that Kirsten still in the picture? Besides, she'd not be here forever. She was in New York to paint, to make valuable contacts in the industry, to experience living alone and, in another city, before going on to visit Paris or Rome. One day she'd eventually return to Australia. Possibly when her money ran out...

She sighed and watched the city lights flash by. Her paintings had to sell. She wanted this so badly, to be a successful selling artist. Could she do it? The idea of failing chilled her, depressed her.

Thoughts of her dad filled her mind. And the ache of losing him consumed her once more. Had she done the right thing coming here so soon after his death? Was her mother right and she should have waited more than a month after the funeral to leave?

She didn't know the answer. All she knew was living at home with her mother became more unbearable each day.

The silences between them were stretching longer and longer each day. Without her dad to be the buffer between them it was difficult to hide their true relationship.

No, she couldn't go back to Sydney, to the memories of what she'd lost. She needed to travel and experience the world, at least for a while, and concentrating on finding her feet here and her painting was enough. She had to be sensible. She needed to build up her portfolio, make contacts in the art industry. That's all she should focus on. Her art. To work hard. Create a reputation. Sell her work. Make her dad proud.

As she entered the building and walked up the flights of stairs she paused only briefly on the landing to Ronan's apartment. What was she to do about him though? She yawned. Now wasn't the time to ponder on him.

She was curled up in bed reading a book on modern artists when the soft knock came at the door. She guessed it to be Ronan but dressed in her pyjamas she didn't want to see him or discuss the disastrous dinner. After another knock it all went silent, and Antonia snuggled further down into her pillows. She'd have to face him sometime, but not now. He wasn't important.

___ell___

The next day, although chilly, was bright with sunshine which flooded through the large windows into the apartment. Having bought an easel, canvases of assorted sizes and new paints the second morning after arriving, Antonia decided today was a perfect painting day. She wore old jeans and a baggy grey sweater and set up the easel on the terrace. She had enough food in to last a few days. A habit she'd acquired was buying plenty of food that would keep awhile, vegetables, tins, rice and pot noodles because once she was in the painting mood, she didn't like to stop for mundane things like grocery shopping.

Putting on the local radio for background noise, she got to work. Painting for her was an extension of who she was. She couldn't imagine life without it. Her father had painted, although in a different style to hers, yet it was one of the many things they had in common. Antonia admired her father's talent, he worked in oils, whereas she preferred a mixture of oils and watercolours. Her father had painted for a hobby, but he encouraged her to go to art school, to make a career out of it. She had trained to be an art teacher at the local high school. She had graduated and spent a year as a teacher, but her heart wasn't in it to teach kids that didn't really care for art. Her dad had understood that. Her mother hadn't. But then her mother didn't understand her at all. As a medical researcher, her mother was methodical, introverted and self-sufficient. To have a whimsical child that flowed through life not being profoundly serious in her career goals was, in Antonia's mother's mind, a disappointment. At least that is how Antonia saw her mother view her.

Painting fast to capture the changing light of the Manhattan landscape from different angles, Antonia worked well into the late afternoon. Several canvases were propped against the furniture inside drying. She was placing another smaller canvas of the Hudson River onto the kitchen bench top to dry when knocking sounded on the door.

Without thinking she opened it, a paint brush still in hand, her mind lost to a world of colour, shading and light.

Ronan stood there holding a large bunch of white and pink roses. But there was no lop-sided smile, just an expression of guilt on his face. 'Hi.'

'Hi.'

'I bought you these, to apologise for last night.'

'Oh. Er...thanks.' She took them from him and stepped back to allow him inside. 'You didn't have to.' She shut the door and walked through the living room to the kitchen. A nervous flutter of her stupid heart made it awkward for her to make eye contact with him.

He pushed his hands into the front pockets of his jeans. 'Last night was a disaster and I'm sorry. I did try to follow you but when I got outside you had vanished.'

'A cab was right out front.' Not knowing what else to say, she placed her flowers beside the little painting and started hunting in the cupboards for a vase. 'You know, I might not even have a vase...' She kept her face from him, embarrassed by the discomfort of the situation.

'I should have thought of that. I should have bought chocolates instead.'

'No, really, it's a nice gesture. Thank you.' She finally located a dusty glass vase in the cupboard above the fridge and grabbing a small folding stool managed to reach it.

'You've been busy.' Ronan strolled around studying each canvas.

'Yes, a day's work.' She busied herself in filling the vase with water and arranging the flowers.

'And I've interrupted you, sorry. You must think me such a pain in the ass.'

'No, not at all.' She smiled at him. 'I appreciate your thoughtfulness in buying me flowers and apologising. I probably over-reacted last night...'

'No, you didn't. They were rude. I rang him this morning and told him exactly what I thought about last night.'

'They were drunk. It's fine.'

Ronan walked around the room. 'These paintings are really good. I like them. You're definitely talented.'

'Thank you.' She was never easy with people praising her work.

'Have you had time to eat today? Perhaps we could go for an early dinner, maybe just burger or something?'

She was very tempted to say no. Yet, somehow, she found herself say the opposite even though she wasn't hungry for usually while painting she grazed on finger food, or junk food, it helped her concentrate.

'We could grab a hot dog and walk in Central Park until the light fades if you prefer?'

She smiled. 'I went for a walk in the Park the day after I arrived but didn't have a hot dog.' She looked at him properly for the first time since he'd entered the apartment. Again, his rugged handsomeness stole her breath. He wore black jeans and a thick red sweater that looked warm. 'Do you work full time where you teach?'

'Yes, Monday to Friday.'

She glanced at the clock and realised it was past five o'clock. 'I didn't realise the time. Hours mean nothing when I'm in the zone. I'll just go change.'

'It's cold in the shade. You'll need a jacket.'

With the apartment only two blocks away, Antonia and Ronan were soon walking along the park's meandering paths. The cool breeze whipped up the falling leaves of gold and amber.

'I understand why Americans call autumn, the Fall.' Antonia said, hands in her jacket pockets as she strolled beside Ronan. Children ran across the grass, scuffing up the piles of leaves they'd collected. Two teenage girls flew past them on rollerblades, while a slim woman jogged by pushing a toddler in a pram.

Ronan stared into the distance. 'Do you celebrate Halloween in Australia?'

'It's not as bigger deal as in this country. It's more an excuse for kids to fill up on sugar.' She joked.

'So, you won't be having a party?'

She laughed. 'I don't know anyone to invite to a party.'

'You know me.' He gave her a long look before stopping in front of a hot dog stand. 'Ready to try a famous New York hot dog?'

'Why not.'

Supplied with their hot dogs and a large pretzel they continued walking.

'I don't think I can eat all this.' Antonia grinned between mouthfuls. 'The pretzel is so big.'

'Give it ago. Then we can have a coffee afterwards, or ice cream.'

'Are you trying to get me fat?' She grinned, wiping ketchup off her chin with a napkin.

'No, you're perfect just as you are.'

Startled, Antonia glanced at him and felt the heat rise to her cheeks at the compliment. Was he flirting with her? Did he feel attraction too?

He walked on. 'Last night, we never got to finish our conversation.'

'No...' She didn't want to think about last night.

'Again, I'm really sorry for Tyler and them all crashing us like that. They were celebrating Tyler's birthday. He was angry with me because I didn't join them. He'd rung me earlier, you see, inviting me, but...well... let's just say Tyler's parties can get out of control and I'm not into all that. At least not now. We must grow up sometimes, and I guess I'm the first in the group to do so. Besides, it was a Sunday night! I couldn't go to work today with a hangover.'

'I see.' She was tempted to ask about Kirsten but decided against it. What would be the point? It was nothing to do with her anyway.

'Tyler still thinks and behaves as though were eighteen not thirty. It causes tension between us.' Ronan shrugged. 'Anyway, I want to learn about you. Do you have family back in Australia?'

'My mother, some cousins. My father died six weeks ago...' It still seemed unreal to her.

'Oh Christ, I'm sorry to hear that.'

She flashed him a brief smile. Passing a trash can, she threw the rest of her hot dog into it, no longer hungry. It was growing dark as the sun slipped behind the high-rises and the temperature dropped a little.

'How about a coffee?'

She nodded and followed Ronan out of the park and across the street to a busy diner.

They ordered coffee and sat at a table facing the street. For a while they sat in comfortable silence sipping their coffee and watching the people and traffic go by.

'You're brave to come here alone so soon after losing your father.'

'I had to get away. Nothing was the same without him. It was much harder to stay.' She stared out at the people, not wanting to think of her quiet home, of her mother's silent presence. No, she couldn't get out of there quick enough.

'Sorry, didn't mean to make you sad.'

'No, that's all right.' She sipped her latte. 'Would you like to go to the movies tonight?' She was just as surprised as he was by her question. But he was trying to be friends and she could at least meet him halfway.

'I'd really like to, but I have someone coming over later.' He looked apologetic. 'How about I cook us a meal tomorrow night?'

'Um…well…' She felt slighted by his refusal to not go out tonight with her, which was totally unreasonable.

Was Kirsten the person visiting him?

Was Kirsten a crucial factor she didn't know about?

Was she making a fool of herself?

Why did she feel so jealous? She hardly knew the guy. And more importantly, why was she acting so out of character?

'Please. I'd like to cook for you.'

'Okay, sounds good.' How could she not agree when he looked at her with those lovely eyes? Her stomach clenched as he gazed at her.

'Great.' He smiled. 'I'm a decent cook, you know.'

'I hope so!' Laughing, they left the diner. Antonia felt lighter of spirit than she had in weeks. Ronan was good company.

They walked home along the darkened streets, passing shopkeepers as they pulled down the rattling shutters over windows and doors.

Ronan zipped up his jacket as a cool breeze sprung up. 'Are you painting all week?'

'Mostly, but not tomorrow. I've made a few appointments to meet some gallery owners. I want to get a feel of whether they'd be interested in what I can do. I have nothing much to show them that's new, but I've a portfolio of my older stuff that has sold. I'm hoping it's enough for them to take a chance on me when my paintings are ready to be displayed.'

'What are you doing next Saturday?' Ronan asked as they reached their building.

'Probably painting. Why?'

'If you fancy a break, we could spend a few hours together if you want? Visit some museums, or something?'

'Actually, I'd like to visit the Statue of Liberty. I've not done that yet. Would you like to come with me?'

'Absolutely. I've not been there in years.' He grinned, opening the front door of the foyer for her.

'Oh, Ronan! I've been waiting ages.' A beautiful woman wearing a fire engine red pant suit and gold heels stood next to the desk chatting idly to old George, the doorman, who was never at his post during the day but usually further down the street talking to pensioners sitting out on the sidewalk. On spotting Antonia, the woman's almond shaped eyes narrowed, and her smile became an icy grimace.

'Kirsten. I thought you were coming at eight thirty?' A muscle jerked in Ronan's jaw.

'I'm early for once, darling. You should be glad. It gives us more time together.' She kissed him on the lips, before linking her arm through his and giving him a wide smile of invitation.

Ronan pulled back slightly. 'Antonia, this is a friend of mine, Kirsten Stevens. Kirsten, Antonia Deakin. Antonia just moved here from Australia.'

'Good lord, you're Australian?' They way Kirsten said it made it sounds as though it was Hell itself and Antonia's hackles rose.

'Shall we go up?' Ronan virtually pushed Kirsten towards the stairs. 'Goodnight, Antonia.' He went to say more, but Kirsten stepped between them.

'You really should move somewhere more upmarket, Ronan, the elevator never works in this building. I've already taken my bag up, George helped me.'

As their voices faded up the stairs, Antonia sagged a little at the instant rejection. Feeling foolish, she glanced at George, whom she'd met the second night after her arrival and liked him instantly.

'Don't you be worried about Ronan liking her too much.' George's look of sympathy didn't help her dejection. 'She had her chance and blew it. She's not good enough for him, even if her family is one of the wealthiest in the city.' He grimaced; his white teeth stark against his dark face.

'Really?'

'Oh, yes. Miss Stevens treated Ronan like he was her bit of rough, but he didn't take it for too long and realised she wasn't worth his time. Not sure why she's sniffing around again.' Old George settled down on his chair and switched on the small television set under the desk. 'Care to watch a game with me?'

'No, thank you, George. I'd best be going up.'

'I'll have that elevator fixed tomorrow even if I have to tie the repair man to it to do so!'

'Thanks, George. Goodnight.' She climbed the stairs slowly, saying hello to Mrs Bowden on the second floor, who was letting herself into her own apartment. They'd bumped into each other on the stairs the day before and chatted about the weather before introducing themselves.

The flat was cold and dark when she let herself in and it matched Antonia's mood. She turned on the lamp in the corner of the living room, then the heating, before going through to run a hot bath. She added scented soap to make lots of bubbles, before going back into the kitchen to pour herself a glass of white wine and grab her smartphone.

Relaxing in the bath, she played music on her phone and checked Facebook and contacted friends with updates. A love song began, and Antonia laid there thinking about Ronan, who was right now entertaining his girlfriend one floor below. She didn't understand why it would bug her so much. She'd only just met the guy. They were mere acquaintances. Yes, she was attracted to him, and liked spending time with him, but she had no reason to feel jealous. She just had to be smart. This Kirsten woman wasn't out of his life, that was clear, so she needed to keep away from him and let him sort it out. She refused to be a fill in, or a rebound, or anything at all.

Did she even want to get involved with someone?

Climbing out of the cooled bath, she towelled dry, and then changed her music to more upbeat dance songs. She instantly felt better. Slipping into comfortable clothes she headed for the kitchen and refilled her wine. Although not terribly hungry she needed something on her stomach with this second glass than the half-eaten hot dog. A toasted ham and cheese sandwich was sufficient for her to munch on while she studied the paintings dotted around the apartment. They all needed touch ups, some more than others. One small painting she didn't like the composition at all, but another one looked promising. She'd done too many too soon.

Patience, she had to learn patience with her painting. Each canvas needed her time, her focus.

A knock on the door interrupted her critical musings and half-heartedly she went to open it. Ronan stood there, hands in pockets. 'Oh, hello.' She was surprised to see him.

'Hi.'

'Is something wrong?'

'Yes, very much so.' He looked downcast, totally fed up.

'Come in.' She walked towards the kitchen. 'Would you like a drink, wine, coffee?'

'Wine would be great, thanks.'

She poured him a glass and waited for him to speak, but he didn't seem keen to break the silence. 'Ronan?'

'Sorry.' He sighed heavily, staring into his wine glass. 'I've just had a god-awful argument with Kirsten. She didn't take it well that I don't want her anymore. I haven't for a while, nearly a year I guess.' He shrugged as though it was of little importance. 'I've just allowed it to drag along…'

'No one likes to be told they are no longer wanted. She's hurting.'

'Only her pride. Not her heart. She's incapable of loving.'

'Really?' Antonia invited him to sit on the sofa with her, it was the only comfortable seating she had, but there was easily enough room for two.

Ronan gave her a gut twisting smile. 'She's a spoilt rich girl. I always knew it. I enjoyed it at first. Everything was so intense with her. She is impulsive and crazy. She loved to fight and bitch about everything. She demanded and expected whatever she wanted, and usually got it. Money buys you so much.'

'She must have had good points too.'

'Not many, but some, yes.' Ronan drank from his glass. 'I've nearly forgotten what they are though simply because lately she has become someone I don't like. I've drifted away from her, from her pettiness, her selfishness, her attention seeking. Having a rich, powerful girlfriend pales after a while when you realise there's no substance underneath.'

Sipping her wine, Antonia didn't know what to say in response. Why was he telling her this?

Suddenly he stood, giving her a soft smile. 'I'm sorry. I shouldn't have come. You don't need to hear all about that.' He glanced at the paintings. 'You're busy. I'll go.'

'I didn't mind listening, I'm good at it. At this time of the night, I didn't paint, especially not when I've been at it all day.'

He started walked towards the door. 'Kirsten stormed out before I could finish my side of the argument. I guess I felt I needed to talk to someone, to get it out of my system.'

'Has it helped?' She lightly touched his arm, the first time she'd touched him. 'Do you feel better?'

'Yes, thank you. I'll leave you in peace now.' He opened the door and took a step. 'I'll see you tomorrow for dinner?'

She nodded, smiling. 'See you tomorrow night.'

He hesitated for a moment, his gaze not leaving hers, and then he turned sharply and went downstairs. Closing the door, she leaned her forehead against it.

Did that mean he was now free?

And did she want him to be?

⁓ℓℓ⁓

Ronan observed Antonia without her knowing. She stood waiting at the rail of the boat gazing up at the Statue of Liberty as they docked, ready to disembark onto the little island. She was beautiful, he couldn't deny it, but not in the superficial way like Kirsten. Antonia's beauty was more subtle, innocent. Nor could he deny his attraction to her. She wasn't like any of the girls he usually fancied. He normally went for leggy long-haired brunettes, girls with attitudes and confidence ball breakers. Antonia was nothing like that. She wasn't very tall. Her hair was shoulder length goldy brown. Her slender body was compact, no false boobs, no fake tan and no over the top make up. After a lifetime of city girls, he'd met a suburban girl. He admired her toughness to move from another country, but he sensed vulnerability about her too. She fascinated him. Everything about her was understated and that only intrigued him more. He enjoyed her company, loved listening to her talk, and felt that time rushed by with incredible speed whenever they were together.

After cooking dinner for her on Tuesday night, he'd seen her every evening since. They talked about so many topics and ate and drank wine, sometimes in her apartment or sometimes in his. She told him about the appointments with two galleries, her eagerness to make a good impression. It must have worked for they asked her to bring some new work in when she was ready. Her joy had been intoxicating and he had trouble stopping himself for swooping her up and kissing her senseless. All week he wanted nothing more than to take her into his arms, yet he knew it was too soon.

Being October, the crowds were smaller than in the height of summer, and so they could stroll at leisure without the hustle of hordes of people. It had rained earlier in the morning and the sky was still pewter grey and threatening.

'Do you want to go up to the top?' He pointed up to the crown where people stood on the observation deck of the statue.

'No, not this time.' She scrunched her nose up in disappointment, which he found such a cute thing she did. 'I think the clouds are closing in. Visibility won't be great, will it?'

'Shall we walk, until it starts to rain? Then we can go into the museum if you want?'

'Okay. We should have picked a better day, but I can always come back another day, when the weather is better.'

They followed the paths, strolling in comfortable silence. He liked that about her. She didn't feel the need to fill silences with nonsense. That was a tick in her favour, but then she had a lot of ticks in his mind.

How did she feel about him though? She obviously liked his company. It hadn't helped that their first dinner date was a disaster, nor Kirsten turning up unannounced. And what had processed him to talk to Antonia about Kirsten like he had done last week? He'd felt an idiot afterwards, back in his own apartment drinking beer to finish a terrible evening. Kirsten was out of his system and out of his life. It was long overdue. He knew that. The relief was immense. What shocked him more was the way Antonia had crept under his skin and consumed his every thought. Was he even ready to be with someone else?

A few drops of rain hit them, and they exchanged smiles and mutually headed for the museum. Inside there were more people and their progress was slowed as the rain came down heavier outside and other like-minded tourists came into the building.

They spent an hour in the museum, chatting about what they saw, but Ronan felt a little frustrated. He wanted Antonia to himself, he wanted to talk to her and a public space full of tourists wasn't ideal. Sometimes, he believed she was holding herself back from him and he wanted to change that.

How could he do that without frightening her off?

Later, back in his apartment, he started preparing another meal he'd promised to cook for her. She assured him she liked steak with roasted potatoes, green beans, caramelised carrots and a red wine sauce he was going to cook them. While he chopped vegetables, Antonia went up to her apartment to change and returned wearing black tailored trousers and a jade-coloured shirt. She looked amazing and smelt even better. He poured her a glass of wine and stood staring at her. She'd put on some light makeup and her eyes captured him.

'You're staring at me!' She laughed at him. 'Have a smudged my make up?'

Suddenly he could stand it no more. He took her glass from her and joined it with his on the table, before slowly taking her into his arms. He bent his head and kissed her gently, softly, testing her resistance and when he was met with none, he pressed his lips harder.

He wrapped his arms around her tiny waist, and he could feel her breast squashed against his chest. His groin tightened in response. When she lifted her hands, and entangled her fingertips into his hair, he felt his heartbeat kick up a notch. She was kissing him back now, firmer, more assured.

As she paused for breath, he swooped her up into his arms and carried her over to his big leather sofa. Cradling her in his lap, her kissed her neck, her ears then back to her mouth as his hands lightly roamed her body. Although he wanted them both naked, he had to go slow and not blow his chance.

Time had no meaning, everything was lost to him as her hands and fingers touched his body, she pulled his shirt up over his head, her nails lightly tracing a meaningless pattern over his chest and shoulders. He was on fire for her. His need so great he thought he'd not last another minute, he leaned back and took a deep breath, smiling at her as she gazed at him with lust drugged eyes.

'There are no words to describe how bad I want you right now,' he whispered against her lips.

'Then take me.' She climbed off his lap and held out her hand.

'You sure?' He led her to his bedroom and hoped to god she'd not say no.

'I know my own mind. Life is too short.' She stepped into his arms and kissed him, her tongue seeking his own.

He unbuttoned her shirt and drew it off her shoulders, letting it drop to the floor so he could concentrate on her breasts clad in a blue lace bra. He kissed the exposed skin of her cleavage before whispering his tongue over the satin covered nipples. She shuddered in his arms and gave a soft moan. Encouraged, he laid her on the bed, taking his weight on his elbow so he could gaze down at her. His fingers had a mind of their own and he kissed her. The rest of her clothes soon joined the heap on the floor, and he knelt on the bed by her feet. 'You are beautiful.'

'Thank you.'

He liked that she blushed but didn't hide her body, there was no need. To him she was unbelievably hot, and she was driving him mad. His penis was rock hard and throbbing to be inside her. He kissed her flat stomach, using the tip of his tongue to draw circles around her bellybutton. She wiggled, laughing at him, and then suddenly she was pulling him up to her and kissing him passionately, turning him inside out with need and want.

Antonia drew back, a little out of breath. 'I know we should take our time and explore each other but it's been so long since I've been with someone and if I don't have you inside me soon I might just cum without you!'

Her words were all he needed. He reached over to the bedside table and opened the drawer to grab a condom. Antonia took it off him, opened it and gently applied it to his penis. He stilled, not breathing at the touch of her fingers on him. Every muscle tensed as he concentrated on not blowing his load.

'Ronan?'

He opened his eyes and smiled. 'Have you any idea what you do to me?' He kissed her deeply, his tongue dancing, tasting hers. She shifted into a better position under him and lifted her hips to him, he needed no more clues she was ready for him. A small nudge with the tip of his penis and her hands grabbed his bum. She guided him into her tight wetness, and he nearly lost his mind. Gathering her close to him, he moved deeper inside her, kissing her as his hips thrust to meet hers.

'Oh...' she moaned into his mouth, her hands moving up along his back, digging her nails into his shoulders before moving down to grip his bum again, driving him harder. She came quickly, her breath catching. Ronan watched her face; he kissed her closed eyes and she opened them to smile at him. Her smile was honest, sincere and he gave another quick thrust for his own climax and shuddered, straining to give it all, to feel everything from her body, take everything she was willing to give him.

They lay quiet. Entangled. Their panting the only sound.

Ronan, not wanting to crush her, withdrew out of her and rolled to the side. 'Do not move.' He gave her a wink and went to the bathroom. He was quick to get rid of the condom and get back to her. She'd crawled under the covers, and he climbed in beside her, drawing her against him, kissing her.

'That was pretty good,' she murmured, snuggly closer to his chest.

'Pretty good?' Shocked, he tried to see her expression. 'Just pretty good?'

'Wasn't it for you?' She looked at him wide eyed. 'I know it didn't last for long that was my fault.'

'I thought it was freaking awesome, actually!'

Relaxing, she laughed. 'Yes, it was.'

'I'm glad you enjoyed it.'

'Enough for a repeat performance, I'm sure.'

He grinned. 'Perhaps. If you're lucky.'

She punched him playfully. 'You need to feed me first, I'm starving.'

Chuckling, he pushed her onto her back and kissed her thoroughly. 'Your wish is my command.'

They got dressed and went into the kitchen. While he cooked, Antonia drank her wine and set the table. He liked the ease in how they just got along.

'Do you know, we've talked so much about so many things except you.' She bit into their long overdue steak.

'What do you want to know?' He was ravenous. He couldn't remember the last time he felt so happy, so content.

'Everything.'

She grinned and he wanted to kiss her again. She did something to him that just filled him up inside with warmth and another hunger that had nothing to do with food. 'Well, I was born in New England. My parents are from Ireland.'

'Really?'

'With a name like Ronan Kelly, could you think anything else?' He laughed and sipped his wine.

'Why did your parents come to America?'

'For work. My dad is an engineer and was offered a good contract to work in Boston. So, they packed up and left. It was incredibly stressful, so my mom tells me. They left all family and friends behind, but we had cousins here on both sides. Irish people have long been immigrants to the US.'

'Yes, that's true. From the time of the Potato famine.'

His eyes widened. 'You know about that?'

'I do know some history. I actually like history, and I studied art history in university,' she sipped her wine, 'plus I read a lot.'

Ronan cut into his steak, thinking that Kirsten wouldn't have a first clue about general history. It was so refreshing to enjoy a meal with someone who was also intelligent. It'd been too long for him. 'I'm glad you read. There's nothing worse when you want to read, and another person resents you escaping into an enjoyable book.'

'Yes. My mother is a great reader. As young as I can remember she's always had books in the house, and after dinner her evening would be spent reading while my dad and I watched rubbish TV.'

'Don't get me wrong, I enjoy rubbish TV too.'

'I'm so glad!' She laughed again.

'I like your laugh.'

'I feel as though it's been years since I laughed, everything has been so serious in my life.'

'I'll lighten you up. No more seriousness.'

'That would be wonderful, thank you.'

He leaned over and kissed her, then settled back in his chair to continue eating.

'This steak is delicious. Go on, tell me more about your family. Brothers? Sisters?'

Ronan nodded. 'So, my parents arrived, and my mother found out she was pregnant with me. A few years later she had my brother, Sean. We had the perfect childhood and my brother and I are great mates. We are a close family.'

'That's nice. I am an only child. I don't think my mother wanted any children at all. She had a baby for my father's sake.' Her eyes clouded over a little at the turn of subject and Ronan hated the thought of her being sad.

'No, nothing serious remember, at least not tonight.'

'Yes, you're right.' She gave him a wide smile and he felt his body respond to her again. Leaving his chair, he went around the table and pulled her up and into his arms. 'I want you.'

'Again?' She laughed up at him.

'Yep.'

'What about our dinner?'

'I'll order pizza later if were hungry.' He frowned. 'Unless you don't want to stay the night?'

She reached up and kissed him. 'What a silly question.'

He groaned as the kiss deepened, he pulled her against him, his hands moulding around her hips. She fitted perfectly to his body. He kissed along her jaw, nibbling her earlobe, before kissing down her neck.

Taking a deep breath, he paused to smile at her. 'I'm so happy you came to New York, to this building.'

'Me too.' She placed her palm against his cheek, and he turned to kiss it. 'Take me to bed.'

'I might never let you out of it.' He laughed.

⁓⁓ *ele* ⁓⁓

The streets of Manhattan were turning into a kaleidoscope of autumnal colours as the mid October weather cooled the city. Outside, the rain pitted against the bedroom window. Antonia turned over in Ronan's bed and watched him sleeping. He was so handsome, not just in looks but in personality. She studied the shape of his nose, the curve of his eyebrows. His morning stubble shadowed his jaw and she ached to place her lips on his kissable mouth. She resisted the urge to touch him, not wanting to disturb him as they'd been late to finally go to sleep last night. Their sex life was incredible, so many times she would just stare at him and not believe her luck.

For the last few weeks, Antonia painted solidly through the days, and the evenings she spent enveloped in Ronan's arms. They took it in turns cooking at each other's apartment or they would go out for dinner at various restaurants in Hell's Kitchen. Thankfully, Ronan's friends didn't come around and spoil their time together.

She'd grown comfortable in his presence, surprised how easy and quickly the relationship developed and how familiar Ronan had become. They shared a love of music and food, art and history and books. He'd watch TV or prepare for his classes while she painted, and she grew to expect to see him every day.

It worried her a little that Ronan impacted on her future decisions. Surely it was too soon to think long term? Nearly half of her time in New York was over, but she tried not to think about leaving for France in six weeks. Of course, she had the option to stay in New York and lease the apartment for another few months, but by early spring she was meant to be in either Rome or Paris.

Was she mad to even consider staying?

Meeting someone was not part of the plan. But could she walk away from Ronan? She was falling in love...

'Why are you staring at me?' he suddenly whispered, startling her.

She kissed him quickly, nibbling his bottom lip. 'Go back to sleep.'

'I can't.' He lifted the sheet to show her his erection.

Laughing, she caressed it, making him groan. 'I'm hungry.'

'Mmm, me too.' He rolled her onto her back and kissed her neck and breasts. 'Very hungry.'

She opened her legs for him and moaned as he entered her. Matching his rhythm, she dug her fingers into his back as her body built towards climax. She came first and he kissed her as her nerve endings exploded and soon, he was shuddering in release with her.

In the quiet of the bedroom, her stomach rumbled and they both grinned. 'You need food,' he said yawning.

'And you need more sleep. Stay in bed, I'll go make a coffee.' She slipped out of bed and pulled his black jumper over her head and padded into the kitchen to put the kettle on. It was just past nine o'clock. She needed food. A knock at the door startled her. It was probably George, as the elevator was being temperamental again yesterday.

She opened the door only enough to pop her head out with a ready smile that soon froze on her face as she stared at Kirsten. 'Oh.'

Kirsten's eyes narrowed to mere slits as she barged in. She looked Antonia up and down with a sneer. 'What the hell are you doing?'

'I beg your pardon?' She blinked at the venom in her voice.

'Why are you here?'

'That is none of your business.' Aware the jumper only just covered her private areas; Antonia merely raised her chin in defence. 'What do you want?'

'I want to see my boyfriend.'

'He isn't your boyfriend anymore. He's mine.'

'Really? We'll see about that!' Kirsten pushed past Antonia and headed straight to the bedroom where she flung open the door.

Hurrying after her, Antonia grabbed her jeans and put them on, watching Kirsten who stood at the end of the bed staring at Ronan as he slept with his back to them. She turned to Antonia. 'Get out,' she whispered.

'No. You can't tell me what to do.'

A look of pure hatred crossed Kirsten's heavily made-up face. 'I am pregnant. Ronan is mine. Now get out!'

'Jesus Christ!' Ronan turned over to glare at Kirsten. 'Tell me you are lying.'

'I wish I was!' Kirsten sat on the edge of the bed, her back to Antonia shutting her out. 'We need to talk.'

Feeling like the wind had been punch out of her, Antonia gathered up her belongings and left the bedroom.

'Antonia wait!' Ronan, not caring about his nakedness, raced after her, catching her by the front door. 'Don't go. Stay. We'll hear her out and then talk.'

'No. This is your business.'

'You are my business.'

Treacherous tears gathered in her eyes but over his shoulder she saw Kirsten come out of the bedroom. 'Not anymore, Ronan. You have much to consider and discuss and…and…' Not able to speak without crying, she opened the door and fled up to her apartment.

Without pause, she stripped off and had the fastest shower of her life, then not caring what she was doing she dressed in clean jeans and shirt, before throwing on a jacket and boots.

Within ten minutes she was walking swiftly along Broadway, not knowing or even bothered where she was headed, just needing to get lost in the crowds. Saturday shoppers thronged the streets, getting ready for the holidays season. Halloween, Thanksgiving and Christmas were only weeks away. Antonia hated the thought of Christmas. Her first Christmas without her dad, and now not likely to be spent with Ronan. Life was just crap.

After buying a coffee, she kept walking, trying not to think or feel. She didn't want to process the reality that Ronan was lost to her. The one good thing she'd found in her life was gone, just like her father, and she felt a raw pain eat at her insides like a crazed beast.

She couldn't cry, wouldn't cry! It was her own fault. She'd come to New York to paint, not fall in love.

Straightening her shoulders, she strode out, determined. She had years ahead of her to fall in love, but right now she needed to focus on her career. That's what she wanted, wasn't it? To be an artist? To sell her work? To experience the world? Yes. It was her plan. Granted, she'd become a little distracted and had lost focus, but all that would change now. It was time to get on with it. After all, she couldn't allow her mother to be right, could she? She had to make a success of it. And if tears dried on her cheeks as she walked, she ignored them.

ele

Ronan, fully dressed, switched on the coffee machine. His hands were shaking. His stomach roiled and he wondered idly if he'd throw up in the kitchen sink. He'd yanked on a pair of jeans and the shirt he'd worn last night, and which smelled of Antonia's perfume...

'I didn't mean to tell you like that.' Kirsten stood leaning against the counter.

'What burst into my bedroom and blurt it out in front of Antonia, like that you mean?' he spoke to the window, not even daring to turn around for he could feel a deep rage burning in his brain and was frightened of the consequences if he gave into it.

'I'm hoping you don't mean what you said last time I was here, that we are over because everything has changed now. We can start again. Be a family. I'm not asking you to marry me, but we can still be together and bring this baby into the world as a couple.'

'No.' Was she insane?

'But why? We used to have so much fun, you can't deny that.'

'Yes, years ago when we were fresh out of college.' He made the coffee but didn't ask her if she wanted one. He needed her to go. Why was this happening? He didn't even like her.

'I want you to be in this child's life.'

The way she said child was like a stab to his heart. It sounded like a life sentence in prison. He didn't want a child, not now and definitely not with her. 'Are you sure you're pregnant because it was months ago when we last...' He couldn't even remember when they'd last done it. For the last year it had been few and far between and merely body release for him, not like how it was with Antonia...

He fought the urge to retch. 'It's been at least four months or more,' he barely got the words out.

'That's how far along I am. Four months. I didn't realise, you know how my body is. I skip periods all the time.'

'Yes, because you take the pill and abuse it so you can party all the time.' He turned to face her. She wore jeans and a red coat. She didn't look pregnant, but then she'd hardly be showing yet, would she? He had no idea. 'You said you were on the pill.'

'Ronan, it's done. We need to talk about the future not the past.'

He sipped the scalding hot coffee, trying to settle his stomach. 'I don't want to be a father yet, Kirsten, can't you see? I'm beyond shocked. I'm devastated.'

'This wasn't my plan either, you know. But I love you. I can put everything behind us and just concentrate on us and the baby. You can too. We can make it work.'

'How? How can we make it work when I don't love you?'

She smiled thinly. 'I have enough love for both of us.'

'I don't want your kind of love. I've tried it before, and it doesn't make me happy.'

'This time it'll be different. We'll be parents. We'll have a baby to love. It'll change us and bring us closer.' She stepped closer to him and rested her head against his shoulder. It was the first tender thing she'd done in an awfully long time.

He tried hard not to shudder. 'How long have you known?'

'I've just found out. Taken a test. I came straight over.'

'Okay... Well, we need to go to the doctors.'

'I'll book an appointment for next week.'

'And it's mine?'

'Of course!' Her tone was adamant.

He sagged, feeling the life drain out of him. 'I'll support you, Kirsten, and the baby, but I'm not giving up Antonia. She's in my life now.'

She thrust herself away from him. 'You hardly know her! She's been here all of five minutes!'

'She's been here long enough for me to know that she's important to me.' He ran his hand over his face, feeling like death. Poor Antonia. Poor him! His parents will be shocked. They weren't keen on Kirsten, never had been. She always behaves as though her family is above his, and yes, they were richer than his but there was more to life than money. Kirsten's parents had affairs that weren't very well hidden, at least his parents still were in love. Something he wanted to have one day too...

'I won't be pushed away because of her, Ronan.' Kirsten folded her arms, determination written across her features. 'Our baby comes first.'

'We will just have to figure it out as we go along, but there will be no talk of you and I being a couple, do you understand?'

＿＿ℓℓ＿＿

Antonia took a sip of her coffee, musing at the painting

before her. She dabbed lightly at the cobalt blue paint and applied it with a gentle sweep of the brush. The Hudson River took on a deeper hue, she'd have to adjust the sky colour, it wasn't right. Nor was the shade of grey of the buildings on the opposite bank. White highlights needed to be added to reflect the sun. The coffee forgotten she concentrated on altering aspects of the painting, adding lighter hues and painting over bits she wasn't happy with.

Her phone rang. She ignored it. She'd rung her mother yesterday and with that duty done, there was no need for her to answer any calls or texts. They were all from Ronan anyway. For five days he'd rang and text and knocked on her door, but she refused to open it or even listen to the dozens of voicemails he left on her phone.

She'd only left the building once since Kirsten's announcement when she knew he'd be at the college he taught at. She reported to George at the door, that she was busy working and didn't want to be disturbed by anyone or anything. With enough food, canvases and paint to last her for weeks, she had no wish to see Ronan or any living soul. Hiding away was cowardly, she knew. Ronan didn't deserve it. Yet, the thought of seeing him, of saying goodbye to their relationship before it was given a chance to completely flourish hurt too much. To shield away from that pain, she threw herself into her work.

On Saturday she was going to set up a stall at a market she'd been given the details for from one of the gallery owners. He encouraged her to show off her paintings and see what she could sell. Although he had mentioned for her to show him on Friday the best of what she had first, so he could display them in his gallery. The thought terrified and excited her at the same time. The rest of her paintings she was going to hopefully sell on the stall.

Suddenly tears filled her eyes. This was the biggest step forward of her new career and whether she succeeded or failed, she had no one to share it. A silly stupid traitorous tear rolled down her cheek and she wiped it away angrily. She wouldn't cry. She ached for Ronan's arms, and to see his smile, but she wouldn't back down.

They were over.

Banging on the door startled her. She looked at the time. Quarter to two in the afternoon. Ronan would be at work. Confident it was only George at the door, she opened it and died on the spot when Ronan stood there, his hand ready to bang again.

'Oh, so you are alive then? George assured me you were, but I wasn't sure.' Sarcasm dripped from him.

'I've been busy.'

'You've been hiding!' Anger replaced the sarcasm. 'God Antonia, I thought you were an adult! Do you think I need you behaving like this on top of everything else?'

'No, I guess not. I was giving you time,' she lied.

'Time for what? To go stark raving mad? Because believe me, I'm nearly there.' The emotions played on his face, hurt, fury and sadness all at once.

'I'm sorry.' She shrugged, fighting to hide her feelings. 'I didn't know how to handle this. I was shocked and well…'

'Do you think I don't know?' He stepped inside but didn't try to come any closer to her. 'I never wanted to be in this situation. I just wanted you.'

She closed the door and walked away from him. 'I don't know what to say or do, Ronan.'

'Say what you feel.'

Absentmindedly, she picked at the dry paint on her fingers. 'That's just it. I don't know what to say or what I feel. All I know is that I thought I had you in my life and now I don't.'

'You can. This doesn't change us.'

'Don't be naive!' She glared at him, taking her frustration out on him. 'You went from her to me in a matter of months. I hate that. I hate that she's having your baby. I hate that I was finally feeling like I'd met someone I could…I could…'

'Fall in love with?'

'Yes!'

'And it's ruined.' He finished for her.

'Yes, it is ruined. You're going to be a father, with her. You're going to experience things, happy things with her, and I can't sit by and watch that. Jealous would eat me away. I can't do it. I wish I could, but I can't. I'm sorry.'

He nodded, looking pale and drawn and totally unhappy. 'I know.'

Her heart was crumbling, slowly, piece by piece.

He took a step back, towards the door. 'So, that's it then. Over before it began.'

'Yes,' she whispered choked by tears she refused to let fall.

'Okay.' He nodded. 'I will try to understand but I don't want this. Just so you know. I want you. Us. I have fallen in love with you. This last week without you has been a nightmare.' He opened the door and hesitated. 'You know where I am if you change your mind.'

When he left, Antonia stayed standing where she was for a long time. If she moved, she believed she'd fall in a heap and never get up again. Apart from her father, no man in her life had said they loved her. Ronan loved her. He wanted her.

In a heartbeat she was racing out of the apartment and down the stairs to his door, only to skid to a halt at the sight of Kirsten walking to his door, her hand raised ready to knock, all the while talking loudly on her phone.

She sneered as she saw Antonia and took the phone away from her ear and ended the call. 'He doesn't want to see you. You're making a fool of yourself.'

'You know nothing of what he wants.' It annoyed her how stylish Kirsten always appeared, as though she'd just stepped out of a fashion magazine. Kirsten and Ronan did make the perfect model pair.

'Is that so? I've known Ronan for years, unlike you.' From her enormous Gucci bag, she pulled out brochures and waved them at Antonia. 'We're house hunting. Did he tell you that? Somewhere with a garden for the baby.' She stepped closer and lowered her voice. 'He will forget you, and any other little tart that thinks she can have him. Don't you realise there are girls at his college throwing themselves at him on a daily basis? You and they will not win. He's always been mine.'

'He loves me.'

'He'll love me again the minute this child is born. I'll make sure of it. Ronan is a decent guy. Loyal. Do you think you can stand by and watch us be a family while you're always on the outside looking in? I feel sorry for you. I won't let you have a moment's piece of mind. You'll wonder where he is and what he's doing every minute of the day. Even when you're with him, I'll ring and text him with excuses to see me and the baby. It'll drive you crazy. Is that what you want?' Kirsten tilted her head, a pitying expression on her face. 'It's nothing personal, you understand. It wouldn't matter who the woman was, no one will have Ronan but me. It's been like that since we were in college. Find someone else. Go back to Australia. You're pretty, you'll meet someone else.' She turned on her high heel and knocked on Ronan's door.

Not wanting to be seen hanging about, Antonia fled upstairs back to her sanctuary. She stood at the kitchen sink, her hands shaking as she gripped the edge. Part of her wanted to march back downstairs and tell Kirsten where to really go! Yet, another part of her, the bruised, wounded part, kept her still. She wasn't the type for confrontations.

She hated arguments. And deep down she knew Kirsten was right. Antonia would always be on the outside looking in at the three of them. She'd envy Kirsten giving Ronan his first child, sharing all those firsts together. She'd be a distant third in the line up wanting Ronan's attention.

She couldn't do it.

Sighing, acknowledging the truth, she picked up her phone. It was time to change her plans.

ele

Paris

Antonia turned the corner away from the studio where she took her art classes. Today's lesson had been particularly challenging, and her head throbbed from trying to please her instructor. A terrible lesson had topped off an awful day, for some of her paintings had been rejected by an owner of a trendy Parisian galley.

She hurried along, her cape flapping out behind her like a bird's wings and not keeping her warm or dry at all. Rain lashed down and she was thankful her canvases were in a protective waterproof case. She crossed the bridge over the canal and strode along Quai de la Loire towards her apartment.

She'd been living in Paris for two months and, apart from missing Ronan, she enjoyed the lifestyle of Parisian art scene, mainly due to her new friends. She'd been accepted by a group of people who lived in her apartment block, most were artists of some kind, painters like herself, but also actors, models, sculptors, photographers and writers.

Unlike Manhattan, her arrival in Paris was harsher, the apartment she'd impulse booked lacked any comfort. Its only redeeming feature was its large windows looking out over the canal and the building's proximity to galleries and being in the centre of the current art area.

A frosty winter gripped Paris and Antonia missed the warmth of the sun of Australia. But she felt that by having to struggle at first, had helped her to try and forget the comfort of Ronan's arms. By having to concentrate on finding her way around a strange city and not speaking fluent French, by meeting new people, by taking art lessons, all contributed into her getting through the weeks after leaving New York and not losing her mind over the breakup.

The day she left to go to the airport was still etched in her mind and heart. Ronan had stood outside of her door, not leaving until she came out. When she did, he held her tightly, kissing the top of her head, but saying nothing, then he helped her to take her bags down to the taxi. Again, he kissed her wordlessly. There were no words to say.

How she missed him. All of him, his smiles, his humour, his cooking, his tender loving looks, and the great love making.

Entering the foyer, she stopped to check her post box, but as usual it was empty. She'd hoped to hear from some of the galleries in New York where she'd left some paintings, but nothing. Her instructor told she had talent, and she had to believe him, but it was tough at times to keep her confidence up. It was only her mother's look of 'I told you so' which was stopping her from returning to Australia.

Depressed, cold and hungry, she waited for the elevator. Reports suggested there'd be snow tonight and shivering in the draft of the doorway, she believed it.

Antonia stepped back as the elevator door opened and Maree and Patsy came out. 'Hello.'

'Bonjour, Antonia!' Patsy smiled, an Englishwoman who was in Paris to study art like Antonia. 'My, you looked sodden.'

'I am.'

'Do you want to come out with us?' Maree, a tall, thin Belgian photographer, puffed on a stylish pink e-cig. Maree shared an apartment with Patsy and a guy called Sean, from Ireland, a writer or sculptor, depending on his mood and state of intoxication.

'I'm damp and a mess.' Antonia shook out her cape.

'We'll wait for you to change.'

'We're off to Jason's apartment,' Patsy added. 'He's putting on a mini show.'

'I would say yes if I'd not spent last night drinking at yours until the wee hours.' Antonia laughed.

Patsy grinned. 'What is wrong with that?'

'You are tired. No food today?' Maree tilted her head to peer at her. 'Go to bed. Eat, then bed. Yes?'

'Yes, I think so.'

Maree nodded; her short slick-backed black hair never moved. She wore a black and white pin-stripe suit and appeared effortlessly elegant. She was the most fashionable person; Antonia had ever met. And by comparison, Antonia looked and felt like a drowned rat.

'How was your lesson?' Patsy asked, while checking her phone.

Shrugging, Antonia adjusted the canvas under her arm. 'I think I'm making progress. Monsieur Benaud says, I have talent...talent that is hidden but it will emerge, even if he has to break me in half to find it!'

'He sounds delicious!' Maree laughed.

'He's seventy if a day, and permanently squints.' She stepped into the elevator, laughing.

'Age is but a number, Cherie!'

Antonia shook her head at her and chuckled. 'Have a wonderful night. I want to hear all about it tomorrow.'

'Eat! Bed!' Maree shouted as they left through the front door.

Antonia let herself into her apartment. It was cold, the heating a hit and miss affair. She sighed, wondering if she should have gone with the girls. Getting blind drunk might have been a fitting ending to an awful cold day. She didn't know what she'd done without those two women. She'd spent the first weeks in Paris feeling lonely and upset that she and Ronan had split. Painting had saved her sanity, but at night when she was alone in a cold bed in a freezing apartment away from everyone she knew and loved, then the images of Ronan making love to her would haunt her, make her long for him with an intensity that either made her sob into her pillow or bash the pillow in anger for being such a fool to let a man come before her work to start with!

Maree and Patsy had zoned in on her heartbreak and insisted they become friends. The pair of them made sure she had one of them checked on her every day. Their apartment became an extension of hers, and for once, instead of hiding away she welcomed the company. Sean, too in his own crazy-man way helped. The four of them would spend many nights sitting on big cushions in front of the temperamental heater wrapped in blankets and eating take away food and drinking cheap wine. They discussed every topic they could think of, they laughed and playfully argued. Christmas and New Year came and went in a drunken haze. The four of them cooked, and played cards, watched movies and sang Karaoke in dingy bars.

Antonia thought the world of them, these three strangers who'd lessened the ache of missing Ronan. For her they suffered endless trips to galleries and museums, of listening to her talk of art and painting, of gazing at books of the renowned artists of history.

But as much as she loved going out with them and meeting new people, she was starting to tire, her work suffered because of it.

This morning's rejection stung. Mediocre. That's what the gallery owner had told her. The word replayed in her head like a broken record. His cutting remarks as he flipped through her portfolio deflated her. She wasn't fluent in French, but she knew enough to understand his remarks and the tone in which he said them.

Thinking about it now, she made the decision to take more lessons with Monsieur Benaud. Mediocre wasn't her. She had to be better than that! She would keep taking lessons until that label had been wiped from Monsieur Benaud's memory.

Turning the heating on again and hoping it'd stay on this time, Antonia then opened the small fridge. There wasn't much in it. Cheese, sliced ham and eggs. It'd have to do. After a hot shower and dressed in a warm tracksuit, she cooked scrambled eggs and ham with melted cheese on top. A cup of coffee washed it down. Her paintings were stacked around the living room and a fresh canvas was on the easel waiting for her attention, but she ignored it. Tomorrow. She'd start afresh tomorrow. Be more determined and focused tomorrow. No more messing about.

Tonight, she needed to rest, recharge the batteries. Eating a bar of chocolate, she flicked on the TV, searching until she found a movie she knew and could watch and nearly understand. It was a way to help her learn the language. Her phone bussed and she answered a text from her cousin in Australia. Facebook took another hour of her time, and as the snow fell outside her windows, she snuggled deep into the sofa and drifted off to sleep.

She dreamed of her mother, arguing with her dad, telling him Antonia would never settle down. She thought her dad was banging on something, but suddenly opening her eyes she realised the banging was on the door to her apartment.

The TV was still on, and thankfully the heating. The time on her phone read twenty past eleven. Yawning, she opened the door to reveal Sean. 'Hi, is something wrong?'

'Yes, there's some guy wanting to see you and he won't leave my door until I tell him where you are. Have you a stalker?'

Antonia blinked, clearing her fuzzy mind. 'A Stalker? Don't be ridiculous.'

'Antonia! At bloody last!'

Staring past Sean, she gaped at Ronan, who'd come around the corner from Sean's corridor. 'Oh my God.'

'You know him then?' Sean asked, 'Is he a maniac?'

'No, he's not. It's Ronan.'

'The guy you go on about, who broke your heart?'

'Yes, thanks for spilling that, Sean.' She blushed in embarrassment.

'I'll go then.' Sean and Ronan swapped places and Antonia, on shaking legs, walked back inside.

Ronan shut the door behind him, and they stood staring at each other. Her heart broke again at the uncertain expression on his face. He'd lost weight. His clothes didn't fit him right.

'How are you?' He finally asked

'I'm fine. How did you find me?' she asked, shocked that he stood before her. For two long months she had wanted nothing more than him being here with her and now he was she didn't know what to say or do.

'On Facebook.'

'Facebook?' She tried to think what she had put on the social website.

'I know you don't post on there much, I've checked your page every day hoping you would. You never reveal your location, but yesterday, I think it was yesterday, or the day before, I saw a picture of you. Someone called Maree had tagged you in on it. She wrote that you were on your way home as the sun was rising and, in the background, was a street sign Quai de la Loire. I jumped on the first plane to Paris, got a taxi from the airport to this street and then started asking around. A guy in the café on the corner said an Australian woman lived in this building. So, I started on the first door on the first floor and kept knocking until I found Sean and he said he knew you.'

Antonia couldn't believe he had done all that to find her. She ached to hug and kiss him, but she stayed where she was, for he seemed a little fragile. 'And here you are,' she murmured.

'Here I am.'

'Why?' she whispered, finding it unbearable that they were standing yards apart.

'Why am I here?' He shrugged and she saw the raw pain in his eyes as she had seen it in her own staring back from the mirror. 'I couldn't live without you.'

She smothered a sob. 'We've been through this. Before I left. We agreed it was for the best.'

'Kirsten isn't pregnant. She never was.'

Antonia gasped. 'Not pregnant? I don't understand.'

'She was lying all along. She didn't develop a big stomach. The weeks went by, and her stomach didn't grow.'

'But she said she was four months along. Why would she lie?'

'She lied because she thought she could win me back, like in some bloody movie. Kirsten didn't want me to be with you, or anyone. She had to control me.'

'How did she think she was going to get away with it?'

He shrugged. 'I don't know. I think she thought that I'd believe her when she said she'd miscarried.'

'Yet you didn't?'

'No. It all conveniently happened when I was at work. I got a phone call from her saying she'd been to the hospital, lost the baby and was at home. I called in at her place to see her and she didn't look like someone who'd lost a baby. She wasn't unduly upset.' He took a deep breath. 'I got back in my car and on my phone, I googled what happens when someone loses a child in their sixth month. I read that she would have been in labour, kept in hospital at least twenty-four hours... There were other things, no scans, no gaining weight, no queasiness, she'd say she went to the doctor when I was at work. She didn't look at baby books or buy baby things. Suddenly I realised it was all an elaborate lie.'

Antonia sagged, shocked. 'How could anyone do such a thing? It's evil, cruel.'

'People can do all sorts of things... I've found that out first-hand.'

'Are you okay? You must feel betrayed, or used... I don't know... That isn't how you behave when you love someone. That is all about control, thinking only of yourself.'

Ronan wiped a hand over his eyes. 'I feel nothing but relief. It's been the most awful, shittest time of my life. We fought and argued. She wanted us to be a couple and I couldn't. I didn't want that. How could I when I loved you so much and missed you so bad, I thought I'd never recover from it?'

'Oh, god.' Tears slipped down her cheeks.

'She put me through hell over losing you. For nothing. For her own selfish needs. I never thought she could be that manipulating.'

'Is she gone for good now?'

'Oh yes, very much. We hate each other. I feel free at last.' He tucked his hands into the front pocket of his jeans as though he didn't know what to do with them. 'I'm sorry. You've no idea how sorry.'

'It wasn't your fault. She was lying to you. You did what you thought was best, the honourable thing.'

'I shouldn't have let you go.'

'It wasn't your decision, it was mine. I knew I couldn't cope seeing you both together with a baby. I did what I always do when things get tough, I run.' She glanced away from trying to gather her thoughts. 'Perhaps I should have trusted you more, but it all happened so quickly. You and me, and then her bombshell. After losing dad as well, it was all too much. Do you understand?'

'Of course, I do. But you leaving was the worst thing that had ever happened to me.' His voice broke. 'I've never loved anyone as much as I love you. To me, you were exactly what I wanted and needed in my life. I have never been as happy as I was when I was with you. It was like a kick in the gut every time I thought of you, knowing I could never be with you again.'

'I've been feeling the same.' She gave him a watery smile, the tears brimming on her lashes. 'I never expected to fall in love.'

'It's a killer, isn't it?' he joked. Then he straightened, his handsome face becoming serious. 'Is it too late for us?'

She shook her head. 'No.'

She ran into his arms and felt the breath squeezed out of her he held her so tight. 'We have the rest of our lives.'

About the Author

AnneMarie Brear was born to Yorkshire parents but grew up in Australia. Her love of reading fiction started at an early age with Enid Blyton's novels, before moving on into more adult stories such as Catherine Cookson's novels as a teenager. Living in England, she discovered her love of history by visiting the many and varied places of historical interest.

AnneMarie is currently only writing historical novels, mainly set in Yorkshire and Australia in the eras covering from Victorian to WWII. Her books are available in ebook and paperback and audio.

For more about AnneMarie Brear and her books visit her website where you can sign up for a newsletter.

http://www.annemariebrear.com

https://www.facebook.com/annemariebrearauthor

https://twitter.com/annemariebrear

Printed in Great Britain
by Amazon